THE
HOPE
VALLEY
HUBCAP
KING

THE HOPE VALLEY HUBCAP KING

SEAN MURPHY

DELTA TRADE PAPERBACKS

Sean

07/12

For Jana, who will
complete her book
one day soon —
—Sean

THE HOPE VALLEY HUBCAP KING
A Delta Trade Paperback

PUBLISHING HISTORY
Dell mass market edition published November 2002
Delta trade paperback edition / February 2004

Published by
Bantam Dell
A Division of Random House, Inc.
New York, New York

ISBN 0-385-33782-5

Manufactured in the United States of America
Published simultaneously in Canada

BVG   10   9   8   7   6   5   4   3   2   1

Dedicated to Dr. Henry Leroy Finch Jr.
for his boundless inspiration and encouragement,
and to Maggie and the entire Finch family.
And to my parents, Ruth and Harold Gardner,
for their love and unswerving belief in me.

ACKNOWLEDGMENTS

The people who helped in one way or another in the process of writing this book are truly too numerous to mention. I'll just have to do my best and attempt a partial list:

Boundless appreciation goes first to my wife, Tania, whose love, encouragement, and sharp editing skills were essential in finishing this book (finally!), and in keeping my body, soul, and mind alive in the process. Great thanks go to my parents and to the Finch family for encouraging, helping, feeding, coaxing, and cajoling, and anything else that seemed necessary at any given time.

Great gratitude also to Malachy McCourt for reading and commenting on the book and providing such wonderful quotes, and to Natalie Goldberg for the countless ways in which she has assisted and encouraged me. And to my editor, Liz Scheier, and my agent, Peter Rubie, for believing in the book and fighting so hard on its behalf.

To my Zen teacher, John Daido Loori, and the community at

Zen Mountain Monastery, and to Gerry Shishin Wick, Maezumi Roshi, and many others in the White Plum Sangha, to all of whom I owe whatever brief moments of clarity may appear in this work.

To my many writing teachers, especially Keith Abbott and Bob Potter; and to Mike Smith and Sarah for doing my first promotional materials for free.

To the more than 600 members of the Great Peace March, in whose company, on our nine-month trek across the continent, the seeds of this narrative began to germinate.

Finally, my deep appreciation to the many friends who have read and commented on the manuscript at various points in its evolution, or who have helped in other ways, including: Roy Finch and Susie Landau; Robert Johnson and Dana O'Neill; Cathy Black; Laura Monagan; Joe Kinczel and Lori Graff; Fiona Thompson; Sky and Greg Johnson; Lisa Smith; Jeanne Ward; Jim Gallagher; Liz Schoofs; Patty Loughrey; Brian Galvin; Valarie Schwann; Liz and Peter Gifford; Paul Sowanick; Kimmer Macarus; Aubrey Carton; Tina Brandt; Mirabai and Jenny Starr; Miss Christy Bright; and Richard Freeman and Mary Taylor. I hope you will find the results worthy of your efforts!

And to anyone else I forgot, thank you, thank you, and please forgive me.

PROLOGUE

Bibi is dreaming again. Amidst the haze of heat and pain, the squeal of tires comes to him once more. He again sees the man with the pallid, moist face, panting from his place behind the wheel, again feels the arc into space and the shuddering end of that arc.

He groans, moves, nearly surfaces. Words come into his mind, strange, yet familiar:

Terry Cloth?

The scene shimmers, shifts; memories twine about him like damp sheets. Next come his ancestors, as in his childhood, brooding down at him from their places on the living room wall. Larger than life—though, one would have to say, not so large as death—and each bearing that same look of sorrowful perplexity, they stand shoulder to shoulder, casting grave and watchful eyes upon his every action. He again feels the weight of their history, as though all the gravity of the world were pressing in upon him.

A field of light, of spinning orbs, appears before him: Hub-caps?

And as the pain sweeps in once more, penetrating even the depths of his dreaming, he feels again the weight of the decision he has carried throughout his life: to follow the fate of his ancestors, or to go his own way.

1.
TINY
BLUE MOONS

He was no more than a child when the unreality of the world began to impress itself on him. His earliest memories were of moments when perspective went out of kilter, and foreground and background shifted without warning. Once, during a picnic at the waterfront, his mother bent forward to pass a plate of quartered dill pickles, and the river behind her appeared to freeze in place, while its banks drifted upstream. Another time, as he ambled along a city sidewalk holding his father's hand, the cars seemed to glide to a halt, while the buildings coasted along behind as though on an unseen conveyor belt.

On one occasion he spent an entire afternoon staring into his reflection in a neighbor's fish pond. "My face, Daddy," he cried, as his parents finally led him away, "I could stick my hand through it. I could drink it!"

He'd wriggled about so much in the womb his mother finally complained to her obstetrician: "Doc, can't you give him tranquilizers or something? My insides feel like a jungle gym!"

Once he learned to crawl he roamed the house ceaselessly, up and down stairs, in and out of closets, cabinets, the basement. A moment's inattention by his mother and he was gone; following a panicked search, she'd find him in the cellar, staring at a spider building its web, or a scrap of insulation that had come loose from the pipes and drifted to and fro with every draft. After he began to walk he struck off for wider territory. Out a window, through a door left ajar; once his father found him teetering at the edge of a bluff overlooking the river, face jutting into the wind like the figurehead on the prow of a ship.

A family friend remarked that the child had all the quickness and agility of a greyhound. The resemblance did not stop at that; for he was long and lean-limbed, with streamlined, forward-pointing features, and the way the hair swept back from his brow gave the impression of constant motion.

"And those eyes," the friend cooed. "So blue and round, like little moons. Tiny blue moons, I do declare!"

He'd been christened Frederick G. Brown II, but from the time of his birth he was known, for no reason anyone could ever ascertain, as Bibi.

"Pronounced BB," his mother explained to doctors, teachers, and anyone else who balked on seeing the name in print. "You know, like the gun."

One morning in his fifth year, Bibi was skating in his socks across the kitchen floor when he collided with a kettle of scalding water his mother was taking off the stove—an event that caused his already wide eyes to open wider than ever and which, his mother later claimed, caused their blue color to deepen permanently by several degrees. The child was left with a nasty burn on the back of his left wrist; and in the next days he did little but stare at it. It was as though by peering into his wound Bibi was seeing, for the first time, into himself. He gazed for hours into that translucent pink expanse, imagining the intricate workings of blood cells and capillaries, and wondering in his childish way: *Is this all I am?*

"Bibi," his mother told him, "go out and play! It's not normal to sit around all day staring at that thing!"

But her words had no effect. The burn eventually healed, leaving him with a mark shaped roughly like the continent of Australia, and the child resumed his wandering ways—but for years after, whenever he was worried or unable to sleep, Bibi's parents would find him sitting in the corner of his bedroom, staring into the roughened, puckered surface of his scar, and rubbing his fingers across it again and again.

Bibi's dawning perception of the world's unreality was accompanied by a deepening sense of the strangeness of time. The Fourth Depression had reached its lowest ebb by the time he entered school, and whenever he and his mother drove into town they'd pass crowds of jobless men in front of liquor stores and movie marquees, beneath billboards announcing:

BELIEVE IN AMERICA

"Mom," Bibi asked on one such visit, "what are those men doing?"

"Just killing time, I suppose," his mother shrugged, smiling at her son's curiosity.

Bibi said no more, but her words stuck with him. What a notion! All those people standing around, killing time—yet time never seemed to die. Bibi spent hours afterward imagining what the world might look like following the death of time: but the closest he could come was a chaotic mishmash where everything happened at once, like a dream in which the details always eluded him.

Then there was the uncertain nature of love. Love was something Bibi often felt coming from other people toward him—

when his mother, for instance, brushed her way through his dark, tousled mat of hair in the morning, kissed him on that prominent forehead, and sent him off to school saying: "Make Momma proud!" But he was never entirely sure he could feel anything going in the opposite direction. To find out, he undertook a series of experiments. Bibi reasoned that the best way to figure out whether you loved someone was to see how you'd feel if something awful happened to them. With this in mind, he began a program of visualizations in which he imagined his parents in all manner of horrifying circumstances: tumbling from precipices, flattened by steamrollers, sinking in storm-tossed seas—all the while examining his own responses for any glimmer of regret. The results were inconclusive. He was unable to stimulate a single feeling he could confidently label "love." Bibi liked many people—in fact, nearly everyone he met—but of love he was never certain.

Thus Bibi wasn't sure what he felt when, on an otherwise ordinary day in his eleventh year, his father killed himself. The event, to be sure, was hardly unexpected; Bibi's father was the twelfth firstborn son in the last dozen generations of Browns to take his own life.

Bibi's grandfather, Harrison Humbert Brown, a noted university professor and scholar, had hung himself from a crossbeam in his garage nine years earlier, leaving a note that read: "Life was better before I knew so much."

Bibi's great-grandfather, Nate "West" Brown, a social reformer and labor organizer, had leapt from the Sears Tower during the Third Depression, leaving the message: "The future is bright, but I never seem to get there."

And Bibi's great-great-grandfather, G. Larson Brown, a well-known scientist and inventor, exited the world via a deliberate laboratory explosion, leaving the comment: "Life was the death of me."

The eight remaining generations of deceased Browns will be arranged in list form to simplify presentation:

Vladimir Estragon Brown, hobo and philosopher. Intentional self-starvation:
"God stood me up."

Willy "The Zip" Brown, Dadaist and performance artist. Had himself cast in a seven by nine foot block of Lucite on a nationwide TV show:
"Life is a Naugahyde seat cover with no stuffing."

Quentin Sartoris Brown, physician and researcher. Intravenous self-injection of curare:
"At last I've found the cure for all life's ills."

Chandler Phillips Brown, private detective. Willful ingestion of seventy-three .45-caliber bullets:
"I haven't got a clue."

Ernest "Rhinoceros" Brown, big-game hunter and explorer. Ritual self-disembowelment by buffalo horn:
"When all is said and done, I'm just like everybody else."

Gregor Samson Brown, failed writer and bodybuilder. Overdose of DDT. Left behind seven unfinished novels, the theme of which might best be summarized as: "Why bother?"

Andrew Philifor Brown, ruined gold miner. Drowned self in Placer River after the great rush:
"Dad gum-it!"

Ulysses Bloom Brown, land baron. Drove horse and carriage off West River Bridge:
"I'm just plain bored."

"Twelve generations of Browns," wept Bibi's mother after his father's funeral, dabbing at her face with a mascara-streaked handkerchief. "Gone, all gone."

"Thirteen," Bibi corrected, holding one hand in the other and scratching along the edges of his scar.

"Well, yes," his mother responded. "There *is* you." And she broke out crying all over again.

Bibi's father, an amateur table tennis champion, had ended his life via the unconventional means of inhaling a Ping-Pong ball, which had lodged just above his epiglottis, asphyxiating him. Bibi and his dog Buster found the body when they scrambled beneath a rosebush in the garden to retrieve a lost toy. The victim's eyes were open and bulging, as though in surprise that his method had produced the desired effect. Although his father was the first dead person Bibi had seen, he was not to be the last; and the image of those permanently startled features would trouble his dreams for years to come.

The note left by Frederick G. Brown senior read simply: "Is this all I am?" Ironically, it was the same question his son had been asking himself not long ago, one that would continue to haunt him for much of the rest of his life.

As Bibi grew older he took to roaming the city by bus, and asking questions of those he met. He once, for instance, asked a woman on the Thirty-nine Northbound about the nature of gravity.

"Er . . ." she replied, peering at him over a pair of teardrop-shaped bifocals, "it's a form of suction, I suppose. Like that chewing gum on the floor over there. Just think of gravity as a wad of gum dropped by God that we've all stepped in—and now we're stuck!"

Another time Bibi asked a man on a park bench about death. "Death?" the man responded, pushing greying hair back from his face and tossing crumbs to the gaggle of pigeons at his feet. "Why, people are dying all the time. Here we are talking, and they're out there switching off like lights. Going down like ships. One for every word we say, one for every syllable. Poof! Just like that. If you ask me, death's become a habit, like smoking—one we're not likely to give up, even though it can't be good for us." He laughed, then scattered the birds with a wave of his hand. "Poof," he cried, as they flapped off. "Away with you!"

As Bibi entered adolescence, his obsessive tendencies deepened with the discovery of a new and irresistible subject matter: the feminine sex. Every day on his way to school Bibi passed beneath a billboard for Protectobane automobile finish, in which a smiling, bikini-clad model leaned against a red sports car, grasping a cylindrical, round-tipped Protectobane bottle with what seemed to Bibi to be an unusual degree of delight. It was twilight in the picture, and a full moon rose over a cluster of palm trees in the background. The message read:

THE MOON MAY WAX, THE MOON MAY WANE, BUT YOU DON'T HAVE TO WAX WITH PROTECTOBANE!

Bibi had passed beneath the sign every school day of his life, but as he grew older the image took on new meaning. It wasn't as though he had no other pictures of women to look at: there were magazines the boys passed around at school, movies and television, and plenty of other billboards. But there was something special about this one, though at first he couldn't say what it was. He stood for hours below it, enraptured; his schoolmates taunted him, and he was often late for class. Then one day Bibi discovered the source of his fascination. He was passing by with a neighbor boy when he stopped in mid-stride.

"Aw, Bibi," whined his companion. "You're not gonna stand there and stare at that thing again, are ya? You'll make us late."

His friend finally went on without him. What Bibi had noticed was a small thing: a detail the photographer had overlooked, or found too insignificant to retouch out of the picture. Both of the woman's hands were clasped around the Protectobane bottle, which was held just below the level of her navel—in a rather unnatural position, if Bibi thought about it. Her fingers were only partly visible, as her hands had been placed toward the rear of the bottle so the label might be more fully exposed. But when Bibi looked carefully at the second finger from the bottom, the ring finger of her left hand, he could just barely make out that part of it was missing. All the others were complete, but through some mishap or accident of birth this particular digit ended between the second and third knuckle, leaving a small but discernible stub.

And there was something about this partial finger that moved Bibi deeply, more deeply than anything had moved him before, moved him all the way through his flesh and into his bones and through his bones and into the marrow and through his marrow to whatever lay on the other side. It was a compassion for what he imagined she'd suffered, but also an excitement over her hidden difference, a difference he alone could recognize. His insides quivered so he could scarcely breathe and he felt as though he were attached to something from within, something he couldn't see but which tugged and pulled unceasingly now from some buried center of his being. He didn't understand it, and he certainly couldn't have explained it; but he suddenly felt as though he'd found something for which he'd been searching a very long time.

What bliss his fantasies of the Nine-fingered Woman brought to Bibi's solitary nighttime recreations! Her ivory skin, the golden tresses spilling across her shoulders, those long, perfect fingers—fingers with a space between them, like parentheses, just waiting to be filled by his boundless, overflowing love. Her caresses! Those perfect, partial caresses, all the more complete for the space inside them. And when, in the love nest of his mind, he gave her his own private Protectobane bottle to hold, what indescribable ecstasy!

In the newly sunlit world of his fancy, Bibi spun anguished, heroic tales in which his beloved found herself in precarious positions where he alone might be of assistance. An interview, for example, at a modeling agency:

"I'm sorry, ma'am, you are without a doubt the most beautiful woman I've ever met, but with that missing finger—" The interviewer, a big-city type with suit and cigar, leans back in his chair.

"Please, sir, I've been to every agency in the city. I wouldn't ask just for myself, but my mother is sick and I—" The Nine-fingered Woman's sea-green eyes well up with emotion.

"I'd like to help you, ma'am, I really would, but—"

"Hold on just a minute!" shouts Bibi, who happens to be waiting in the next room for an appointment on some unrelated matter. He shoulders his way through the door to face his darling's tormentor. "Are you looking for just another pretty face, or someone who is truly unique?"

"Well, I—"

"Do you mean to tell me you're going to turn away the most beautiful woman in the country because of a single trivial defect?"

"I, well—"

"One that will inspire in the hearts of those few who notice it only the greatest sympathy, love, even admiration—"

"That is—"

"Admiration for a woman who doesn't fear to set her own standards of beauty, an inspiration for women everywhere who are tired of living up to impossible ideals of perfection, women who will emulate her, model themselves after her, purchase the products she represents with such undeniable candor and charm—"

"Enough, enough! We'll sign her on. We'll do it today!"

"Thank you, kind sir," says the Nine-fingered Woman, turning to Bibi with moist, grateful eyes as they descend the front steps of the building. "I don't know how I could ever thank you enough."

"Dinner?" replies Bibi, with impeccable savoir faire. "French Cordon Bleu?"

He even went so far as to imagine their wedding day, that magical moment when the priest would ask for the ring and Bibi, taking his beloved's hand in his and caressing what was left of her ring finger, would lovingly slide the band on the next digit over. Oh, she was perfect, flawless in every detail but one; and her partiality imposed a tortuous bondage on his love-smitten soul.

After a while, having grown into a relatively normal fifteen-year-old boy, Bibi felt the need for actual flesh-and-blood companionship. There being no young women in the neighborhood with missing digits, he had to settle for what was available. Though he could hardly have been called handsome, with those elongated features and that dark maze of hair which, do as he might, stubbornly maintained a mind of its own, Bibi's bright intensity and his unblinking, blue-eyed gaze brought him more than his share of admirers.

He went through the usual series of adolescent romances, but after the thrill wore off he found something lacking in all of them. One girl laughed too loudly; another, not enough; a third, at the wrong things. One had a peculiar nasal quality to her voice; another, the irritating habit of repeating everything he said; the next, an unsettling tilt to her profile when viewed from a three-quarter angle. One way or another Bibi always had the sense that something was missing. He became distant; and at this point his young lovers often found him staring with strange intensity at their hands. In these moments the world felt more unreal to him than ever, and he despaired of ever understanding love.

Bibi slipped into a period of adolescent doldrums. Tall for his age, with gangly, oversized limbs that no longer quite seemed to belong to him, he roamed the city for hours—these were boom years now, the street corner crowds had vanished, and time no longer seemed in imminent danger of dying. He covered block upon block in lean, long-legged strides, face thrust into the wind, body tilting forward at the waist as though yearning to get on with it all—through the business district and into the suburbs, the mansions of the lakeshore and the tenements of the lower west end. He passed billboards, multiplied threefold since the election of the new president:

AMERICA: THE DREAM IS ALIVE. AMERICANS. BETTER THAN THE REST. MAKE MONEY, BE HAPPY: AMERICA!

He watched mothers with their children and farmers in their fields, executives and secretaries and shopkeepers; and he despaired of ever finding his place in it all.

"Mom," Bibi asked one morning, after one of his increasingly frequent nights of unsettling dreams, "aren't there *any* men in our family who didn't kill themselves?"

"Well," his mother took a faded black-and-white photo from a shoebox and handed it to him. "There is your crazy Uncle Otto. You remember him, I bet. Stopped by that summer on his way back from the Himalayas. You were probably six or so." She smiled, pulling a strand of hair back from her face and pinning it into her neat, newly-greying bun. "I suppose he's still in one piece, though I haven't heard from him in ages. He traveled the world for years, then made a fortune investing in futures on the money market, and finally went to prison on some kind of tax charge. Word has it he's moved out onto the Frontier, a place called Hope Valley, and started a junk farm. They say folks out there call him the Hope Valley Hubcap King. Apparently he's surrounded himself with a bunch of cranks and misfits who think he's some kind of holy man."

"The Frontier?" Bibi studied the picture. A large, rugged-looking fellow with sandy, disheveled hair and a hooped earring dangling from one earlobe stood grinning at the camera, arm draped across the shoulders of a much smaller Asian man dressed in a robe.

"That's Otto when he was in Mongolia or Tibet or someplace, trying to learn to levitate or some such thing." His mother sighed, studying the photograph. "Do you remember him?"

"He's not the kind of guy you forget."

Later that evening Bibi pulled the atlas from its place on the shelf and spent several hours poring over the two-page spread titled "America." But he was unable to find any trace of an area known as Hope Valley. His mother couldn't remember any more, and though he questioned everybody he knew on the subject, no one else could help him either.

Nearing his sixteenth birthday, Bibi entered a period of obsessive reading and deep thought. He considered the theory of continental drift: he could almost sense the plates of the earth shifting beneath his feet. He pondered notions of duality and opposition, left and right, right and wrong, and concluded that each was a side of a coin—*and you've got to have both,* he told himself, *before you can spend it.*

He reflected on the four-dimensional model of reality—he could practically feel the hole snipped out of space and time to accommodate him, and he informed anyone bold enough to ask that God, if He or She existed, must be something very much like an enormous pair of scissors.

To those who asked what he planned to do with his life, he replied: "I would like to understand Time, the Universe, and America."

But simple thought was not enough. In his attempts to know himself, Bibi dove to the innermost pit of his being where, groping about in the dark, he came upon the oddest, most chilling objects: clammy, fleshy nothings that had no names and were entirely beyond the realm of understanding. And having gotten there, he went deeper. He sensed an infinite openness just beyond the reaches of his perception, as though his mind were a single lighted room in a vast and darkened wilderness.

Somehow, he felt this openness was his true home.

He tried out his new insights on his companions. He and his latest girlfriend were sitting by a pond in the park when Bibi pointed out a water strider skating across the surface.

"See," he told her, "we're like those bugs, coasting along the surface of life, pretending it's solid, never dreaming there's another point of view from which, if we stopped even for an instant, we'd fall right through and drown."

"Bibi, you're weird." She tousled his jungle of hair. "Kiss me."

He did.

When he was a child he roamed the neighborhood; as an adolescent he roamed the city; on the day he turned eighteen he left home and began to roam America.

Bibi's mother embraced him as he stood upon the doorstep, face pointed into the wind, rucksack in hand.

"I don't know what you expect to find out there"—her hands twisted about the hem of her apron—"but whatever you do, don't kill yourself."

"Don't worry, Mom, I won't."

"Promise?"

"Promise."

Bibi kissed his mother's cheek and, with a gallant wave of his hand, was off. With no career prospects and no worldly goals to distract him, he'd become possessed in the past months of a fierce, new sense of certainty.

He had to find his Uncle Otto's hubcap ranch.

2.
BABIES
AND DEAD MEN

Bibi stopped on his way out of town to look up the cousin who'd given his mother her last news of the Hubcap King, but arrived to find the house empty and windows boarded up.

"Yeah, I remember her," a neighbor told him. "Married a lumberjack, went off to live on the Frontier."

"The Frontier?" said Bibi. "Do you know any more than that?"

"Only thing I remember is the guy had a foreign name, ended in -ski or something—and he must've stood nearly seven feet tall."

Bibi shouldered his rucksack and headed for the edge of town. Where the houses thinned out he found a pothole-ridden road that ascended into the foothills, and stuck out his thumb. After twenty minutes or so a battered pickup braked to a halt. The driver, a drooping, sallow-faced man, greeted him without much enthusiasm: "Where you headed?"

"The Frontier," answered Bibi.

"Pointless destination. But then, aren't they all?" The man paused, as though needing to summon his strength, then leaned over to unlock the passenger door. "Got business out there?" he asked as Bibi climbed in.

In answer, Bibi pulled out the photo his mother had given him. "Ever seen this guy?"

The man shook his head.

"He's my Uncle Otto," Bibi said as they pulled onto the blacktop. "The Hope Valley Hubcap King. I'm trying to find him."

"Hope," responded the driver, "does not exist."

They rode in silence for a while after that. The road climbed and twisted; Bibi watched as the town shrank to a child's toy and ravines with rushing streams opened beneath the edges of their tires. The pickup coughed and sputtered.

"Know much about the Frontier?" Bibi asked.

The driver shrugged. "It's a dangerous place. Wild animals, trackless wastes, cults—who knows what all." Bibi couldn't help but notice that the man's breath whistled every time it came in or out of his chest, and his tight, thin lips seemed to part reluctantly, enough to let each phrase out and no more.

"But then, the whole thing's dangerous, isn't it?" the fellow went on. "Why, the moment we come into this world we start dying. Mothers kill children by giving birth to them. Ever wonder why babies are always crying when they're born? They know the score." Bibi wasn't sure how to respond. A sheen of sweat was forming on the man's brow, and he couldn't help but think that his pale, almost jaundiced skin had an unusually coarse texture. *A soggy face,* thought Bibi, *a terry cloth face; a face for wiping one's hands on and throwing away.*

"That's why anytime I see a baby"—the driver yanked the pickup around a curve—"all I can think is, 'you may be cute now, but you're going to get old and ugly and mean—and then you're gonna die.'" The tires emitted a squeal of protest and a passing semi sounded its horn.

"But surely," Bibi objected, edging as close to the passenger door as he could, "you must believe what happens *between* birth and death might be of some value—"

"Ha!" The man fixed Bibi with his pale, fierce gaze. "Do you have any idea what happens to us at the moment of death? We lose all control of our bodily functions!" His lips curled to a snarl. "From the womb to the tomb. Want to know what kind of world this is? Ask babies and dead men."

They rode the rest of the way in silence, save for the whistling of the man's breath, until they pulled over beside a clay lumber road and the driver said, "This is as far as I go."

"Thanks," said Bibi, relieved to find himself stepping down from the cab onto firm ground. He could find no way to avoid shaking the fellow's outstretched hand. It was like touching a damp washcloth, or a fish.

"Good luck," said the man. "You're going to need it."

"By the way," Bibi asked as he was about to pull away, "have you ever met a lumberjack, seven feet tall, name ends in -ski?"

The Man with the Terry Cloth Face looked at him. "They all end in -ski," he said mysteriously, then pulled back onto the road, pickup backfiring and spitting smoke.

Bibi walked ten miles along the logging road through deepening forest, relieved to be on his own, yet unable to shed a lingering feeling of unease, as though the Terry Cloth Man had left behind a sort of residue that clung to his skin. Late that afternoon he came out onto a hilltop. Land stretched before him, ridge upon ridge folded into infinity. He could feel the vastness, the sheer unknown of it, making a hollow place in the pit of his stomach. *The Frontier!* Surely Hope Valley lay somewhere among those hills and forests, waiting to be discovered.

Bibi watched as the shadows lengthened, until the sun slipped over the horizon and the last light swirled slowly down behind it like water into a drain. The stars came into existence one by one and the smooth flat disc of the moon glided into the sky without making a sound. At last he fixed a meal of bread and peanut butter, spread out his bedroll at the edge of a stream, and lay down to sleep.

But a breeze blew up, with a wind behind it, and more wind behind that. The trees swayed back and forth, trunks creaking, branches rattling. The sounds blended with the rush of the stream, and in the commotion Bibi began to hear voices: chuckles, cries of children, distant shouts. Breath tightening in his chest, he raised his head to look, but all he saw was forest and moonlight. The wind intensified, hurling the treetops back and forth, branches twisting like gnarled fingers trying to pluck the moon from the sky. He tried methods to calm himself, but even his fantasies of the Nine-fingered Woman were of no use. More than once he dozed off, only to drift into a world of uneasy dreams, where the trees shook so violently they appeared to be laughing, and disconnected words reverberated again and again through the darkness:

babies and . . .

             dead men

      babies

            and dead

                 men

lights and ships and . . .

                is   this

         all I am?

  just killing

        time I suppose

              life was the death of

me

why

bother?

o

l

d and ugly and mean old and ugly and mean old ugly

            better before I knew so much

       and   and   and . . .

die?

Bibi awoke with a start just before dawn, roused by the silence that came in the wake of the storm, and surprised to find himself still in one piece. A receding dream, like a wave sliding back to sea, left a single image stranded in his mind: the face of his father as he lay beneath the rosebushes, twin orbs of his eyes staring upward, merging inseparably into Bibi's own. Bibi lay there for a long while, edging his fingers over the roughness of his scar in the darkness, before he rose at first light, packed his gear, and pushed on into the wilderness.

Bibi used the next days of solitude to expand his investigations into the nature of things. He hurled sticks toward the heavens and noted how they always fell to earth. He studied flora and fauna and geologic formations. He pondered time, existence, and destiny, keeping track of his insights in a journal he'd brought along for the purpose.

Imagine, he wrote, *if dead people were as useful and long-lasting as dead trees. If like old oaks, they still stood in place twenty years after the event, so a visitor might point to the figure in the front yard and ask, "who'd that used to be?" and you'd answer, "Mr. Smith, the mailman," or "my Aunt Sarah."*

What if we could use these former friends and relatives, like trees, to construct our homes? What was once Cousin Charlie could be a mantelpiece or a door frame—a far more productive use of the dead than to put them in the ground where they do nobody any good!

Below that he noted: *If twelve generations of Browns wasted their lives, at least they would not have wasted their deaths.*

A notion even the Terry Cloth Man might appreciate!

In the evenings, as he lay with his rucksack beneath his head and watched while the stars did nothing in particular, Bibi's thoughts often turned to the Hubcap King. He'd light a candle stub and, fishing the old photo from his pocket, study it for a long while in the flickering glow. Images assembled in his mind as he lay there, like snapshots fallen from his mother's shoebox:

His father and mother, side by side on a red velvet divan. A much younger Bibi, seated on the carpet at their feet. Above, eleven portraits of Brown ancestors tremble against the wall as his Uncle Otto, weather-worn and red-faced, far too large for their living room, paces about, waving his arms, spinning an assortment of tales too outlandish to disbelieve: treks over the deserts of Senegal and Afghanistan, expeditions across Borneo, skirmishes with smugglers and brushes with pirates. Once he was carried for weeks on a litter through the jungles of New Guinea after losing one of his planar digits in a misunderstanding with a crocodile; another time he narrowly escaped death by riding out of a Nepali blizzard on a stolen yak. Rumor had it—and Otto himself hinted—that he stumbled on schools of hidden knowledge in his travels, and trained for years with masters of the occult, the arcane, and the esoteric.

Bibi recalled the celebratory mood of that visit: never had he seen his mother so vibrant as when she danced the Maori fire dance with his uncle across the living room rug; and never again (but once) would he see his father's eyes so wide as when he accepted his brother's homecoming present—an enormous stuffed anteater from the Gobi Desert.

Later, he remembered, there was a sort of magic show, in which the inimitable Otto demonstrated his mastery over the causal plane by dematerializing and rematerializing various household objects: a pen, a spoon, and finally, one of Bibi's mother's treasured diamond earrings—though this last item, to her dismay, the magician was never able to restore to earthly existence.

Otto ended the evening by reading everyone's palms, a skill he learned from an Iraqi sailor in Maricopa. Bibi could no longer recall what he'd told his mother and father—but his own fortune swept back to him now across the intervening gulfs of time. His uncle, after studying the boy's palm for a long while, had looked up with his blue eyes glittering, lamplight dancing from his single hooped earring, and pronounced: "You are destined to become a very wise man, or die a very violent death, or both."

.   .   .

One afternoon, perhaps a week after he'd entered the wilderness, Bibi rounded a bend in a trail and came upon a man lying facedown on the ground. The stranger was sprawled before a mound of stones nearly as tall as Bibi was, with his arms stretched toward it as though in a gesture of supplication. Identical mounds, spaced every ten feet or so, extended into the distance as far as he could see.

At first Bibi thought perhaps the fellow had been hurt and was unable to move; then he noticed his head lifting and dropping ever so slightly as he lay there, and it became gradually clear that he was speaking:

"Oh Keeper of Granite," he seemed to be mumbling, "Lord of Stone . . ."

Bibi edged closer.

"We who are but ore in your veins . . ."

"Excuse me—" Bibi began.

"Pebbles to your grandeur!"

Bibi wondered if the fellow was perhaps ill, and had fallen into a delirium. "Mister?"

"Minerals of righteousness . . ."

"Are you—?"

"Paleomorphic . . . igneousness of mercy—"

"Pardon me—"

Abruptly, the man leapt to his feet. His face was twisted into a snarl of fury. He glared at the intruder and emitted a fierce, guttural cry. Then he seized a rock from the pile and hurled it point-blank at Bibi's head.

And the world was gone and Bibi dropped to the ground like a stone.

Bibi swam back to consciousness through a sea of disconnected images: hubcaps . . . clock faces . . . the moon—the world shivered, shook itself, and hardened back into its accustomed shape. He awoke to the sound of a woman's voice and the feeling of a damp cloth against his forehead. There was a swollen area close to his right temple, and he winced when she touched it.

"There, there," she told him, face folding into a network of furrows as she swabbed at him. "Sit quiet while I clean this up." She spoke to someone whom Bibi couldn't see. "That's an awful nasty knock he's got, Clifford. You've got to learn to control that temper."

"I hit the boy with The Source," Bibi heard a voice come back in a mournful tone. "I shouldn'a done that."

"No, you shouldn't have."

"But he snuck up on me all of a sudden—how was I to know he wasn't one of them government geologists, or some danged prospector?" The voice dropped to a sulky drawl. "Aw, Mae, you know how I get when I'm genuflecting. I didn't mean to hurt the boy."

"Well, next time you don't mean to hurt somebody, I suggest you hit them with a softer manifestation of The Source than the one you chose." The woman stood back to examine her handiwork. "Lucky he's young and hard-headed. Ought to be fine in a couple of days."

The man came closer and looked down at Bibi. "Sorry, kid. You kinda startled me."

Bibi was surprised to see that the fellow actually had a rather kind face, with crinkled-up eyes and a grey mustache that swooped low above his lips as though threatening to engulf them. Through the collar of his shirt Bibi glimpsed a neckband of uncut stone. Then a sort of white mist came across the scene, and everything went blank once more.

Idleness did not suit Bibi's nature, but for the next few days, whenever he tried to stand up he fell down again. The man and woman were kind to him. Mae brought him soup, and Clifford made a point of coming in every few hours to see how he was doing. Still, time might have hung heavily upon him but for the one compensation of his condition: the strange dreams it brought on.

In one such vision, Bibi was driving through a graveyard in a black limousine. On a grassy hillside along the road were gathered hundreds of white cats. As he watched, the animals arranged themselves into letters, white against green, spelling out the message:

WELCOME BACK SOCIALITES

Bibi asked the driver to pull over, but he scrambled up the hill only to find the creatures turning into scraps of paper and blowing away.

In another dream, Bibi found himself in a library where he'd been told there were books with the answers to every conceivable question; but on pulling the volumes from their shelves, he found they were written in a variety of unfamiliar languages, none of which he could decipher.

But stranger than any dream was the scene below Bibi's window, beside which he often sat as he became stronger. His room looked down upon a village square, lined with buildings of rough-cut stone; along the streets were mounds of rock like those he'd seen along the path, but spaced more closely, so passersby could scarcely thread their way between them. And whenever any of the citizens came abreast of one of these, they prostrated themselves before it. As a result, it took them forever to get anywhere. Bibi would nod off and emerge from another dream only to see the same people who'd been beneath his window a half hour earlier, now just a few yards further along.

"What on earth is going on?" he asked Mae one afternoon.

"In times past," she explained, "we didn't have The Source gathered together like we do now. In those days we used to bow before every manifestation—each rock, stone, or pebble we came across, no matter how small. Why, in some places The Source was so thick upon the ground our people had to crawl along in constant worship. We rarely got home for meals. Folks were chronically malnourished—some even died. At last our elders came up with the notion of gathering all manifestations of The Source together in certain key places; and in a few years our way of life had been revolutionized. Oh, we still make pilgrimages to outlying areas to gather those particles that may have strayed and wish to return home. But in the main, our work is done. We pride ourselves on having found a practical means of carrying on our faith!"

After several days Bibi was back on his feet. Mae and Clifford, who'd grown fond of him during his visit, tried to convince him to stay.

"Y'see," Clifford said, "we don't have any kinfolk of our own—"

"And with that hard head of yours," finished Mae, "you're practically a manifestation of The Source yourself!"

But Bibi explained that he was on a search of his own.

"Hubcaps?" responded Clifford. "Some people have the most peculiar notions."

That evening the three sat on the back porch of the cottage, drinking sarsaparilla tea and looking out over the night.

"Y'see those stars?" asked Clifford, gazing into the spangled sky. "Thousands of 'em. Millions. Count 'em sometime." He took a long pull from his drink. "Now no one can say for sure whether there's life on any of the worlds out there. But one thing's certain—there's rocks. Rocks are the building blocks of the universe!"

The next morning Bibi rose early and bid a rather wistful farewell to his hosts; for during the course of his stay he'd grown fond of them, too.

"Guess you're not the kind to gather any moss, are you?" Mae said as she kissed him on the cheek.

"You'll find that Hubcap fella of yours," Clifford told him. "I'm sure of it. Remember—with The Source on his side, David overcame Goliath!"

With that Bibi embraced them both, hoisted his rucksack onto his shoulders once more, and moved on into the Frontier.

As the weeks went by, Bibi became more and more familiar with the wilderness, and ever more comfortable with his life there. Sometimes he'd be taken in for the night by a woodcutter and his family; or he'd come upon a native village, or a fur trapper's cabin, and share a meal in exchange for his company and news of the outside world. From these people Bibi learned to live off the land, to thread his way through the labyrinth of the forest without getting lost, to walk without making a sound. He became so quiet he could hear the trees breathing; so peaceful he could hear the moon rising. He finally grew so at home in the wilderness, and so silent, that he was able to hear the long slow thoughts of stones, which every hundred years manage to produce the single insight: "Here I am." At last he'd penetrated so far he could no longer find a trail, and days passed without a sign that humans existed at all.

Bibi was wandering through the forest on one such afternoon, as day tilted slowly toward evening. He strolled in the late, slanting sunlight across meadows and over streams, past trees whose trunks burst from the earth like barked, muscled arms, or the legs of titans: trees that had been here before the first of his ancestors, twelve generations ago, had come to America, and would remain long after the last Brown had vanished from the planet. And as darkness began to fall, a deep, indefinable ecstasy came over him. He'd seen stars ripple in a pool when a stone was tossed amongst them; tonight he felt he could ripple the stars in the sky, if only he could throw a stone far enough.

Bibi had just begun to think about stopping for the evening when he saw a light coming through the trees and decided to investigate. He'd walked no more than ten minutes when he emerged at the edge of a clearing, filled with men and machinery and high-intensity lamps that hurt his eyes.

As his vision adjusted, Bibi was stunned to find every trace of foliage removed from an area larger than many of the villages he'd visited in the past weeks. Bulldozers roved back and forth, uprooting stumps; men ran about with measuring tapes and instruments for gauging the lay of the land. Bibi finally found someone who wasn't too busy to talk with him: a tall man with an affable manner and a bit of tissue paper dangling from the end of his nose.

"What's all this?" Bibi asked.

"New development." The man drew a tissue from his pocket and emptied the contents of his sinuses into it. "Why, once we're finished, this is gonna be the largest shopping mall for miles."

"A mall?" Bibi stared at the clearing. "All the way out here?"

"Darn tootin'," said the man, then sneezed ferociously. "It's The Boom. Can't find enough space in the cities to put 'em all. Can't find the time, either. That's how come they've got us working all night in the middle of nowhere."

"Who's 'they'?" Bibi watched as a bulldozer moved into the space behind the man and slammed into a stump.

"Government Rural Renewal Project, of course. Why, this program's going to create jobs and homes for thousands!" The man wiped at his nose. "Doggoned hay fever. Hate these outdoorsy projects."

"Homes?" Bibi persisted. "But there aren't even any roads out here."

"We're building 'em." The fellow pointed to a growth of cattails at the clearing's edge. "Once that swamp's gone, this'll be one of the most exclusive communities in the country. 'Marshland Gardens' they're gonna call it."

Bibi noticed that the bulldozer behind the man had ground to a halt. He watched as the operator felt under the side and came up with his hand dripping with oil. "Dang!" he exclaimed, and walked over to a group of men at the edge of the site. They gesticulated spiritedly.

"Marshland Gardens?" repeated Bibi, not feeling altogether certain the forest needed renewal. But his companion had turned away to watch the action on the other side. The men, carving the air with near-frantic motions, had produced handheld radios from somewhere and now shouted into them with excitement.

Bibi's heart felt like an anvil in his chest. He turned to go, but then thought of something else. "I don't suppose you've ever run across a seven-foot-tall lumberjack, name ends in -ski?"

The man laughed. "Get a grip, buddy. There's no lumberjacks out here anymore. You've been in the boondocks too long!"

"What do you mean?"

"It's all being automated. They got these new machines, just mow the stuff down like grass." The man made a buzzing sound and passed the flat of his hand along the tree line at the far side of the site. Meanwhile the crew had driven another bulldozer over and were attaching a hook to the disabled one.

"Wait," Bibi called as the fellow walked off to join them. "Where'd all the lumbermen go?"

"Seems like I heard something about relocating them all to the desert. Big industrial projects out that way. If you're smart you'd head there yourself. Jobs with a future—it's the new Frontier!"

Bibi watched him walk away. The men around the bulldozers were upset. They'd hooked the second machine to the first, but now loud groaning sounds were coming from its engine. As Bibi looked on, the second bulldozer emitted several piercing squeals, then a bang and a cloud of smoke, and relaxed into position beside the other.

"Dad gum-it!" Bibi heard one of the men shout through the night.

Which, as one might recall, was identical to the message left by Andrew P. Brown, failed gold miner and Bibi's distant forebear, who'd drowned himself in the Placer River at the end of the great rush. "Dad gum-it," his note read simply, in a large looping scrawl pressed onto a scrap of paper with a burnt match head. "Sincerely yours, Andrew Philifor Brown."

3.
GOD

All along the western reaches of the forest echoed the hum and grind of machinery. Rights had been traded; leases had been negotiated; agreements had been reached. Roads stretched across the back country like strands of an enormous web. Acres of woodland fell like grain before the scythe, and in their place appeared shopping establishments and townhouse developments with names like "Frontier Estates" and "Le Bog." There was nothing for Bibi to do but move west, with heavy heart, onto the barren lands of the flats toward the Great Divide, which nobody wanted—yet.

"Wouldn't head that way on foot if I was you," the foreman of a road crew told him, as Bibi passed into the thinning western boundary of the forest. "Flats go on for hundreds of miles—not a town or a tree or a road in sight. If the coyotes don't get you, the Bushes of Boredom will."

"Bushes of Boredom?" repeated Bibi. He'd come too far to let folk tales stop him now.

"Believe me if you like, but they've been the ruin of many a more intrepid traveler than yourself. If I were you I'd take a bus."

But Bibi had no money for a bus and besides, if he stayed on the highway he knew he'd never really see anything. And how did he know Hope Valley wasn't somewhere out on the plains, waiting to be discovered?

As he moved west the forest thinned to groves separated by meadows, then to green ribbons along riverbeds, then to nothing but grasslands. Days passed without a hillock or hummock, a single dale or dell breaking the perfect three-hundred-and-sixty-degree expanse of openness. Bibi lived on crayfish he found in creekbottoms, groped for roots and tubers in the dark loam of the earth, roasted grasshoppers over fires of antelope dung while the moon hung in the sky like a great silver ball—and never for an instant was he bored. Strange, he thought, that the man seemed so concerned. When one had the delights of nature, plenty of food for thought, and all the time in the world, what was there to fear from boredom?

Then the bushes began to appear. First one, then another: waist-high, brown, and thoroughly unobjectionable. In the beginning, in fact, Bibi rather enjoyed the variety they gave to the formerly undifferentiated prairie. But then they began to multiply. Every day there was less grass and water, and more heat and dust; and soon the bushes were everywhere. The sky filled with a haze that made everything blend together; the sun burned more fiercely by the hour. Every step became an effort, and Bibi's head filled with a daze as thick as the bushes, those endless identical bushes that now filled every scrap of space from horizon to horizon.

At first he sought methods of distraction. He tried counting bushes, but found himself unable to concentrate after the first five hundred or so. He tried fantasy, but even the Nine-fingered Woman could do nothing to arouse his interest. He constructed theories on the nature of monotony, but became too bored to follow his own line of thought.

Finally life became so tedious Bibi could scarcely make the effort to lay out his bedroll at night. Long after dark he'd find himself still standing in the same place he'd stopped at sundown. If by some act of will he forced himself to a horizontal position, it took hours to get back on his feet in the morning. Time passed; he moved in such a state of ennui that he had no idea how much ground he was covering, what direction he was headed in, or why. Days passed when he was unable to remember his own name.

At last the afternoon came when Bibi stopped moving altogether. He had not an atom of will remaining, only a boredom as vast and omnipresent as the bushes themselves. He stood in place through that night, till his legs gave out and he sagged to earth; and he lay beneath the sun all the next day, with only an occasional parched and dreary thought staggering across the landscape of his consciousness to let him know he was still alive:

> *Now I'll never find the Hubcap King.*
>   (Long pause)
> *So who cares?*
>   (Longer pause, punctuated by a groan)
> *I guess I'm going to die.*
>   (Interminable pause)
> *Ah, well. Death can't possibly be any more boring*
>   *than this.*

And here Bibi's story would surely have ended, if not for a dream that came upon him in the early hours the next morning. He was drifting through a netherworld of shapes and shadows, of twilight and spirits, a cobwebby land where light itself was unheard of, when all at once a tremendous crash reverberated through the darkness. There came another crash, and another, so powerful the earth trembled with the sound. Then a series of flashes lit up the universe, a roar washed in like a cataract, and

Bibi awoke to find himself in the middle of—water! Wet, wonderful water, flowing across his body, soaking into his skin, penetrating all the way, it seemed, to his bones.

Wetness, he thought. *I am wet!* He rolled onto his back and let the rain run into his mouth.

Suddenly, more than anything he'd ever wanted, Bibi wanted to live.

When sunrise came Bibi rose, covered in mud and soaked through from one end to the other, and there it was: the Great Divide. The mountains stood in a jagged line across the horizon, looming above the plains like the spires of gothic novels or of dreams. In the early light they stood out with startling clarity, as though transmitted directly to mind without need of the senses. They seemed so close Bibi could practically hear them ringing out like bells beneath the hard blue; so near he could almost smell the pine upon their slopes.

A day of walking brought him into the foothills. Piñon appeared on the hillsides, thickening to forests of spruce and ponderosa; then the ground tilted to vertical and Bibi found himself climbing into the sky. And when at last he emerged into the high country above tree line, a profound enchantment overtook him. Bibi watched from cloud-wreathed summits as the sun sank to the horizon and the sky, turning colors it had never imagined, startled itself with its own boldness and blushed a deeper red. He watched the moon rise, immaculate as bone china, felt his mind stretching out to enclose the entire star-strewn universe. Out here he could feel the earth turning, the law of gravity, all the invisible, ineffable mysteries of the world; and he often had the sense that his mind was hovering just at the edge of understanding, and anything—a thunderclap, a shout—might make it all drop into place.

·   ·   ·

Bibi had been in the mountains no more than a week when his progress was halted by an enormous wall of rock that extended as far as he could see in either direction. A thousand feet high, composed of pure granite, it was strangely free of fissures or other handholds that might allow him to climb it. He roamed its base, finding almost invisible cracks and protuberances that provided a temporary grip; once he even managed to make it halfway up its face, to hang giddy and exuberant five hundred feet above the valley floor. But these avenues always gave out and he found himself again making the perilous descent to the ground below.

Bibi sat one morning, several days after he'd reached the impasse, at the edge of a pond at the foot of the cliff. Munching at the clump of mugwort that was to be his only breakfast, he was reflecting on the words of Gregor Samson Brown, failed writer and bodybuilder, whose last message to the world had been: "Why bother?" For the first time in his life, Bibi felt his ancestor might have been right.

He sat a while and mused in this vein, rubbing along the edges of his scar, and watching a small waterfall at the base of the cliff empty itself into the pond. It was one of those flows that do not drop down the full face of a slope, but burst from the surface partway: in this case, through an aperture scarcely wider than a man's shoulders. And all at once it came to him: *Rational thinking has done nothing to get me past the barrier. The only way out is to take the path of complete insanity.*

Bibi crossed to the far side and scrambled up a scree slope to the crevice. It was late in the season and the water was only six inches or so deep; by lying with his belly submerged he found he could just barely worm his way into the opening. It was slick and dark and cold inside, and thoroughly unpleasant.

Inching his way back out, Bibi wrapped his journal in four layers of plastic bread bags and replaced it in his rucksack, then scrunched the entire arrangement into as small a bundle as possible and wrapped it with twine. Attaching a line five feet in length from his belt to a strap of his pack, he pronounced himself ready to make the ascent.

The crevice slanted into the cliff at perhaps a thirty-degree angle before beginning to steepen. Having no light, Bibi was forced to wriggle upward in absolute darkness, dragging his rucksack on the line behind him. He held position by wedging his arms against the tunnel walls, craning his head back to keep it clear of the flow. Even so, there were moments when the water, cresting over some unseen obstruction, spilled directly into his face, so that for long minutes he pushed forward in gushing, airless blackness without knowing when he might draw his next breath. At other points his body blocked the flow at a turn in the passage till the rising tide threatened to submerge him. Every so often his rucksack hooked on an obstacle and he had to back down to free it; once he lost his grip and slid thirty feet or more down the blackened corridor before managing to stop himself.

Then the cold began to set in. In the beginning Bibi was able to shrug the sensation off; but soon his muscles commenced to quiver, and then to shake; and before long his entire body was quaking uncontrollably. His teeth clattered and pains shot through his muscles, as though white-hot icicles were being forced into them. Before long he was sliding two feet back for every three he went forward.

It was at that point that the lethargy overtook him. First Bibi's muscles grew numb, turning to icy blocks of stone he dragged along by sheer will. He became relaxed; and oddly enough, all he wanted to do in that clammy cavern in the heart of the earth was to stop and take a nap. But every time he faltered his face dropped into the frigid flow, or his body lost its grip and he slid backward in darkness, and he'd have to command his sodden will to take hold of his reluctant limbs and thrust him forward once more.

This had been going on for some time when the hallucinations started. Bibi glimpsed sudden flashes of light, like a Fourth of July display; then sinister, hovering shapes that blocked out the brightness. His father's face appeared, eyes bulging and distended; then his grandfather's; then that of every ancestral Brown, reeling back through the ages. Finally, and most horrifically, there came the leering, tortured image of the Man with the Terry Cloth Face, looming wetly above him. Remembering the photo of the Hubcap King, which he'd wrapped securely in several sandwich bags and placed in his breast pocket, Bibi touched his fingers to the spot; this seemed to restore his strength. And so he pushed on.

After a time the scene became suffused with a comforting glow, so that for a moment Bibi thought he was glimpsing the gates of eternity. But then the passage began to level out and the light focused to a luminous oval at the center of his vision. As though propelled by some unseen force, Bibi thrust his way into it.

He tumbled out the other side, to land in the middle of a stream in the impossibly bright and blinding sunlight. Rising to his feet, Bibi experienced a brief moment of triumph and exaltation. Then he staggered to a nearby sandbar and collapsed into a sleep as black and deep as the cavern itself.

Sometime near sunset, still shivering and wearing every bit of still-damp clothing he owned, Bibi clambered up a rocky slope to see where he was. He paused by an outcrop of boulders to take in the view, and found below him the most splendid valley imaginable. Twin ridges swept down like tree-covered arms to embrace its verdant floor. A meadow, dotted with clumps of aspen and laced with meandering streams, lay cupped in the bottom. And at the center was a town, made miniature by distance, topped by two high-steepled churches.

That night Bibi dreamed of a land of no shadows. Nowhere—not under trees, or beneath stones, or even in mine shafts—was there the slightest trace of darkness.

•   •   •

Fall was in the air. The wind was up, and it had a bite to it; and as Bibi sauntered down the incline into the valley he noticed the first aspen beginning to change color. He was passing through a grove of them, all green and gold and shimmering with light, when he came suddenly upon a man on his hands and knees beneath the trees. The fellow held a magnifying glass in one hand and a pair of tweezers in the other, and examined the leaf litter with such fearsome concentration he scarcely seemed to notice Bibi's arrival.

"Good morning!" Bibi exclaimed, for it was a buoyant day and he was in a buoyant mood.

The fellow paid him no mind. He wore a black greatcoat, split at the tails, and as he rooted through the leaves he reminded Bibi of nothing so much as an oversized insect—a beetle, perhaps.

Bibi tried another tack. "I don't suppose this is Hope Valley?"

The man emitted a sigh, laid his magnifying glass on the ground, and turned to face the intruder. His eyes were bulbous, and they peered from beneath dark, beetled brows; it took very little imagination for Bibi to picture a pair of antennae waving about his head.

"No, it is not," he replied shortly, and went back to his examination of the humus.

Bibi sat back on his heels and watched. Every so often the man found something of interest. He picked up such items, invisible to his onlooker, with his tweezers, examined them through the magnifier with a scowl, and dropped them into a vial he produced from a pocket in his coat. After a time Bibi's curiosity got the better of him.

"What are you looking for?" he asked.

"God, of course!" snapped the man, without looking up.

Bibi watched a while longer, but as there seemed to be no more information forthcoming, he rose to go. He'd traveled no more than a few steps, however, when he heard the fellow's voice call out: "Hold on just a minute!"

"Excuse me?"

"Strangers are not allowed in town without an escort." The Beetle Man stabbed at the soil with his tweezers. "Aha!" he cried, and lifted another invisible morsel into the vial.

"I just wanted to get some supplies," Bibi explained. "I'm looking for my Uncle Otto, you see, and I—"

"There's no Ottos here." The man glared at him. "How'd you find your way in here anyway?"

"Through an underground stream channel."

"I thought they'd gotten those all sealed up." The fellow's jaws worked back and forth like a set of mandibles, as though he were chewing up all the leftover words he'd thus far avoided speaking. He sighed. "All right. As a man of God I suppose I'm obliged to be charitable. I'll take you into town and get you what you need if you promise to leave first thing tomorrow morning."

Bibi followed as his guide led the way through the aspen grove and over a stream, then scuttled out onto a hillside where the wind flapped his coat so violently that for a moment Bibi imagined he was going to fly away. The village was visible now, a tidy collection of red and black buildings tucked into a fold between hills—almost too tidy, Bibi thought.

"What's the name of your community?" he asked.

"*We* call it Smallville," answered the Beetle Man.

"Who is 'we'?"

"The Church of God the Minuscule, of course." He paused long enough to grace Bibi with an ironic bow. "Reverend H. R. Small, at your service." Then he was off again.

"God the Minuscule?" Bibi persisted, trotting to keep up. "But—could you tell me something about your beliefs?"

"Beliefs?" exploded the reverend. "Other religions deal in beliefs, son. We deal in certainty!" He glared at Bibi from beneath brows as dark as thunder. "Our creed has been verified by years of research. We are now certain, beyond the shadow of a doubt, that the reason for God's apparent absence on this planet is that he's too small to be perceived."

"Too small?" replied Bibi. "But then . . . why do you go on looking?"

"As an act of faith, of course. Surely you believe in faith?"

"Well yes, but . . ."

"There you have it."

Bibi wasn't quite sure what he had, but he was fated to carry on in ignorance, as the Beetle Man dismissed all further questions with a contemptuous wave of his hand.

After ten minutes or so they topped a hill and came once more in sight of the town. As they drew nearer, Bibi again had the undeniable sensation that there was something wrong about the place, though he could not have said what it was. Then all at once it came to him: not only were red and black the dominant colors of the buildings—they were the only colors, and never did they mix. Each was clustered with others of the same hue in an erratic checkerboard pattern that extended throughout the village. Not only that, but as they approached he could make out light-colored strands, like bits of spiderweb, that seemed to stretch in and along the streets; and the walls of the houses, on closer inspection, were marred by an assortment of odd marks or smears.

Then they rounded a curve and passed through a stone entryway; and Bibi stepped into a town divided. The strands he had seen from above proved to be a bright webbed fabric, like a tennis net but higher, that stretched along the center of the main avenue, splitting it into halves. Similar barriers wove in and around the side streets, separating red buildings from black; and as they drew nearer the marks on the walls resolved into words:

Minis Eat Dirt!
Humos Go Home!
God Is No Small Matter!
God Is No Big Thing!

"Spiritual graffiti!" exclaimed Bibi.

"Damned Humos." Reverend Small's eyes narrowed.

"Humos?"

"Church of God the Humongous." The reverend pointed to the nearer of the two churches Bibi had spotted from above. Through the maze of nets and buildings Bibi glimpsed an enormous telescope that jutted through the roof, pointing to the sky. The Beetle Man snorted. "The morons believe God is too big to be detected!"

They walked on along the avenue. The buildings on Bibi's side were small, squat, and uniformly dark, save for spatterings of light-colored graffiti. They hugged the ground like anthills, with tiny windows scarcely a hand's width across, and doorways so low the owners had to stoop over at the waist to get through them. There were businesses and eateries—the "Small Beer Tavern" and "Mustard Seed Cafe" seemed to Bibi to be the most popular. The citizens were dressed in dark cloaks and wraps against the fall air, and they strode along the sidewalk with as much intensity and sense of purpose as did their minister. The men wore undersized bowler hats that they doffed as they passed, mumbling "Afternoon, Reverend Small," but that otherwise perched uncertainly atop their heads, threatening to slide off at the least provocation.

The other side of the avenue was a different story. Through the maze of webbing Bibi glimpsed tall buildings of red brick, with broad windows and entrances that looked wide enough to admit a horse. Their denizens were clad in colors ranging from maroon to scarlet; and the men wore oversized tophats that they had to push back constantly to keep from slipping over their eyes. Horsecarts hurtled down both halves of the street, drivers on one side never so much as glancing at those on the other; while pedestrians, separated by millimeters of fabric, passed one another without a nod.

After a short walk the reverend halted before the Church of

God the Minuscule, distinguished by the monumental sculpture of a microscope in the square before it. An inscription on the platform read: "Deus Magnificus Ne Documentatus."

"What does it mean?" Bibi asked.

The Beetle Man assumed a reverent tone. "Even the greatest of lenses must fall short in the magnification of God."

He led the way up the steps. "You'll receive sanctuary here for the night. My daughter will pick up whatever supplies you need. You'll be escorted to the edge of the village in the morning; after that, I cannot be responsible for your safety." He graced Bibi with another bow. "I must leave you now. May your thoughts be small."

He scrambled down the steps, coattails flapping behind him, and was gone.

Stooping in through the low doorway, Bibi found he had the church all to himself. At first glance the place seemed ordinary enough—there were pews and altars and windows in all the usual places. But when Bibi looked more closely he realized the amorphous shapes on the stained glass were actually protozoan designs; and in a museum case along one wall he found an odd array of items, including a collection of antique buttons and thimbles, an assortment of stuffed hummingbirds, and thirteen pairs of bronzed baby shoes. Above the case was the inscription:

THOUGH THE MILLS OF GOD GRIND SLOWLY, YET THEY GRIND EXCEEDINGLY SMALL.

On a wall nearby was a portrait of Napoleon; on another, William Blake. And mounted to the back of each pew Bibi found a microscope, with a text no bigger than a matchbook attached to it by a string. When he squinted closely he was able to make out a title, *The Still Small Voice*, printed along one of the spines; but the words inside proved too tiny to read until he realized they were meant to be examined beneath the eyepiece.

Placing a page under one of the lenses, he turned a knob at the side, and the words came into focus:

For His invisible qualities are clearly
seen from the world's creation onward . . .

Bibi skipped a commentary on how many angels could fit on the head of a pin, and another on how many camels could pass through the eye of a needle. At the back of the volume he found a collection of hymns, with titles including "Behold Thy Diminutive Glory" and "O Tiny and Righteous." On the last page was the quote:

The little one will become a thousand, and the small
*   a mighty nation.*
Praise to the king of eternity, incorruptible, invisible,
the only God, be honor and glory forever and ever. Amen.

Beneath was inscribed:

The small shall inherit the earth.

It was only then that Bibi realized there was someone looking over his shoulder.

"Uh . . . hi," he said, putting the little text back in its place.

The newcomer was a woman, about Bibi's age, with flowing reddish-blond hair and vibrant green eyes. A medallion with an amoebic design dangled from a chain around her neck.

"Gloria Small," she said, extending her hand. Her voice was low and husky. "Looking for God?"

"Bibi . . . um, Brown," explained Bibi. "I was looking, but I'm not sure I was finding anything."

"Good. That's exactly what we like to hear. Now come along and I'll show you the laboratory."

She led him up a winding staircase to a low-ceilinged room

filled with piping and an assortment of flasks that overflowed with bubbling, undefinable substances. At its center was an ornate microscope that looked to Bibi as though it might have been left over from the Renaissance.

Gloria dipped some fluid onto a slide and placed it under the lens.

"Observe," she said.

Bibi did. All he saw were a bunch of flecks, oozing and tumbling beneath the eyepiece.

"What do you see?" Gloria asked him.

"A bunch of specks moving around a lot."

"What's between them?"

"Other, smaller specks."

"And between those?"

"Well," Bibi replied, after a pause, "it's hard to say. Between those specks are smaller specks and between those even smaller ones. But if you look closely enough beyond that I guess you see . . . nothing."

"That's it," exclaimed Gloria. "You've got it!"

"Got what?"

"Beyond the smallest specks you see nothing, because what is there is too small to be perceived. You've just proven the existence of God!"

Gloria went for supplies, the two spread a tablecloth on the lawn in the church garden, and for the first time in weeks Bibi ate his fill. Afterward he basked in the sun while Gloria filled him in on local culture.

"This ridiculous quarrel between the Minis and Humos gets worse every year. We're a small community, but we have to pay for two police forces, two hospitals—why, we're going bankrupt!"

"Sounds like everyone's making mountains out of molehills," responded Bibi, as he reached lazily for another handful of sesame seeds.

"Actually," replied Gloria, "molehills are far superior."

"But isn't there anything you share?"

"The asylum. It's too far up the valley to worry about and they're all too crazy there to care, anyway. Sometimes to decide matters of special urgency my father and the other reverend hold a joint tribunal. Never works out very well. Other than that, we're a divided people."

She looked extraordinarily compelling, Bibi thought, stretched out on the lawn with the sun in her hair and her green eyes gazing across at him. He found himself staring closely at her hands.

"What's it like," Gloria asked him, "on the outside?"

"You've never been there?"

"No one has. Other than a few passageways they keep filling up, there's no way in or out. You're the first visitor we've had in years."

"Well," said Bibi, "I'm not sure you're missing much. The mountains are beautiful, and the forests, but you've got all that here in the valley. There are cities with lots of excitement, but the people there never seem satisfied. Lots of them end up destroying themselves, if not outright then by drinking—or worse, by just not caring about anything. I have yet to meet anyone who is truly happy."

"Sounds pretty much the same as it is here."

"It's bigger," Bibi said. "Probably easier to be left alone."

Gloria cracked a hard-boiled egg carefully at the small end. "What do you want," she asked, "more than anything else in the world?"

"I'd like," answered Bibi, "to understand Time, the Universe, and America."

"I'll have to take *that,*" Gloria responded, reaching across his lap for the shaker, "with a grain of salt."

Shortly after dark Bibi retired to the room Gloria had made up for him, but the cot seemed to have been sized for a child, and he tossed about for a long time, while thoughts of his hostess's graceful form, blended with that of the Nine-fingered Woman, twisted around him like tangled sheets. He was just climbing up the stream channel again, pale ghostly crayfish scrambling across his flesh, when he was awakened by a faint knock at the door.

"Bibi," hissed a husky voice. "Open up. It's Gloria!"

"Huh? . . ." groaned Bibi, rubbing his eyes. "Is it time to go?" He reached for the lamp.

"No lights!" The door opened a crack and Gloria slipped in, more beautiful than ever, carrying a candle in an old-fashioned holder. Bibi's heart did somersaults, and for a moment he thought all his fantasies were about to come true. But then the door opened further and a man stepped into the room behind her, overturning an end table with his foot.

"Shhh," Gloria warned. The stranger stood erect and smoothed his clothes. "Bibi," she said, "I'd like you to meet my fiancé, Hugo."

There was something about the name that bothered Bibi, though he couldn't put his finger on it at first. "Bibi," he said, extending his hand. "Bibi Brown."

The man was powerfully but awkwardly built; he wore his body as though it were a suit of clothes several sizes too big for him. Horn-rimmed glasses made his eyes seem larger than they were, and his brows were knitted in a perpetual expression of consternation. He took Bibi's hand and squeezed so enthusiastically Bibi wasn't sure he'd ever have use of it again.

Bibi retrieved his mangled member and repeated the man's name, half to himself. "Hugo . . ." Something was still bothering him.

"Yes," confirmed the fiancé mournfully. "I'm a Humo."

"We thought," said Gloria, "you might like to see the telescope."

In the blackness of early morning the three slipped through the city. They clawed their way over netting, scaled walls, scrambled beneath hedges. They slid into a drainage ditch, scarcely daring to breathe, as a Mini police patrol passed. They cowered in a culvert while a Humo vigilante group prowled by. They dove into a trash bin as a Mini graffiti gang assaulted the Chamber of Commerce, and quivered beneath a carriage while a Humo group defaced the Department of Justice. They fled through backyards after Hugo knocked over a stack of trash cans and a succession of chihuahuas and great danes were unleashed upon them. At last they reached the Church of God the Humongous.

Hugo hustled them through the side door with a passkey—"Reverend's son," he grinned—then up a stairway, until they reached a room dominated by an immense telescope that jutted through an aperture in the ceiling. Taking a seat at its base, Hugo peered through the eyepiece, reached for a nearby joystick, and pulled it toward him. The platform revolved clockwise.

"Dang," exclaimed Hugo. "Wrong way!" He pushed the stick away and the platform revolved in the opposite direction. When it came to rest he stepped from his place and motioned to Bibi.

"It's all yours," he said.

Bibi peered into the eyepiece. Strangely, Hugo had picked a rather empty piece of sky to focus upon. Except for a few bright stars around the perimeter and an indeterminate number of faint ones receding into the distance, there was mostly darkness.

"What do you see?" Hugo asked him.

"Well," Bibi replied after a moment, "it's hard to tell, since between the stars are smaller ones, and fainter ones beyond, till you can hardly tell where they leave off and the sky begins. But if I look hard enough beyond it all, I guess I see—nothing."

Hugo leaned so close he was practically speaking in Bibi's ear. "Gloria and I are convinced," he said, "that the nothing you see here is exactly the same as the nothing you saw beneath the microscope."

"Meaning—?"

"Meaning," explained Gloria, "that God is both too large *and* too small to be perceived, and the Churches of God the Minuscule and God the Humongous are identical in their beliefs."

"Incredible," said Bibi. "Wait till you tell them. The two of you, through your love, will save Smallville!"

"Largemont," corrected Hugo.

"Are you crazy?" replied Gloria. "They'll put us away forever. We've got to get out of here."

"We want you to take us with you," said Hugo.

"To the outside?"

The two nodded solemnly.

"I'm not sure how I'm going to get there myself," replied Bibi. He thought for a moment. "I'll help you," he told them. "I'll show you how to get out the way I came. But I'm going to find a way down the other side."

The three slithered through the night to the outskirts of town, and there they parted ways. Bibi had drawn the lovers a map with detailed directions to the stream channel; from there they would be on their own. Bibi was more than a little sorry to see the pair go—in the course of the evening's adventures he'd grown rather fond of them. But their decisions were irrevocable. The three shook hands and split off into the darkness.

For the next few days Bibi hunted along the west end of the valley for a way out. He crept into crevices, crawled into caves, lowered himself down rock faces, and at each turn was met with frustration. On the third morning he awoke to find himself surrounded by two groups of men: one in red uniforms, the other in black. Struggling to an upright position, Bibi rubbed his eyes and blinked at the intruders. He wasn't sure what their presence indicated, but he was relatively certain it was not going to be to his liking.

The leaders of the groups cleared their throats, paused for emphasis, and announced simultaneously:

"WE HEREBY PLACE YOU, BIBI BROWN, UNDER ARREST FOR AIDING
AND ABETTING THE DISAPPEARANCE OF VARIOUS MEMBERS OF
OUR CITIZENRY, AS WELL AS ACTS OF HERESY, TREASON, AND
DIMENSIONAL INFIDELITY!"

With that, one took him by the left arm, and the other by the right, and they led him away.

Bibi had never been in jail before. He was placed in a cell without a window, furnished only with a rickety cot and a galvanized bucket for bodily excretions; and there he languished for more than a week.

The police had confiscated Bibi's journal with the rest of his possessions, and he had little to do but lie on his bunk and dwell on his misfortunes. His spirit alternately soared with wild, irrational hopes, then sank to the darkest caverns of despair:

> *One of the jailers will turn out to be my cousin's lumberjack husband, who'll orchestrate a breakout and set me free!*

> *I'll be tortured and convicted, and die an old man in prison without ever having understood a thing about anything.*

> *Hugo and Gloria will slip in under cover of darkness to release me!*

> *I'll be beaten, starved, and executed at dawn.*

When he was unlucky enough to slip into sleep, Bibi found his dreams populated by the panting, perspiring figure of the Terry Cloth Man, and the pop-eyed ghost of his father—not to

mention the rest of his unfortunate ancestors, in various states
of decomposition and dishevelment. To relieve his anxiety, Bibi
counted the stone blocks that made up his walls; 135 on the
south side, 144 on the west. He lost himself in continued fantasies in which Gloria Small and the Nine-fingered Woman had
merged into a single body. He formulated theories on the nature
of justice and retribution; but these respites were brief, and he
always returned to find himself in the same dank, inescapable
reality. In the end he spent hours simply tracing the outlines of
his Australoid scar with one fingertip, studying it as though he'd
never seen it before.

On the morning of the eleventh day, Bibi was awakened by
the rattling of keys at the barred door of his cell. Two guards
had arrived, one in a red uniform and the other in black. As
Bibi looked on the two, standing at either side of the door, and
without so much as a glance at one another, attempted to in-
sert their keys simultaneously into the lock. Their knuckles
crashed together. They scowled at each other in silence, then
tried again. Once more their knuckles intersected; this time
they frowned so fiercely Bibi thought they were going to come
to blows. At last the black guard stepped back and, with exag-
gerated courtesy, gestured toward the lock. The red one smiled
with equal irony, motioning the other forward. The first
scowled and gestured back. Then both dashed for the door.
Crashing into each other, they bounced backward and fell to
the floor. A spirited scuffle ensued, as each clawed his way toward the lock. Finally the black guard, pressing the other's face
to the ground with one hand, managed to get his key into the
aperture, and the door clicked open. With that the two scrambled to their feet, brushed themselves off, and announced simultaneously:

"HIGH TREASON SUSPECT BIBI BROWN IS HEREBY
SUMMONED TO TESTIFY BEFORE THE

SMALL (GUARD ONE)   LARGE (GUARD TWO)

VALLEY CITIZEN'S TRIBUNAL!"

The room in which Bibi's trial took place was the most out-landish he had ever seen. Half was painted red; the other, black. Strands of webbing divided the space, but for a narrow central corridor, in half. A separate audience sat on each side; one group in child-sized chairs that could have come from a kinder-garten; the other in seats so enormous they might almost be called thrones. There were two juries, two clerks, and two sets of guards with identically impassive faces; and at the head of the court stood two judge's benches of opposing hues.

After a moment the clerks rose to their feet and announced as one:

"LADIES AND GENTLEMEN, THE HONORABLE
H. R. SMALL!   J. B. BELLERUS!"

Doors opened at either side of the courtroom and in strode the justices. From the left entered Reverend Small, looking as irascible and insectile as ever. Through the other door shuffled a gangly, misshapen man who looked to Bibi like some enor-mous, wounded bird of prey. The two sat at their benches, pounded gavels simultaneously, and announced:

"COURT IS NOW IN SESSION!"

Bibi's attention was taken by the second judge. He was sur-prised to see tears streaming down his face, forming rivulets on either side of his prominent, beaklike nose. The man rocked back and forth in his seat, and at first Bibi thought with a pang that he must be mourning terribly for the loss of his son. But then he noticed the magistrate clutching one thumb in his hand as he rocked, and realized he must have bashed it in bringing down the gavel. *Like father, like son,* thought Bibi, reflecting that with the new frontal perspective, and the grotesque grimaces that accompanied his pain, the poor fellow looked even more like some huge, broken-winged bird than he'd first imagined.

The trial dragged on for hours. Bibi was questioned as to the night in question, the fugitives in question, and whether he'd ever questioned the consequences of his questionable activities. And as morning melted into afternoon and the air in the courtroom became increasingly stuffy, Bibi found it more and more difficult to keep his attention on the proceedings. As in his school days, he drifted into reveries wherein he correlated the arrangement of wood grain on his tabletop with the gestural patterns of those who spoke. He considered the layout of the floor tiles, and even initiated a small and very private study of the footwear of court officers.

Meanwhile he continued, near as he could tell, to answer those questions that were addressed directly to him; but as the afternoon wore on, a part of him became increasingly detached, as though he were a diver on the surface of a sea, staring down with bemused interest on the proceedings below. The sunlight slanting through the windows grew thick and greenish, the atmosphere dreamlike; and the people seemed to swim past with grand and fluid gestures. Clerks scuttled crablike across the floor; juries huddled in their boxes like clumps of oysters; judges sat motionless at their benches, mouths opening and closing in an even, carplike rhythm.

Now the clerkfish drifted over to the judgefish and handed each a sheaf of papers; and after some time had passed, words began to bubble forth from their piscine mouths.

"We have here," burbled the Beetlefish, "some selections from a document found in the possession of Mr. Brown. I wonder, sir, if you would mind clarifying some of these passages for the court?"

"Certainly," Bibi heard himself reply.

As the magistrate began to read, Bibi recognized, with a certain remote interest, an excerpt lifted in its entirety from his journal:

The sun! It looks so small we can block it with a finger.
Hold up a quarter and you can eclipse it entirely. But stare
at it for any length of time and it will burn your eyes out.
This should tell us something about the nature of power.

The words bubbled to the surface and burst against the ceiling; in his newly aquatic state Bibi found them to be the most peculiar and incomprehensible sounds he had ever heard.

"Well?" babbled the Beetle, eyes rolling and bulging; but Bibi did not rise to the bait.

"Well what?" gargled the submarine defendant.

"Perhaps you'd be so kind as to tell us what it means?"

"I have absolutely no idea," replied Bibi.

"You wrote it," interjected the Eaglefish, "didn't you?"

"Yes, but that doesn't necessarily mean I understand it."

The briny Reverend Beetle broke in. "Please," he said, in a tone slithering with condescension, "allow me to continue:

Time asks questions of us. Time is a speed-typing test, and
we are the countless monkeys who must somehow come up
with 'Hamlet' before our allotted span runs out."

"J.B.," he dribbled, addressing his colleague directly for the first time, "do you understand any of this?"

His associate shook his head.

"Nor do I," said the Water Beetle, "—at least, not in its current form. I submit that it is not in fact possible to understand it, for what we have here is actually a coded plan for the overflow—er, throw—of Smallville!"

"Largemont," corrected the other.

The juries recessed for deliberations. By the time they re-turned evening had begun to fall, the atmosphere had fresh-ened, and the spell that possessed Bibi that afternoon had passed. The room was once more filled with mere air, and the two Bibis had again joined into one, a new Bibi brimming over with fresh and unshakable resolve. A hush fell upon the court as the justices reentered. There was a pause as the foremen of the juries rose to their feet. The two cleared their throats and announced at the same moment:

"WE FIND THE DEFENDANT TO BE:
GUILTY!   NOT GUILTY!"

The foremen looked at one another in consternation.

The judges glanced at each other nervously.

The Beetle Man's eyes bulged, and his jaw worked back and forth.

The Eagle Man's nose twitched, and he wrung his hands.

"Well," said Justice Beetle, finally.

"Indeed," said the Honorable Eagle.

"In a situation of this nature . . ."

"Clearly the proper course of action . . ."

There was a long moment of silence.

"Um . . . let the judges decide!" the Eagle Man burst out in a triumphant tone.

"Exactly!" exclaimed his associate.

A murmur ran through the courtroom, for this was the first time the magistrates had ever been heard to agree on anything.

"Go ahead, H.R." said the Eagle Man. "You first."

"No, no, J.B.," replied his colleague. "After you."

"But I insist," urged the Eagle.

"Really—" rejoined the Beetle.

They glared at one another. There was a moment's pause, then the two shouted as one:

"NOT GUILTY!   GUILTY!"

"Not guilty?" repeated Reverend Beetle, in an incredulous tone.

"Well," replied the Eagle Man, "I don't think, to tell you the truth, H.R., that we have clearly proven criminal intent as defined in section 11a, paragraph 23 of the criminal code—"

"Intent!" cried Reverend Small in a strangled voice. "J.B., Hugo's your son!"

"So? Gloria's your daughter."

"But *I* judged the defendant guilty."

"Oh," replied the Eagle Man after a moment. "You have a point there. Well, in that case, why don't I just reevaluate my—"

"Excuse me, Your Honor," interjected one of the clerks, fumbling through a leather-bound book on the desk before him, "but it is my duty to inform you that according to the criminal code a judgment once made by a licensed magistrate cannot be recanted, retracted, or—"

"So," interjected the Beetle. "Well, then."

"Indeed," replied the Reverend Eagle, "in a situation of this nature . . ."

"Clearly, the proper course of action—"

"Excuse me," interrupted Bibi, whose patience had been utterly exhausted by the proceedings. He rose to his feet. "Might it help if I made a statement of clarification?"

The justices looked at one another, then shrugged.

"I believe we've been missing the point entirely. Your side, sir"—here Bibi pointed to the Eagle Man—"believes God to be infinitely large. Yours, sir"—he indicated the Beetle—"believes God is infinitely small. Now surely we must agree that infinity, being infinite, must extend indefinitely in both directions. Logically speaking, therefore, if God is infinite and infinity has no end, then Ipso Post Facto there must be no end to God. Your beliefs are identical."

"Ah!" cried the Beetle Man, and the Eagle shouted at the

same moment: "Eureka!" The justices looked at one another and grinned broadly. The Eagle Man rose from his bench and strode toward his colleague. The Beetle stood to meet him. The two shook hands and gazed at one another in solemn acknowledgment. Then they turned to face the assembly, and in a single voice announced their verdict:

INSANITY!

4.
INSANITY

The first thing that struck Bibi as he entered the asylum was the dense odor of popcorn that permeated the place. The second was the maxim engraved on an archway over the entrance to the main hall:

**INSANITY IS MERELY THE
MISAPPREHENSION OF THE DIVINE**

"You're just going to love the other group members," gushed the head nurse, Wanda Baker, as they followed the echo of their footsteps down a stone corridor. "They're just the loveliest people even if they are, well—a trifle confused. Let's see, there's the General, he fought in World Wars A and B; and Rhonda, used to be an actress, has a few problems, but I'm sure you'll get along splendidly; and the Professor, of course, always up to one experiment or another; and Peter, he was in the money market, they used to call him Peter the Wolf; and—oh well, here we are, you can see for yourself. We were just getting ready to discuss our dreams, and I guess the best thing is to carry right on."

They stepped from the hall into a grim room which had at some point in its past been painted a cheerful orange. Seven patients were seated in a semicircle around a chair in the center, on which Miss Baker took her place. Bibi felt fourteen eyes follow his every movement as he entered; and as he took his seat at the end of the row, a man leaned forward and cried in a lively tone: "Goody, goody, a new heretic to play with!"

"Now, Mr. Sphere," said Nurse Baker, "we must be kind to our new guest. He's just been through a rather difficult ordeal."

"Harrumph," replied the man, who as Bibi was soon to discover, was known to the others simply as Sphere. He fit his name extraordinarily well, Bibi thought, being a short, rotund fellow, ruddy as a plum. In addition to those mentioned by Nurse Baker there were two others: a tall, morose man who had a problem with excessive earwax, and a nondescript fellow, body slumped like a wrinkled suit of clothing, who watched the earwax man's every movement and imitated it exactly. These two Bibi would come to know as Adam and Abram.

"Well," issued a voice from several places down as Bibi settled into his seat. "He's certainly tall enough." The voice belonged to the only female in the group, a slender, pallid woman with dark circles under her eyes who looked very beautiful from certain angles. Perhaps in her mid-forties, she had a faded, wispy quality about her, as though her beauty was peeling away in tiny flakes and when it was gone there would be nothing left to her at all. She reached her hand across several laps in his direction.

"Rhonda," she breathed in introduction. "Rhonda . . . Voux."

"Bibi Brown," replied Bibi politely. He found her grip to be as pale as her flesh.

"All right now, patients," announced Nurse Baker. "I think it's high time we got down to work. Mr. Sphere, would you tell us about your dreams?"

"Oh, yes," exclaimed Sphere. "When I dream, I dream of round things: of clocks and cantaloupes, moons and merry-go-rounds, discarded tires, human skulls. The sun is round, and so is the Earth—and life is round too, if you think about it; birth, then death, and the seasons going round and round."

Rhonda broke in. "In my dreams, it is always night. Other people may have gay, sunlit dreams, all daffodils and spring-time. But in my dreams, darkness rules. Why, I once dreamed of a night so dark it swallowed up all sound. I once dreamed of a night so black the stars turned to stones and fell from the sky."

"I," interjected Sphere, "once dreamed of a night so cold my goldfish froze solid in its bowl!"

"Even in morning," Rhonda went on, "I feel the nightmare within me. At twilight, as day crawls toward oblivion, darkness moves inside me and I am pregnant—pregnant with horror. Oh, I know I'm ravishing on the outside, but inside I'm filled up with blood and guts and the most awful things. Why, sometimes I can just feel the excrement slithering around inside of me. Sometimes—"

"Thank you, that's quite enough," interrupted Nurse Baker, whose face had begun to turn a peculiar shade of grey. "General?"

"Yes!" answered the old soldier, snapping to attention. "Over the years, the oxidation of fancy . . . our dreams, like birdcages left in the elements, begin to rust away! You've got to be Number One Man. When you're walking into the brightness of the sun, sometimes you can only see one step in front of you!" With that he mumbled off into confusion; the lights that were his eyes went dead and he looked about in a muddle, as though try-ing to figure out who it was that had been speaking.

It went on like that. The Professor dreamed he'd burned all his belongings: first notebooks and old photographs, then fur-niture, and finally anything that had his name on it—check-books, honorary degrees, even monogrammed towels. "What do you suppose it all means?" he kept asking Nurse Baker, making meticulous notes on her replies.

Peter described a dream where he was inside a liquefying body while its organs disintegrated and flowed away, and enormous birds of prey materialized from the ooze and flapped off into the heavens. Finally Adam shared a dream in which the streets had turned to water with porpoises jumping in them, and Abram related a very similar experience in which the streets had turned to milk with cows drifting down them.

At last it was time for dinner, and Bibi joined his group at their table amidst the noise and tumult of the cafeteria.

He couldn't help but notice, when he looked down at his plate, that the single potato he'd been served was shaped almost exactly like a human heart.

It was on the third day of his enforced insanity that Bibi solved the riddle of the popcorn smell that pervaded the asylum. Though confined to their rooms at night, inmates were free to wander as they pleased during the day; and one afternoon Bibi followed his nose down one corridor and up another until, when the smell was so thick he could almost swallow it, he found himself standing in the basement before a half-opened door. He peered in to see a man bent over a hot plate from which the crackle of popping corn was at that moment being emitted. The fellow's back was turned so Bibi couldn't see his face; nevertheless, the strangeness of his appearance was inescapable. Greying hair stood out in all directions from the back of his head, as though each strand were straining to get as far from its companions as possible. His shirttails were tucked in on one side but not on the other. His belt, though fastened in the vicinity of his waistband, had failed to negotiate several crucial loops and appeared to be preparing to mount an attack up his flank. And beneath the crumpled cuffs of his trousers were a pair of argyle socks so mismatched it made Bibi's eyes water to look upon them.

As Bibi watched, the man lifted a single kernel from a skillet and placed it on the tray of a scale. He scribbled an entry on a yellow pad, took the dimensions of the morsel with a set of calipers, and placed it to one side. Then he leaned back in his chair, fixed his gaze on the wall, and began to grope about his pockets. Coming up at last with a pipe, he attempted to stuff a wad of tobacco in the bowl. The receptacle, however, proved to be upside down, and the mixture spilled into his lap. Regarding the implement with mild surprise, he righted it and, after an ineffectual attempt to brush the debris from his clothing, began the process once more.

About this time Bibi leaned a bit too heavily against the door, and the hinges emitted a rust-laden groan. The man, now in the process of applying a match to his pipe, turned in his chair. It was, of course, the Professor.

"Why, young Bibi," he exclaimed. "Do come in—that is, er . . . Ouch!" He dropped the match and shook his fingers vigorously. "What I mean to say is—welcome to my laboratory!"

The two spent the next several hours engaged in a spirited inquiry into the nature of existence. Bibi shared with his new friend all of his theories about the universe, time, and reality—and never, he thought, had he met with a more astute or attentive audience.

"Discursive thought," the Professor announced, when Bibi finally ground to a halt, "is the gateway to the universe. The scientific mind takes reality apart so its pieces may be put back together in a more orderly fashion. It is the highest path to knowledge!"

With that the scholar went on to delineate his numerous discoveries. "I have isolated," he informed his listener, "seven dimensions of logic, eleven levels of infinity, and thirteen different categories of nonsense!" Indeed, he quickly proved himself capable of discoursing in five of the seven logical dimensions at once, though once he rose above the third Bibi found his insights admittedly a bit difficult to follow.

But the Professor was no mere theoretician. "A discovery without an application," he announced, "is like a stillborn infant." With that he drew the veil from a pedestal at the center of the room to reveal his latest and greatest invention:

"The Electric Shoe!"

"Electric Shoe?" repeated Bibi, feeling that the conversation was moving beyond the realm of his comprehension.

His host nodded sagely. Bibi watched as he pressed a tiny button above the heel and placed the device on the floor. Slowly, with a great deal of dignity, it strode unassisted across the room.

"Soon," the Professor asserted, "humanity will have no need of feet."

"But where," Bibi asked, "does the popcorn fit in?"

"Ah!" said the man of thought, holding one finger in the air. "I am, even as we speak, on the brink of a revolutionary insight into the nature of fate. As you've undoubtedly noticed, there are a number of possible relationships between human beings and destiny: seventeen, to be exact. Those with consistently good luck, those with consistently bad luck, those who expect good but are met with bad, those who expect bad but encounter good—"

"And the popcorn?"

The Professor motioned Bibi to the hot plate. "As you've no doubt observed," he said, reaching into the fluffy mass with his forceps, "in every batch of corn there are some kernels which, though exposed to the same conditions as the rest, go through the process unchanged." He selected an unpopped kernel and held it up for inspection. "In the same way some people, though experiencing the same circumstances as others, exhibit an atypical response to them. It is my hope that by studying the varying effects of chance on otherwise identical kernels of corn, I will one day be able to apply the same laws to human beings!"

• • •

To keep his spirits up, Bibi initiated a program of systematic inquiries throughout the various wards of the asylum, in hopes of finding a clue to the whereabouts of his Uncle Otto, or the cousin and lumberjack husband who'd been the last to see him alive. But at every turn he was met with disappointment. In the mania clinic Bibi met an ex-trucker who called himself the "Mudflap King," and in the delirium division, a "Prince of Axles and Steel-belted Treads." In the melancholia wing he encountered a sad old Lithuanian shoemaker who claimed to be Paul Bunyan, and in the monomania ward attended a series of satiric exchanges between two very tall fellows who believed they were Swift and Voltaire.

At last, in the fanaticism annex, Bibi thought he'd struck pay dirt. An old woman slumped in an armchair brightened when he addressed her. "Hope Valley?" she exclaimed, "I know Hope Valley!" For a moment Bibi's heart did backflips. But the woman merely rattled on: "Hope is a Pope. Popes perform Mass. Matter has mass. Therefore, Catholics matter!" And try as he might, Bibi could get no more out of her.

One day Nurse Baker was called away from Bibi's group unexpectedly, and the members had a chance to discuss an officially forbidden topic: the circumstances that had brought them here.

"I," Adam told them, rummaging about his left ear with his little finger, "was the most successful lawyer in Largemont, till I downed a few too many Singapore slings at a civic event and made a rash public reference to 'God, the Whompin'-and-Gallumpin'.'"

"I," chimed in Abram, jiggling a finger in his right ear, "was an up-and-coming accountant for a prominent Smallville firm, till I put away a few too many mai-tais at the Jockey Club one afternoon and made an unfortunate public pronouncement regarding 'God, the Eensie-Weensie.'"

"For nearly a decade after the plane crash which stranded me here," the Professor said, puffing away at his pipe, "I was chief researcher at Smallville University—until I was quoted in a local journal as saying: 'God is dead, and Galileo killed him.' During the trial they kept demanding I produce my Italian co-conspirator."

"In an interview shortly after the ballooning accident that marooned me in this cultural backwater," sighed Peter, "I made the reckless proclamation: 'God is time and time is money. Therefore, money is God.'" He laughed. "On the outside they would have made me president!"

"I," said Sphere, "merely remarked to the counterman at the local Magna-Burger that God was no doubt 'circular and palatable.'"

"And I," breathed Rhonda, "after being abducted from the set of my last film, *"A" Is for Adulteress,* by a deranged skydiver who perished in the jump into the valley, commented to the ambulance team that 'God is beauty. Beauty and death.'"

Even the General, who no longer had any idea how he had come to be here, roused himself from his torpor to shout: "God is America!"

"How about you, kid?" Sphere asked Bibi. "What'd you do?"

"I merely stated," Bibi replied, "that since God is infinite and infinity is endless, God must be both infinitely small and infinitely large at once."

There was a deep silence in the room.

"Some people have the strangest notions," remarked Adam.

"You belong here," said Sphere. "You're dangerous."

Fall crept into winter, and through the window of his room Bibi watched as the leaves dropped from the aspen and the peaks around the valley turned white with snow, while he himself grew no closer to achieving the object of his quest. Sleep became difficult; when he did manage to drift off, he was tormented by visions in which the jaundiced, perspiration-ridden figure of the Terry Cloth Man, generally accompanied by Bibi's father or another of his unfortunate ancestors, tracked him relentlessly across vast stretches of desolation, often stepping precisely in the footprints he'd left behind.

But Bibi soon learned from Peter, who had mysterious connections with the outside world, that following the unprecedented agreement of the judges at Bibi's trial the people of Largemont/Smallville had entered upon a new era of cooperation. Barriers had been removed from select streets, and key businesses opened to all. There was even talk of changing the name of the community to Middlebury.

Bibi was excited by the news. "Maybe they'll realize it was all my doing and set me free!"

His friend laughed. "Are you kidding? Then they'd have to admit you weren't crazy after all. This new arrangement depends on both judges being right, not wrong. They have a tremendous investment in keeping you exactly where you are."

"You mean I may never get out of here as long as I live?"

"Well," replied Peter with a wink, "let's just say they wouldn't let you out—voluntarily."

But he would say no more, and Bibi could only guess at his meaning.

Peter proved to be a valuable resource not only in discovering what was happening outside the asylum but in getting by on the inside as well. Through his growing friendship with the Wolf, Bibi was able to receive extra portions at mealtimes, enjoy extended exercise periods, and even acquire a reading lamp for his bedside table.

Each morning Peter held court at his table in the cafeteria, trading news of the outside world for privileges beyond the reach of other inmates. He spoke in a fierce whisper while his listeners huddled about, his words as fiery as the red hair and close-cropped beard that framed his face. It was through Peter that Bibi learned of the election of the new president, which had come in the wake of an economic slump and a series of executive branch resignations. It was Peter who brought news of the ongoing technological revolution, which was in danger of being crippled by strikes and an unforeseen energy crunch. He regaled them with tales of the American intervention in Borneo and the floundering Tasmanian offensive, which had bogged down amidst heavy ground fire and guerrilla strikes. Peter had somehow made himself privy to information unknown even to staff and doctors in the isolated world of the valley; and even administrators were sometimes seen conferring with him on the outcome of distant sporting events.

"I'm a cynic," he told Bibi once, "and a true cynic feels superior to everything. *I* have developed the unique ability, through criticizing my own attributes again and again, of feeling superior even to myself!" On another occasion, during a game of squash, he turned to Bibi and announced: "It is my ambition never to make a mistake." Although Bibi found his new friend sometimes abrasive, his company was certainly never dull; and he had a hunch that one day the association would serve him well.

It was sometime in early spring that Peter first mentioned the possibility of a breakout.

He and Bibi were playing squash one afternoon when the Wolf arrested the ball in mid-flight, turned suddenly, and whispered, "We're getting out."

"Out?" Bibi repeated, uncertain whether he'd heard him correctly.

"Flying this coop. Blowing this joint. Slipping out on the sly."

"When?" said Bibi. "Who?"

"Soon. Our entire group."

"Rhonda, the General, everybody?"

"They don't know it yet, but they're coming."

"What do I have to do?"

"Don't you worry your little head about that," Peter grinned. "The Wolf's got it all taken care of. Just have your gear ready to go at a moment's notice."

But the weeks went by, and every time Bibi approached his friend for more information, Peter merely put his finger to his lips, pointed in the direction of the mountaintops, and said: "Snow."

As the days grew longer Peter held a series of mysterious meetings with the Professor. Bibi would find them huddled in the basement laboratory, examining charts and diagrams; or they'd station him as lookout while they pounded the ceilings with poles and affixed obscure devices to the walls. At one point Nurse Baker asked the group if anyone knew the whereabouts of certain canned goods and items of linen that had vanished from the storeroom, but the three merely shrugged along with the rest and replied: "No, ma'am."

The plan was kept such a secret that even the other group members remained unaware of their impending liberation: nevertheless there were some heart-stopping moments. One day an inmate known as Xenar, Master of Divination, who was said to hold advanced degrees in geomancy, gyromancy, and numerology, approached Bibi and Peter on the squash court and inquired, "So when are you two fellas taking off?"

Peter hurriedly offered him a place in the escape party in return for his silence, but Xenar reassured him with a smile. "I wouldn't dream of exposing your noble plan," he said. "Besides, I have recently received the prophecy that I am soon to be released, and will go on to become the leader of a small but prosperous Caribbean nation."

"Speaking of prophecies," Bibi said, "I don't suppose you'd

have any information on a place called Hope Valley, or a Hope Valley Hubcap King, or a—"

"I know, I know . . . a seven-foot-tall lumberjack whose name ends in -ski. Hold on while I consult my sources." The Master sat down and concentrated for several moments, forehead resting against the palm of one hand. "Well," he shrugged at last, "they appear to be telling me the usual sort of thing—that you may never find your uncle until you truly come to understand love, that once you're *really* ready you'll find him with no difficulty at all, and so on." He frowned. "But wait—there's something more." His forehead furrowed with concentration. "I see a pale, stooped figure, traveling—searching, just as you are. For what purpose, I don't know. It's as though you had a shadow, a pallid, unhealthy shadow, whose existence you were entirely unaware of."

"But who—?" Bibi began.

"I'm afraid that's all the information I have," shrugged Xenar. "But I do have the distinct impression that you're not the only one interested in finding this Hubcap King."

And although Bibi questioned Xenar repeatedly on the subject, he could get no more out of him.

"Ah, he was probably just speaking symbolically," said Peter later. "—and anyway, you've got to remember that the old guy is a complete lunatic!"

Bibi was inclined to agree with the first part of Peter's analysis, at least. But still the encounter left him with a lingering sense of unease that took many days to fade.

At last, sometime in mid-April, Bibi was awakened in the middle of the night by a voice that seemed to come from nowhere. "Yoo-hoo," it called softly. "Bibi boy!"

Bibi bolted to his feet and stared about in the blackness.

"Bibi," the voice whispered again. "Time to go bye-bye!"

It was then that Bibi noticed a glimmer of light coming from a heating vent in the ceiling.

"Peter?" Bibi inquired of the vent. "Is that you?"

"You get five points for accuracy," replied the voice. "Now let's see how you do on speed!" With that the grate came loose and the unmistakable, red-bearded face of the Wolf, lit by the glow of his flashlight, thrust itself upside down into the room. Bibi grabbed his rucksack, which had stood fully packed at his bedside for weeks.

"I'm ready," said Bibi, trying to remain relaxed despite the squadron of butterflies flapping about his interior. "But I don't see how you expect me to fit through that opening."

"No problem," replied his friend, "with the Professor's patented Ultrasonic De-mortarizer!" Peter drew his head back into the opening and Bibi felt a high, soundless tremor vibrate through the air. Then a section of brickwork shuddered and withdrew itself from the company of its fellows, and this time Peter's entire torso lowered itself into the room.

"Coming?" he asked.

Bibi dragged a chair below the aperture and hoisted himself through. He found Peter and the Professor waiting beyond, in a heating duct just wide enough to enter on all fours. Cobwebs stuck to his face and dust whirled in the glow of Peter's flashlight.

"Nice place you've got here," Bibi said.

"Glad you could make it," replied the Wolf. "Now let's see about the others."

The group had been notified several days earlier to make ready for a sudden departure; but confusion still reigned in the gathering of their forces. Rhonda took one look at the duct and insisted on swaddling her entire body in plastic trash bags before proceeding. "There's dirt up there," she hissed. "Microbes!" The General, who had completely forgotten about the venture, had to be convinced the opening in the brickwork did not conceal an enemy bunker; and they lost precious time as the old soldier collected his scattered war medals. The De-mortarizer stuck briefly in the "on" position above Adam and Abram's room, sending cracks down the walls and into the hallway; and more time still was lost in the creation of the extra large aperture required to admit Sphere.

At last all had gathered in the airshaft. Bibi helped distribute supplies, to be carried in backpacks the Professor and Peter had fabricated from stolen linen. Then, with the Wolf in the lead and Bibi taking up the rear, the eight crawled as rapidly as they could through the darkened veins of the building.

They suffered their first brief delay when the batteries in the Professor's flashlight gave out, necessitating a frantic search through the packs for replacements; and there was another setback when the unfortunate Sphere became lodged at a turn in the shaft.

"Breathe out," hissed Peter, tugging at his arms from the front.

"Think small," urged Bibi, pushing from behind.

"If you don't come loose," threatened the Professor, "we're going to have to starve you out!" At this the poor fellow redoubled his efforts until, with his companions shoving and yanking and a cacophony of gurgles and groans issuing from his abdomen, he managed to wriggle free.

Finally the escape party reached the point where the shaft vented to the outside. Peter removed the grate and he and Bibi stuck their heads out to consider the situation. They had emerged on the third level of the building; directly below them Bibi could see the rectangular bin, perhaps fifteen feet long and as many deep, that served as the repository for the institution's trash.

"Bribery pays off!" exulted Peter.

"How so?" asked Bibi.

"It's no accident the glop box was left directly below the vent. The trashman is now the proud owner of a high-powered radio."

"So that's how you got your information. But how'd you ever manage to keep it a secret?"

"It's one of those miniaturized jobbers you tuck away in the ear canal," Peter grinned. "The trash collector is destined to become a very influential man."

"Well," asked Bibi, "what do we do now?"

Peter looked at him and smiled. "Jump."

Rhonda, flushed and sweating in her trash-bag body suit, slipped up behind them just in time to hear the last of their conversation. She wriggled past Bibi and looked over the side.

"Oh no," she announced, "I'm not leaping into any putrefying pile of slime!"

"You won't have to," said Peter. With a shove of his foot he sent her over the edge, then went tumbling after. The Professor followed, succeeded by the General, who arced through the air like a dried-up bundle of bones. Sphere took a moment to ponder the situation. "Well," he said finally, "I guess there's nothing to fear but Sphere himself!" With that he plummeted from the shaft like a ripe melon. Adam and Abram went next, side by side, and finally Bibi edged his way onto the narrow lip, propped the grate back into position, and plunged into space.

A moment later he found himself lying facedown on a mound of potato skins, coffee grounds, and all manner of indefinable ooze. Peter helped him to a sitting position and handed him a bit of newspaper to wipe his face.

"Nice drop, kid," he said. "You'll make a great bird one day."

Rhonda was crying to herself in one corner of the bin. She held a handkerchief to her nose and made peculiar gagging sounds, while Adam and Abram tried with perfectly symmetrical gestures to comfort her. Peter plucked a banana peel from behind Bibi's ear and patted their sodden substrate fondly. "Trashman left the top filled with nice squishy stuff, just like I requested. What a guy!"

"And now?" asked Bibi.

"Bury ourselves and wait till dawn."

"Bury ourselves?" choked Rhonda. Bibi watched as the Professor handed out three-foot sections of what appeared to be hollow reeds. "Here," the scholar said, passing a length to her. "You'll be needing one of these."

Bibi must have drifted into sleep sometime toward morning, for the next thing he heard was the rattle and clang of a mule team sending their trash-bin refuge into motion. He conquered an initial impulse to cry out, thrash free of the muck, and leap to his feet, and forced himself instead into a state of precarious relaxation by breathing slowly and mindfully through the tube the Professor had given him. He remembered Peter's final words to Rhonda: "Just think clean thoughts," and wondered how the others were holding up. He could sense their motionless forms around him, packed tightly as sardines, and took comfort from the knowledge that he was not alone. But still the skin crept across his flesh with every wobble and dip in the road, and in his bones was a dampness that went deeper than marrow.

As a means of distracting himself, Bibi began to fantasize about his impending freedom. He imagined lying on his back in a field of grass, sky stretching overhead like an upturned lake. Clouds scudded across the tight blue surface like ships. The breeze nuzzled him like a cat; flowers nodded their heads and smiled down on him. The vision became so intense, in fact, that Bibi nearly forgot where he was. The smells that filled his nostrils became the scents of spring; the rubbish pressing in around his body was the gentle pressure of the sun's rays. He was just about to figure the Nine-fingered Woman somehow into the equation when a distant clanking penetrated his reverie. He felt the earth begin to tilt into the air; and the next thing he knew Bibi found himself hurtling down a slick incline, surrounded by mounds of accelerating garbage and the frantic, flailing forms of his friends.

Bibi landed moments later at the bottom of a pit of slime. He struggled to his feet to find himself waist-deep in mire. Overhead wheeled flocks of crows and the hulking silhouettes of vultures. He'd had just enough time to consider his situation and earnestly hope he was still dreaming when there arose from the muck before him the most terrifying apparition he had ever seen. A blackened, inhuman form, it flapped its limbs and emitted several fearsome groans. A pair of apertures blinked open in its faceless skull, and two staring eyes met his. Bibi was just on the point of heading rapidly in the opposite direction when the creature's mouth sprang open and a stream of sounds launched themselves into the atmosphere: "Fun, fun, fun."

The voice was Peter's.

Bibi slogged to his friend's side and helped wipe the mud from his face. "I thought you were some hideous beast," he said.

"You don't look so great yourself," grinned the Wolf. "Don't you ever wash?"

Together the fugitives clambered free and took cover in the forest beyond. But here they found themselves plunged into a deeper mire, for drifts of snow still lingered in the shadows of the trees, all but blocking their passage.

"Well," said Peter, "all one can say at a time like this is 'Thank God for the Electric Shoe.' Right, Professor?"

The scholar looked at him blankly. "I thought *you'd* brought them," he said.

The group kept moving all that day and into the night, but soon discovered that between the snow and the weight of their packs they could cover no more than a mile or so an hour.

"Not enough," the Professor urged them. "They'll have the dogs on our trail in no time!"

All redoubled their efforts, but before long Rhonda was limping terribly in her high-heeled pumps, the only footwear she'd had available. An old croquet injury of Adam's had begun to act up, causing tremendous pain in his and Abram's right knees; and even Peter, feet blistered by his stiff, asylum-issue shoes, walked along in tight-lipped silence. The General did his best to keep their spirits up, crying periodically: "Onward, we're heroes all!", while Sphere serenaded them with a song he'd composed specially for the occasion:

> The world is round
> and so am I
> I'll circle home
> before I die
> Sing Hey, sing Ho
> sing low, sing high
> We'll circle homeward,
> You and I.

Bibi, for his part, was beset by a boundless euphoria at being free once again to roam his beloved wilderness. He ranged ahead in long-legged exuberance, scouting the route for shortcuts, scrambling up cliff faces to check for signs of pursuit. The trees were friends from whom he'd been separated for centuries. The sky, empurpled with the waning day, was more beautiful than he'd ever imagined; even the snow through which they slogged seemed the very embodiment of truth.

By the time they halted for the night, all were too weary to talk much. Over a dinner of canned beans and early mallow shoots Bibi had gathered, Abram tried to point out the beauty of the rising moon to Rhonda, but the actress merely sniffed: "I've never cared much for the moon. Its light is just a reflection!" The General delivered a monologue on how remarkable it was that the hair and fingernails of the dead never stop growing, while the Professor gave a brief discourse on the sensory structure of the amoeba who, having no brain, is one of the few creatures to sense the universe directly.

As the others drifted off to sleep, Bibi made impassioned notes by firelight in his journal, which Peter had miraculously managed to retrieve from Nurse Baker's files before their departure.

Oh, Moon, he wrote, *last time I saw you it was through bars. Was it you who were imprisoned, or I?*

Now we are both set free together!

The next morning the group discarded a portion of their supplies and pushed on at a quicker pace. But as they traveled further from the settled regions of the valley they encountered a new challenge to their progress: the question of navigation.

The Professor had designed for the occasion a device that resembled—and in fact was—a cross between a teakettle, a compass, and a sextant. Dubbed the Navotron, the instrument was designed to measure their position in relation to the Earth's magnetic field, incorporating such variables as atmospheric patterns, barometric pressure, and overall mood of the participants, and thereby deduce an ideal and unvarying course of travel. Peter, on the other hand, whose photographic memory had preserved every nuance of local topography during his ill-fated balloon flight, had developed a series of five hypothetical directions he thought ought to be attempted till one proved successful. Adam, whose grandfather had been chief astronomer for the Church of God the Humongous, had ideas of his own; and Bibi couldn't see why they didn't just find a likely spot at the valley's rim and head straight for it. At last the group reached a compromise whereby the Professor set the morning course, Peter modified it at lunch, and Adam and Abram navigated via celestial reckoning in the evening. In the end, the group spent most of its time traveling around in circles—which was, of course, what Sphere had suggested they do in the first place.

The breaking point came on the second evening when the party discovered their remaining food consisted almost entirely of popcorn.

"We're never going to make it, are we?" moaned Rhonda,

picking listlessly at a plate of fluffy foodstuff. "I should have known. I never should have—"

"There, there," broke in Abram. As Bibi looked on in amazement, he sat down beside the actress and took her hand in his. "Just think, in a few days you'll be free, sitting in a meadow with flowers all around—"

"I can't believe it," cried Rhonda. "I won't. I've pinned my hopes on things so many times they've gotten all full of holes!" With that she collapsed, to Abram's evident astonishment, into his arms and dissolved into tears.

On the third morning Bibi and the others glimpsed a clearing ahead, and emerged from the forest to find themselves standing at the edge of the trash pit they'd left days earlier. Undaunted, they set off again, but clambered out of a gully several hours later only to emerge on the ten-yard line of the Smallville High lacrosse field in the midst of an important game. Fortunately, a goal was taking place at the other end of the field and they were glimpsed only by the nearsighted grandmother of one of the players, who mistook them for a group of cheerleaders from the opposing team. Finally, on the afternoon of the fourth day, they spotted a stone wall through the trees, and the fugitives stumbled out of the shadows to find themselves just outside the south wall of the asylum.

That evening they made camp so close to the building they didn't dare light a fire for fear it would be seen from the windows.

Perhaps because of the unlikely loops and swivels of their progress, there had been up to that point no signs of pursuit; but on the morning of the fifth day the party awoke to the baying of hounds in the distance.

"All right," announced Bibi, whose patience had been completely annihilated by the proceedings. "From here on out we head straight for the rim of the valley!"

No one was in the mood to argue, and as none of them could

come up with a better plan, the group set off as quickly as they could.

But as the day wore on, all became increasingly concerned about the General. Mind addled by sun and exhaustion, the old soldier weaved from side to side, waving his arms and carrying on an endless, incomprehensible monologue:

"Heroes? Zeros. We're all heroes here. Never give up your flag. He who attempts to claim the heavens ends up with a load of babble!" Everyone kept a close watch on him, but the General scarcely noticed their attentions; and his steps only grew weaker as darkness began to fall.

The group halted for a rest at dusk, but as they munched morosely on the last of the stale popcorn, Bibi heard the howling of the dogs spring up anew. It was clear their pursuers had no intention of stopping for the night.

"They've got our scent now," said the Professor darkly. "If we don't push on, they'll catch us in no time!"

Peter, too weary for words, merely grunted in reply. In the rest of the group, a grim silence reigned.

Sometime toward midnight, with cat-eyed Bibi in the lead, the fugitives found themselves skirting the edge of a bog. Too exhausted to think of anything but putting one foot before the other, they clawed through brambles and low-hanging trees that clutched at their hair, while all around echoed the creaking song of frogs and the whine of mosquitoes. Flashlights had been ruled out, and an overcast sky dimmed the moon, making it impossible to see more than one step in front of them.

They had been going on in this way for what seemed hours, when all at once Bibi heard a splash cut through the night, followed by a faint, strangled cry. A frantic search revealed that the General was missing. Within moments the fugitives had fanned out into the brush, battling creepers and slogging through muck; but it was Rhonda who located their comrade, mired to his chest in a pool of mud.

"Leave me," shouted the old warrior. "Let the Cossacks take me!"

"Nonsense!" cried the former star. As Bibi looked on in disbelief, she leapt without hesitation into the pool, to emerge moments later streaked with muck, leading the sodden commander by the hand.

"You're not giving up now," Rhonda scolded, mopping at his face with her scarf. "By this time tomorrow we'll be free—or dead!"

"She saved me," the General mumbled. "The lady soldier saved my life!"

But by now he was so weak he could scarcely walk. After a brief conference they decided to distribute the contents of the General's pack between them, and set off into the night with the old fellow clinging bravely to Sphere's broad back.

Having thrown the dogs off by their passage through the marsh, the fugitives were able to rest for several hours toward morning; but they were awakened at dawn when the baying began anew, closer than seemed possible. Luckily, Bibi had scouted a ravine through which the group might pass unseen almost to the rim of the valley.

"If what you say is correct," said the Professor, poring over a map they'd acquired from a manic-depressive cartographer, "we could reach the top by this afternoon. Then it's over the edge to freedom!"

No one dared ask how they were going to get to the bottom in one piece.

After several hours the group emerged from the shade of the ravine onto a boulder-strewn mountainside. Here the snow had melted, and despite the increased steepness the going was much easier. They moved on steadily over open fields of stone;

but as the sun neared its zenith, Bibi spotted the figures of their pursuers starting up the slope behind them.

As they drew near the top Bibi, the Professor, and Peter pushed ahead to scout for a point from which to make their descent—the possibilities of which seemed gravely uncertain to Bibi, who'd tried the same thing so recently himself. They came out onto a ridge in a fringe of low pines, just below the large peak that dominated this end of the valley. A stream spilled from a source partway up its summit, twisting a short channel through the trees before careening over the edge into space. Bibi squatted at the bank to drink and glimpsed, in a still eddy, an oddly familiar face, peppered with stubble and surmounted by an unruly mass of hair, peering back at him. He stared for a long moment, for it occurred to him that as soon as he turned away, this other Bibi was doomed to be carried off and swept over the brink.

Peter broke the spell. "Come along. You can do your sightseeing later!" Pivoting in place, Bibi caught sight of the others struggling up the slope, followed by a string of disconnected dots that was the pursuit party. He hurried to meet Peter and the Professor at the top of a granite wall that dropped dizzily a thousand or more feet to the ground.

"Here," said the Professor, spilling from his pack a number of small devices. "These are to be affixed to any smooth area of rock you can find." He picked one and held it up. It looked a lot, Bibi thought, like a mechanical mushroom, with a suction-cup-shaped disk on one end and a steel ring on the other. The Professor flipped a switch on the back of the thing and it emitted a humming sound, together with a faint, pulsing light.

"This device," he began, "dubbed the Stone Sucker by our friend the Wolf, operates through my newly discovered principles of Orthomagnetics—"

"Skip the lecture, Dr. Science," broke in Peter, not without a trace of a smile. "We've got a job to do!"

"Er . . . yes," the scholar hurriedly handed several units to each of them. "Merely place the disk against any mineral-laden surface and its magnetic field will harmonize with that of the earth, withstanding an opposing force of up to five G's!" Bibi placed one against a boulder and it clung like a limpet.

The three hurried to install the devices at regular intervals along the cliff top as the first members of their party came stumbling up. Rhonda took one look at the drop, then swayed back and forth with her hand to her forehead and sank to a sitting position on a boulder.

"Oh," she gasped, "I can't stand heights."

"You won't be standing," Peter responded cheerfully. "You'll be flying!"

Sphere staggered up next, every trace of ruddiness gone from his complexion. The arms of the General were still clasped around his neck, while Abram lumbered along behind, holding up the old soldier's feet. As the group gathered on the rim the Professor hurried from one to the next, handing out thick sticks of what appeared to be chewing gum.

"Gum?" gasped Sphere. "At a time like this?" Their pursuers were now in full view on the slope below; Bibi could see the dogs baying and straining at their leashes.

"Let's use those mouths for chewing instead of chatting," urged Peter. "We haven't got much time!"

The eight were soon engaged in spirited mastication, while the Professor, doing his best to talk and chew at the same time, explained the next step.

"Thish shubstanche . . ." he announced, "whisch is so close in appearansche to . . . shhooing gum . . . is in fact a space age polymer designed to ashsist in your shurrender to gravity!" With that he plucked the now-softened material from his mouth and stretched it to a strand several feet long. Attaching one end to his pack harness and the other to the Stone Sucker at his feet, he leapt into space. Bibi rushed to the edge with the others, expecting to see the poor scholar dashed to pieces on the ground below.

Indeed the Professor did fall for several hundred feet, his elastic life rope stretching behind him, till he reached its limit, bounced several times, and rebounded lightly to a ledge far below them.

"He's a human yo-yo!" exclaimed Sphere.

But the dogs were almost upon them, and as Bibi struggled to help everyone fasten their lines to harnesses he heard the report of a rifle and the whistle of a projectile above their heads.

"My Lord," cried Rhonda. "Do they really intend to kill us?"

"They're tranquilizer darts," shouted Peter. "But if they take us back to the asylum we might as well be dead anyhow!" He and Bibi did a last-minute check to make sure everyone was prepared. "All right: it's fly or die."

"I'm not going," protested Rhonda. "Let them do what they want with me. Let them—"

But Peter, eyes flashing, took several steps toward her and the actress, perhaps recalling her compulsory flight into the garbage bin, whirled like a ballerina and dove into the void. The others followed.

As Bibi hurtled downward he had just enough time to think: "So this is what birds feel like," and to earnestly wish he hadn't left his stomach up on the rim. He heard the long, elastic cry of the General, stretched thin by the drop: "I'm fl . . . y . . . ing!", then reached the end of his rope with an unsettling jolt. His digestive organs caught up with him, and for an instant he hung weightless in the sky. Hillsides and meadows swam into focus below; then the line snapped back and Bibi felt himself sailing upward. He bounced lightly to land on the ledge beside the Professor. All around him, like a tribe of enormous grasshoppers, his friends were doing the same.

"Lord-a-mercy," exulted Sphere. "I felt like a . . . flying turtle!"

"I've seen what it is—" crowed Adam, "to be the sky!"

"You know," Rhonda gulped gamely, having just finished expelling the morning's ration of popcorn from her digestive tract, "that wasn't half bad."

But eight hundred feet of naked air still veered below them, and from above Bibi heard a rain of pebbles and a chaos of barks and shouts as their pursuers reached the edge. "What's to stop them," he asked, "from just climbing down the lines after us?"

"Science!" replied the Professor with a smile. With that he produced a device with a blinking yellow light on it, and ceremoniously pressed a button. Nothing happened. Bibi watched as, with a look of alarm, he pressed it again. Nothing. Emitting a strangled cry of frustration, the scholar slammed the unit against the cliff; with a rattle and a clatter the Stone Suckers released their grip, dropped past the ledge, and recoiled to dangle just a few feet below them.

"Onward," shouted the General, teetering like some great bird at the edge of the drop. "We've no time to lose!"

And indeed the pursuit party, having recovered from their initial confusion, proceeded to send a hail of rocks and tranquilizer bullets from above. Hurriedly fixing their holdfasts in position, the fugitives leapt once more into space.

They had to repeat the maneuver three more times, including a stop to replace the batteries in the Professor's failing Stone Sucker control unit, before reaching ground. At last, having moved a safe distance from the base of the cliff, Bibi and his friends embraced in a frenzy of joy and relief, then collapsed in a tangled, exhausted heap upon the earth.

"You know," remarked Rhonda, removing Bibi's elbow from her rib cage, "I could get to like this aeronautics stuff!"

"Let's go back," enthused Abram, "and do it again!"

"How about," Adam suggested, "finding the nearest trash bin and burying ourselves?"

"I," said the Professor, "could do with a swim in a slime pit right about now."

"Is there a swamp in these parts?" rejoined the General. "I'm in the mood for a stroll."

A chuckle spread through the group, which built rapidly to a chortle, and finally, to uncontainable laughter.

But while the others laughed themselves to tears, Sphere rose to his feet and, shading his eyes with one hand, examined the cliff they'd just descended.

"You know," he remarked, swaying back and forth a bit, "I'm afraid I'm not feeling so well." With that he tottered and fell on his back.

"Omigod!" shouted Bibi, rushing to his side.

"Sphere!" cried Rhonda. "Oh Sphere, dear. Come back. Come back!"

Everyone leapt into action. Peter pressed an ear against his chest while the Professor searched for a pulse. Adam splashed water on his face while Abram palpitated his fingers. But it was Bibi who spotted the solution to the mystery protruding from the poor fellow's ample rear.

"Could that be a . . . tranquilizer dart?" he pointed.

All turned to regard their companion's posterior as the Professor withdrew the device.

"He'll be fine in a few hours," the scholar reassured them. "He could probably use the rest, anyway."

"Couldn't we all," sighed Abram. "Couldn't we all."

After a week or so of leisurely downhill travel the party reached the foothills. Here they camped on the banks of a great river, swollen with snowmelt, that wound its way across the prairie. At Bibi's suggestion they used their lifelines to bind together a raft of logs: and thus commenced the most idyllic period of his journeys so far.

For weeks the group drifted along the waterway, plains stretching in every direction like a limitless, grass-strewn sky. Fish were plentiful, as were the eggs of waterfowl; and even Rhonda developed a fondness for steamed crayfish and the succulent tubers Bibi dug from along the riverbanks. In the warm spring evenings Bibi lay on his back on their rocking craft and watched the moon, like a single bright ship, coast its way across the sky. Then, rolling onto his stomach, he'd watch the orb's rippled reflection drift beneath him. The sky was above; the sky was below—and he would have been hard-pressed to say which was real.

His friends, too, reveled in their newfound freedom. Abram and Rhonda had fallen deeply in love, and did little but sit at the edge of the raft, looking into one another's eyes without a word. Adam, for his part, had undergone a remarkable transformation of his own. He gazed into the river for hours at a time, marveling: "I have floated through the sky: now I float upon the water. All things are the same!" The General had completely regained his spirits, and stood boldly through the days at the prow of their craft, surveying the horizon with a spyglass the Professor had fabricated from broken bottle ends, and crying out periodically: "Thar she blows!" Peter had intuited a method of profiting from stepwise declines in the money market during their descent from the cliff, and spent his days scribbling in a pocket-sized ledger, while the Professor calculated the odds against their escape and incorporated them into his theory of destiny. And Sphere, expanding the musical horizons he'd established on their flight from the asylum, had begun a new composition—an epic-length rondo titled "Cycle of the Ring."

Days and nights leapt over one another like the frogs along the riverbank. The travelers came upon herds of antelope, who blinked at them with wide eyes, then bounded away like springs uncoiled across the vast reaches of the prairie. As in a dream, Bibi glimpsed enormous gatherings of buffalo, and distant bronzed warriors who weaved amongst them like dancers. He watched hawks wheel above, saw sunsets that set the very heavens aflame. All was water and sky and a gentle rocking; the days were boats, drifting from one dark shore to another.

One night as he sat alone watching the moon, Bibi became aware of a presence beside him, and heard the quiet whisper of the General at his ear: "They're messin' with time out there. I can feel it."

And on another occasion, when the night had swallowed up all of Bibi's thoughts and he sat alone in absolute silence, the voice of the Professor materialized from the blackness, murmuring: "*We* are the unpopped kernels."

Days flowed together until the travelers no longer had any sense of duration or destination. Time itself had become liquid, and their minds, laying aside all anticipation and regret, grew as tranquil and reflective as the river itself. The Professor put aside his theorizing, Peter laid down his calculations, Bibi gave up his attempts at understanding the universe and simply surrendered to it. As Rhonda put it: "I feel like we are living in a poem, or someone else's dream."

Bibi spent many days staring into the current, until all existence seemed but a river running from source to sea; and there grew in him the conviction that there was a state to which humans could aspire: a condition of transparence, in which one would offer no resistance to life, or time, or events, but would flow between the banks of birth and death unhesitating and unbound, reflecting the world back to itself with scarcely a ripple.

They had been going on in this manner for some time when they came upon the first signs of civilization.

"Peter," called Bibi one day. "Come tell me what this is!" He pointed down the river to where, in the faint haze of morning, a shimmering latticework, like a spider's web, stretched from one bank to the other.

"I could be wrong," his friend replied, "but if we were anywhere near the modern world I would have to say it was a—suspension bridge."

The structure, for all its apparent bulk, hovered there as weightlessly as a vision; and the travelers clustered at the forward edge of the raft, watching its approach with a growing sense of oppression. As they drew nearer Bibi could see a series of bright flashes passing across the span, like flames springing to life and dying out: these proved to be reflections of sunlight on the windshields of an apparently infinite stream of automobiles that spun across it.

"Where on earth are they going," exclaimed Rhonda, "all the way out here?"

No one could answer. As they passed beneath the span, Bibi found he was unable to make out any of the drivers' faces—only dim, identical forms hunched behind tinted glass, so vague as to seem imagined. And if any of the drivers glimpsed the ragged band of travelers drifting below, they gave no sign.

As the journey continued, their surroundings grew only stranger. Bibi glimpsed clusters of houselike vehicles on the shore, and pale, paunchy people with cameras who shouted and gestured as they passed. He saw scattered farms, then picturesque country estates, and finally, tract homes and rows of townhouses. Billboards appeared, urging:

BUY, BUY, BUY!
MONEY = HAPPINESS
ABOVE ALL, SUCCESS!

Their craft was tossed about by steamers, nearly swamped by powerboats; and the tattered party drew suspicious glances from water-skiers clad in the latest bathing fashions. Factories sprouted along the banks, pumping pipeloads of effluent into their beloved river, which grew frothy and dim, and gave forth the smell of rotten eggs. At last they passed into the heart of the city, past tenements with soot-covered doorways and broken windows, and wary dark faces peering from behind fragments of curtain.

The Frontier was behind them.

5.
SUCH
HIDEOUS MASKS

The reentry of the former fugitives into society was followed by a rather emotional leave-taking. At the junction where their river lost itself in the flow of another, greater river, Bibi tied the raft to an abandoned quay and the Professor, who had once been a Justice of the Peace, joined Rhonda and Abram in marriage. The two announced their intention of finding a place where the sky was always blue and the grass always green, and building a better life there than either had known before. Sphere took the opportunity to inform them that he too was leaving. His life, he said, had come full circle, and it was time to go forth into the world and seek his fortune. Perhaps he'd even organize an expedition to discover whether the Earth was, in fact, round. "After all," he told them, "all these years I've been going entirely on hearsay."

"Our new Columbus," smiled Rhonda, tousling the hair over his orbish brow.

Adam, too, announced his plans to strike off and "see if I can discern the essential nature of the universe."

"That's just what I've been trying to do," Bibi told him. "Good luck!"

After many good-byes and fond embraces—the most touching, Bibi thought, being the perfectly symmetrical parting of Adam and Abram—the group parted ways. Their abandoned raft looked as tiny as a matchbox beneath rows of looming warehouses. Bibi stood for a long time, staring at it in silence, before he was able to turn away. He would always remember this as one of the saddest moments of his life.

But he'd decided, along with the Professor and General, to take Peter up on his offer to rest and recover at his family home several hundred miles to the north, just outside the great city at the head of the river. "It's the hub of commerce," Peter told him. "The seat of industry. And if there's any place you can find out about that Hubcap King of yours, it'll be there."

They pawned the Professor's pocket watch and a few of the General's less important medals, and set off by train that afternoon.

It came as no surprise to Bibi to find that Peter's family was immensely wealthy, inhabiting a region of sloping lawns, still lakes, and stately elms just beyond the edges of the city. The travelers disembarked from the taxi that carried them from the station to find a spirited croquet match in progress on the lawn.

"Point," Bibi heard a middle-aged, balding man in plaids shout as they approached. "By God, that's game again!" His companion, a forlorn-looking elderly man with a drooping moustache, dropped his mallet in defeat.

"Irregularities in the turf," he grumbled. "Why, in Sussex—"

"In Sussex I would have beaten you twice as soundly!" cried the other. "Why, in Sussex they wouldn't even allow a player of your caliber—" He stopped in midsentence, having just caught sight of the ragged crew of travelers crossing the lawn toward them. To judge by the look on his face, Bibi thought, they must have presented quite a spectacle. None of them had shaved in weeks. Their hair, despite last-minute attempts at restoring order in the train station men's room, was matted and unkempt. Their clothes were torn and muddy, held together with odd bits of twine; and the soles of their shoes flopped against the ground like the lolling tongues of enormous birds.

The plaid fellow's eyes widened as he regarded the oncoming apparitions. He stepped backward and muttered to his companion: "Good Lord! Call the, er . . . call . . ." Gaze still fixed on the intruders, he lifted one arm into the air as though to tug a bell rope. When he didn't find it, he raised the other. The limbs groped above his head as though possessing minds of their own. Finally he dropped them and, turning in retreat, tripped over his abandoned croquet mallet. Snatching up the weapon, he wheeled to face the invaders. He brandished it about with a hideous grimace, snarled and curled his lip as though daring them to come closer, and seemed just on the point of launching a stream of threats and imprecations in their direction when an odd look crossed his face. He craned his head and squinted into the light, shading his brow with one hand. At last he let the mallet drop to his side.

"Dad," said Peter simply, as he stepped across the turf to meet him.

"Peter," replied his father. "Is it really you? I thought the barbarians had invaded at last. Or worse yet, missionaries!"

There followed an endless round of banquets and celebrations in honor of the travelers. Bibi and the others received fresh suits of clothing for each function they attended: tweed jackets for teatime, riding habits and bathing gear for leisure activities, tuxedos for evenings. The Professor, Bibi, and the General quickly became skilled at vigorous competitive sports such as battledore and rounders; and Bibi impressed the family with his advanced knowledge of squash, acquired from Peter in the asylum. Before supper each evening, the visitors took dance instruction in preparation for the night's events. "You don't want the times to pass you by, now do you, dear?" Peter's mother, Serena, a stylish platinum-haired woman of impeccable grace, coaxed the reluctant General—and all soon became proficient in the latest steps. The Professor mastered the bolero and fandango and was eager for more, while the General became adept at the Charleston and the cha-cha. Bibi, whose elongated limbs were at last beginning to come under his control, specialized in the Latin dances, while displaying a remarkable aptitude for quadrilles and mazurkas as well. At one gathering after another the group was compelled to retell the story of their escape from the asylum, while Peter's father, Leonard, shouted "Splendid!" from the sidelines, and Serena urged: "Tell them the part about the trash bin," or "The popcorn, Peter dear, don't forget the popcorn!" The only time Bibi had for reflection was before he drifted off to sleep at night; and it often seemed to him at these moments that his new life of leisure was more exhausting than all his travels had been.

One evening, during a break in a recital by the Estonian National String Quartet, Peter took Bibi for a walk along the lakeshore.

"You're looking pretty snappy there in that tux, Chief," grinned the Wolf, who'd trimmed back his russet hair and beard and looked, Bibi thought, altogether transformed himself, "—though that hairdo, I must say, could use a little work."

"What hairdo?" Bibi said, running his fingers through the yet-untamed thicket.

"Exactly my point," responded Peter. "Even so—this could be the beginning of a great career in society!"

"I don't know," Bibi shook his head. "It all seems like such a dream."

"It is a dream," smiled his friend. "The best kind—a real one."

They looked together out over the lake; scalloped shards of moonlight glittered on its surface.

"How far does your land stretch?" Bibi asked.

"Eleven square miles. One of the more modest parcels in the area, actually."

"It's hard to imagine it's all yours."

"Well," replied the Wolf, "technically speaking it's not."

"What do you mean?"

"Actually, it's all owned by the bank. We make enormous monthly payments as a tax deduction. Every twenty years or so when the mortgage runs out we refinance it. Why, between business and property expenses, we haven't had to pay a penny's worth of tax in decades."

"You mean," said Bibi, staring about at his surroundings, "you don't have to give the government anything at all?"

"Of course not," replied Peter. "How else do you think we could afford to go on living here?"

Peter's parents proved themselves to be as well-informed and articulate as the Wolf himself. The family's guests consisted of politicians, artists, and intellectuals—the "Creme de la Creme," as Serena put it, or "Movers and Shakers," in Leonard's words—of contemporary society. In spirited after-dinner discussions Bibi caught up on events he'd missed during his travels, and deepened his knowledge of the challenges that faced the modern world. Over cognac and cigars, visiting dignitaries analyzed the differences between the reigning Freedom and Liberty parties, the first of which advocated a free democracy founded on unhindered commerce, and the second, an emancipated republic built on limitless progress. They clarified the causes of the ongoing civil wars in Saskatchewan and Manitoba, and pondered America's involvement in them. They evaluated solutions to the problem of the illegal immigrants, known as "snowbacks," who swarmed daily across the Canadian border. They discussed the ongoing boom, agreed it was likely to last forever, and toasted an era of infinite economic expansion with glass upon glass of imported aperitifs.

Bibi, who was more determined than ever to find the Hubcap King ("after all," he'd said to Peter, "if the Bushes of Boredom couldn't stop me, and the underground passage, and the trial, and the asylum, what could?" "I don't know," responded his friend, "—yourself?") always took the opportunity to inquire of each guest whether they'd happened to run across a hubcap ranch anywhere in their travels.

"Hope Valley?" replied the president of Consolidated Bushings, a stocky man with eyebrows like Velcro and a cigar permanently implanted between his teeth. "Never heard of it—but that'd sure make a catchy name for an industrial park!"

And Leo Fabian, the thin, gloomy artist who was the leader of the Quasi-Revisionist movement, merely responded: "There is no hope."

As Bibi and the others grew accustomed to life at North York, as the family called their waterfront sanctuary, memories of the asylum and their harrowing escape melted into the past. Peter's grandfather, the man with the moustache, who had served in the abortive New Guinean campaign of '37, took to the General with a particular fondness. The two spent hours smoking one cigar after another and analyzing the triumphs and tribulations of modern warfare, until the General forgot the asylum altogether and became convinced he was Peter's lost uncle, recently returned from a tour of duty in Zanzibar. Leonard, on the other hand, who had doubled his family's fortune by investing in applied technology, took a great liking to the Professor, and the two spent many afternoons walking the grounds of the estate, debating the future of science and industry.

But although Bibi was well liked by everybody, he frequently had the feeling that no one, with the possible exception of Peter, understood him in the least. One rainy afternoon when the family had to content itself with such indoor diversions as bagatelle and Parcheesi, Bibi tried to explain his search for the Hubcap King; but although everyone listened politely enough, he somehow had the feeling his words weren't getting through.

"Hubcaps?" Serena remarked, raising her eyebrows slightly. "What a notion!"

And Peter's grandfather shouted from the other side of the room, "You should go into sales!"

"But really," interjected Leo Fabian, who'd come out for the weekend and was always eager for an intellectual debate, "I think what our young friend is getting at is a certain feeling of dislocation, of emptiness; the sense that our lives might be . . . incomplete in some way. Haven't you ever felt that?"

"Well," replied Leonard, after a long moment, "there is the sailboat, I suppose, which will soon need refurbishing—"

"And our expansion of the guest quarters," chimed in Serena. "That, of course, will have to be dealt with."

"And," continued Leonard, growing excited, "there's always my collection of Post-Minimal Sculpturalists to complete—"

"And I've always had a sort of a vision," Serena added, "of the ultimate party—one where the guests *really* have as good a time as they all say they did afterward. Why, when you think about it, there's a world of things—"

"But don't you think," persisted Fabian, "that Bibi has something deeper in mind? A sense of alienation—perhaps even meaninglessness?"

"Why," replied Leonard after a pause, "I should think living the good life is meaning enough. Wouldn't you say, dearest?" He glanced at Serena, but found his wife merely staring into space with a forefinger to her lips, as though trying to remember something she had forgotten a long time ago.

After several weeks of intensive relaxation, Peter and Leonard decided it was time to take Bibi for a visit into the city.

"I want to show you," announced Leonard, "where our family made its fortune!"

Except for a few hours on the afternoon they'd abandoned the raft, Bibi hadn't walked the streets of a city for close to a year; and the concrete and asphalt, traffic and hurrying businesspeople came as a shock to his wide-open senses. Advertisements, each bolder and brighter than the next, were plastered on every available surface. Billboards, installed under the government's new Urban Exhortation Program, shouted out messages in six-foot-high letters:

AMERICA: GET YOUR SHARE
MONEY IS EVERYTHING
MORE, MORE, MORE!

Street vendors hawked their wares along the avenues:

"Souvenirs! Fabrics. Knickknacks!"

"Authentic Zairean Zories!"

"Genuine Hapsburg Homburgs—"

"Don't be fooled by cheap imitations!"

"Buy now, while supplies last—"

"Everything must go!"

"Ah," exclaimed Leonard. "Commerce. Competition! The lifeblood of the nation. But come, you must see the Money Market."

Bibi's head was whirling. He followed Peter and his father around a corner and through an alleyway; at last they emerged in an enormous open-air marketplace with hundreds of stalls, and a crowd of people in business suits running about and shouting in an absolute frenzy.

"This," pronounced Leonard, "is it!"

Amidst the hubbub, it took Bibi some time to figure out what was going on. At the center of the courtyard was an information board covered with numbered placards. Every so often a wizened, bespectacled gentleman ascended a ladder against its face and changed some of the numbers around. Each time he did this, pandemonium erupted in the already manic crowd. Men broke from the cluster at the foot of the board and dashed to a bank of phone booths at the other end of the courtyard. Others gathered in groups, arguing and gesticulating. Still others hurtled through the crowd in a panic, trading slips of paper back and forth at terrific speed.

Fortunately, Leonard was able to explain the inner workings of the system. "What you see before you is the foundation on which our entire way of life is built! Why, our free enterprise system springs from this very center, ensuring the continuance of our exceptional standard of living, not to mention the stability of our gross national product!"

"In other words," translated Peter, "this is where the fat cats come to make the big bucks." But the Wolf's eyes had taken on a gleam Bibi had never seen in them before, and his gaze darted hungrily about as he spoke, taking in every nuance of action in the courtyard.

They followed Leonard to a line of stalls at the far end of the market, where activity was at its most furious. Buyers shouted and mopped their brows; dealers stood on tables with megaphones, making simultaneous announcements from which Bibi was only gradually able to decipher words:

"Get your dollars here, 97 cents!"

"Two bits, 24 cents, step right up."

"Five spots, four-seventy-nine!"

"What on earth is happening?" Bibi finally managed to get out.

"In this sector of the marketplace," explained Leonard, "we have done away with the unwieldy business of dealing in physical objects altogether. In this rarefied atmosphere of pure economics, we deal only with the exchange of money itself!" Seeing Bibi's expression, he went on, "It's quite simple, actually. At this moment the value of the dollar is dropping. Everyone wants to sell. The market fills up with unwanted currency, driving the price lower. When it looks like it's going to bottom out, everyone starts buying again at the better rate. The supply drops, the price skyrockets, and the cycle begins once more. It's supply and demand, cause and effect—human nature in its purest form." He gazed benevolently over the chaos. And indeed, even as Bibi watched, the market began to reverse itself:

"Dollars 99 cents," the dealers cried.

"Tenners, nine-ninety-eight!"

"Quarters, two bits—"

"Dollars one-o-one!"

Bibi turned to Peter. His friend's eyes were ablaze with excitement. "This is it," the Wolf cried. "The real thing. We're not talking abstracts here—we're talking cold hard cash!"

Bibi looked back over the crowd. A fight had broken out, and amid clouds of dust and ties and flying fists he saw the flash of money falling and swirling, with investors diving after lost bills and others struggling against them, till the whole courtyard was a storm and a whirl of fiscal fury.

"Now hear this—" Peter shouted into the frenzy, "you all better watch your butts out there. The Wolf is back—and boy, is he hungry!"

"Ah," chuckled Leonard. "Another day at the market. What do you fellows say we adjourn for lunch?"

•   •   •

Having recovered from his sojourn in the wilderness, Bibi began to consider the notion that finding the hubcap ranch by random means might not be the only way to proceed; and as he became comfortable in his new environment, he dove back into his search with fresh resolve. He took to traveling into the city on his own, prowling through libraries and newspaper archives in search of any reference to his Uncle Otto or Hope Valley. He devoured texts on the history and geography of America, carried home armloads of maps from survey offices, and even pored over the last ten years' death records—hoping, in this case, that he would *not* find what he was looking for.

"Hubcap King?" a woman in the Statistics Bureau responded, screwing her face into a question mark as Bibi explained his mission. "Hmmm . . . somehow that rings a bell." She drummed her fingers on the desk. "You know, it seems to me you're not the only one who's been asking about this fellow."

"But who—?" Bibi was mystified.

"Well, it must have been a couple months back . . . but a Hubcap King, now that's the sort of thing that sticks in your mind."

Bibi stood before the desk, rubbing edgily along the borders of his scar. "Do you remember any more?"

"Only thing I remember is the guy asking was kind of tall— or was he short? Anyway he was awful pale, and he seemed to be having some kind of trouble with his breathing. As I recall he didn't know your hubcap man's last name, so we couldn't help him. He did spend a lot of time browsing through the coroner's files, though. Seemed to enjoy the experience."

The woman's words, strange as they were, rang a distant bell. But although Bibi racked his brain afterward for some clue as to the identity of the other searcher, he couldn't imagine who it might have been. Finally he just had to put it down to another of life's many mysteries; and after a time the question passed from his mind altogether.

At last, while browsing through a stack of ten-year-old issues of *The Global Truth*, Bibi found a headline that caught his eye:

FOUNDATION FOUNDER SENT TO SLAMMER

There, staring back at him from the front page, was the unmistakable face of his Uncle Otto. Dressed in a suit, minus his usual earring, the Hubcap King appeared almost dapper—though his gaze remained piercing, and his short, sandy hair was as undisciplined as ever.

Heart knocking against his ribs like a demented jackhammer, Bibi bent over the story:

> *Otto Brown, founder and chief executive of the idealistic-yet-controversial Wake Up From The American Dream Foundation, was found guilty yesterday on tax charges stemming from the employment of illegal Manitoban and Tibetan immigrants. The organization, whose mission remains obscure, had long been under investigation for sheltering political refugees, as well as the unlicensed import of Oriental scrap metal.*
>
> *"I am entirely responsible," said Brown upon receiving the verdict, "and utterly unrepentant." He has been sentenced to three years in Hum-Hum Federal Prison.*

Having discovered a rough time frame for his investigation, Bibi dove back into the stacks with renewed energy. He unearthed a few articles on the founding of his uncle's organization, which had occurred shortly after his return from Asia ("you might say it's a sort of socio-political advocacy group dedicated to the abolishment of somnolence and languor!" an enthusiastic Otto was quoted at its inception). Bibi uncovered several other stories about his trial, but nothing that would help determine his uncle's current whereabouts. Finally, in an issue dated two years later, Bibi located another article, this one accompanied by a photo of a thinner, tired-looking Otto:

FOUNDATION FELON GETS TIME OFF
FOR GOOD BEHAVIOR

Otto Brown, founder and former chief executive of the Wake Up From The American Dream organization, was released yesterday from Hum-Hum Penitentiary after receiving one year off for good behavior.

"He was a model prisoner," remarked Warden Charlie "Iron Fist" Callahan. "But the strange thing was, it wasn't just him—from the day he arrived it seemed everyone in the joint was exceptionally well-behaved!"

When asked whether he planned to go on working with the foundation, which has expanded its activities in his absence, Brown replied, "H– no! I'm through with politics. I'm headed out to the desert, where I won't have to deal with any of you people ever again!"

Since Brown's release, the prison crime record has returned to normal, with five escape attempts, nine inmate assaults, and thirteen cases of drug trafficking reported in the last twenty-four hours.

Bibi checked in with the other newspapers, but merely found alternate versions of the same stories. And though he spent many more weeks prowling through the stacks, he could find no information from the past seven years at all. The Hubcap King had simply dropped out of sight.

Meanwhile, life at the Yolk had been enlivened by a new arrival, and for a time Bibi was in danger of forgetting his search altogether. The newcomer was Peter's sister, a statuesque and voluble woman of perhaps twenty-eight who worked as an account executive for Joseph K. Cosmetics, and had just returned from a tour of major art centers in Europe.

"My given name was Faith," she told Bibi in introduction. "But I was feeling a bit down after my last divorce so I changed it to Cilantro. Much snappier, don't you think?" With that she flipped a dark lock of hair back from her brow, and fastened her grey-green eyes onto Bibi's with an intensity that made the skin seem to stiffen across his entire body.

True to her name, Cilantro quickly added a great deal of spice to Bibi's life. She introduced him to her friends in the So-So district, center of a burgeoning art scene that was soon to rock the nation's cultural life to its foundations. In addition to Fabian, with whom he was already well acquainted, Bibi met Winston Scallop, the leader of the Intact Rejectionist movement; and they lunched several times with Bambi Poorhall, whose experiments with dropping paint-filled water balloons from skyscrapers had been dubbed Plop Art.

"Neat scar," Poorhall exclaimed, on glimpsing the Australoid imprint on the back of Bibi's wrist. He eyed the mark with an intensity that seemed almost envious. "That'd sure make a great subject for a painting!"

One evening Fabian invited them to an opening at a gallery that specialized in Dematerialism; but to Bibi's astonishment they arrived to find the place bare, with champagne-drinking visitors milling past empty walls, emitting cries of delight. It was rumored that the most radical elements of the new renaissance had attempted to do away with the viewer as well; and indeed, Bibi and his new companion tried one evening to attend an exhibit on Nondirectionalism, but were unable to locate the gallery.

When not frequenting the museums and concert halls of the downtown district, the two danced till dawn in one of the many South Side clubs ("Nobody mambos like Bibi," Cilantro was heard to say) or sat in the smoke-filled coffeehouses of the West Side, talking of art and the meaning of life in America. Focusing onto him with her hazy eyes, flipping her hair back with that characteristic flick of her head, filling the air with grand and extravagant gestures, Cilantro held court in her own fashion, reminding Bibi of Peter's mealtime meetings at the asylum. Bibi listened, with fingers of fascination playing about his insides, while Cilantro shared such family secrets as the identities of Leonard's various mistresses, and Serena's affair with a Saskatchewanian stableboy, whose citizenship she was trying to secure. She told him of their outcast brother Paul, who'd embroiled the family in years of litigation over a series of spankings he'd received as a child, for which he was now seeking compensation, and she shared the stories of her various divorces and the therapies that had helped her recover from them.

Bibi, who had not yet experienced the joys of complete physical intimacy, was captivated—at least, as captivated as it was possible for him to be by a woman bearing a full quota of intact digits. And there would have been more between them than conversation, if not for an odd quirk Cilantro revealed of requiring that her lovers arrive equipped with an assortment of Mediterranean delicacies in order for her to reach a functional state of arousal.

"Did you bring the prosciutto?" she murmured in Bibi's ear the first evening he came to her room, taking him by surprise and making it impossible for either of them to perform; and on a subsequent encounter Bibi, in his confusion, brought along a jar of Beluga caviar, causing his would-be partner to cry: "No, no—that's Russian!" and again ruining the mood of the moment.

"Maybe he really doesn't like me after all," Cilantro lamented to Peter after the "Beluga" incident. "Do you suppose I'm not thin enough? And why do you suppose he keeps staring at my fingers?"

One evening, as dusk seeped between the buildings of the city and the wind, carrying the first bite of autumn, moaned along the avenues, Bibi found himself walking a desolate street in the industrial district. Above, like tilted, ruined windmills, hulked the silhouettes of a dozen or more abandoned factories. An eerie quiet pervaded this region of the city—there was no traffic in sight, no pedestrians foolish enough to be caught out after dark. And as the dusk settled in, Bibi felt an unaccountable sense of peace creep over him, a peace nearly as deep as in his first days in the mountains, or on the drift down the river. For the first time it occurred to him that the city was not something simply created *by* people, but something created through them, with a life and purpose all its own—as natural in its own way as a beehive, or a bird's nest, and no more controllable than the weather. In the gathering twilight not a single object seemed out of place: everything, in the chaos of abandonment, seemed to have ended up exactly where it belonged. In the fading light even the rusted, collapsing machinery seemed shaped by the hand of nature; and all was imbued with the dusky beauty of decay.

Bibi was walking past a mound of trash when he stopped, his eye caught by a movement amidst the rubble. It flickered and fell back into darkness, so that at first he took it for a rat or a mouse. But then it moved again, and Bibi saw an object, the size and shape of a child's shoe, poke from beneath a piece of aluminum sheeting. As he watched, the metal buckled and bounced, and an eye blinked open at an adjacent corner, regarding him with bemused neutrality. Then, with a clattering wham! the sheet slid aside and the smallest man he'd ever seen sprang from the heap to land on the sidewalk. His head reached scarcely to Bibi's waist. He wore a tunic-like garment fashioned from scraps of burlap, on which Bibi could still make out the words "Einstein's Onions." A length of telephone wire held up his pants, which had once belonged to a much larger man; the legs had been cut off at the knee, while the crotch swayed nearly to the ground.

"Ah," exclaimed the fellow. "Naptime's over!" He stretched his arms skyward and arched like a cat. Then he looked at his visitor, and grinned one of the widest, warmest grins Bibi had ever seen on the face of a human being. "Folks call me Nubbin," he said.

Bibi spent the next several hours with his new friend, huddled in the doorway of an abandoned factory, sharing the story of his life and his search. Nubbin listened carefully, added "Uh-huhs" of encouragement and nods of agreement, asking questions to clarify obscure points. When Bibi finally ground to a halt, feeling that at last he'd found someone who understood him, Nubbin gazed for a long time into the deserted street. Then he sprang to his feet and announced:

"You've got to meet the Potato Man."

Through a wilderness of alleys, over abandoned shipyards and fields of tires, through culverts scuttling with rodents, across wastelands of wrack and ruin, all the flotsam and jetsam of a civilization gone mad, Bibi followed Nubbin, beneath a rising moon that shone impartially on it all—a moon, Bibi mused, that was reflected just as completely in a puddle of ditchwater as in the vast and boundless ocean. Finally they came to a highway that thundered with traffic; headlights arced like glowing eyes through the night.

"We're almost there," said Nubbin. "Follow me." He slid down a trash-strewn embankment and over a chain-link fence, then darted, with Bibi behind, into an underpass, across which the road rumbled and roared. The passage turned; they slogged through puddles while moonbeams gleamed through cracks in the mortar and the dank tang of decay invaded Bibi's nostrils. They emerged at last on the edge of the river below an enormous bridge. Bibi saw shafts of headlights and the gleam of hubcaps spinning across the span. The ground shook beneath his feet; moonlight lay on the water like spilled milk. He sensed forms moving about them in the darkness, and knew they were not alone.

"Spud," his companion called into the shadows beneath the bridge. "Spud, it's me, Nubbin!"

After a moment there emerged from the darkness a lumpy white form marked with bumps and carbuncles; a troll-like figure who looked as though he had never seen the light of day.

"Greetings," said the Potato Man. He gently took Bibi's hand, while shapes scuttled behind him in the gloom. "Welcome to our humble abode."

It turned out to be a wild night. Bibi built a fire of old telephone books in a hollow scooped out of the sand, and Nubbin presented the Potato Man with gifts he'd scavenged from trash bins along the way: a bottle of shoe polish and a half-empty can of bathroom disinfectant—from which, to Bibi's dismay, the Potato Man immediately took an enormous swallow.

"Arrggghhh," the fellow cried. "Must be eighty proof at least!"

Sitting by the fire as the traffic screeched overhead, the Potato Man listened to Bibi's story. He took a slug from the disinfectant bottle every so often and, when it was empty, moved on to the shoe polish. When Bibi had finished, the man rose to his feet. He stood, rocking back and forth from one leg to the other, his lumpish figure casting its tortured shadow on the bridge abutment behind him. At last, in a singsong voice, he began to intone:

"I have traveled throughout this great nation by road and by rail. I have slept in weeds and shipping yards and desert canyons, where snakes slid across my bedroll in the night and I lived for weeks on nothing but the flesh of centipedes. I have loved and drank and lusted and adventured and dreamed." He paused to take another swallow of shoe polish, while voices from the darkness urged: "Say it, Spud. Say it!"

"I have cut trees in the forests of the north and grubbed ore from the Great Basin. I've gathered salt from barren flats and rubbed it in wounds caused by loss of love in the heedless days of my youth. I've gulped waters of oceans and eaten snow of the highest peaks. I've carried wine in my hat and varnish in my blood, and spat at the shoes of those who would have consoled me. Even now, as the rats of time gnaw holes in my stomach and worms creep through my bones—"

Voices from the darkness: "Speak it!"

"—I remember all the things I have done in my wild and heedless existence, all those I have loved and betrayed and befriended and drunk beside. And—" The figures outside the firelight leaned closer and Nubbin nudged Bibi with his elbow. "And—" But the Potato Man appeared to be losing momentum. As Bibi looked on, his twisted, rollicking dance slowed to a halt and his shadow merged into the darkness beneath the bridge.

"And," he concluded, sitting down in the firelight with an apologetic sigh, "I'm afraid I can't remember whether I've heard of a place called Hope Valley or not. I must be getting old."

A collective groan came from the bystanders, while Bibi's heart slid wearily down his esophagus to its usual location.

"Perhaps it'll come to me yet," he reassured Bibi. "Meanwhile, you must meet the others."

One by one the Potato Man's companions emerged from the darkness and one by one they told Bibi their stories.

"I have devoted my life," one fellow announced, leaping boldly into the circle and clearing the ground by a good five feet—"to overcoming the force of gravity. Little by little, I have succeeded. Each year I am able to leap some fractions of an inch higher, and stay in the air a few milliseconds longer. In time, I shall be free!" He sprang aloft once more; and indeed, it seemed to Bibi that he hovered in place for the tiniest sliver of an instant before settling back to earth.

Another man, a strange-looking fellow with an oblong face and a tuft of hair that rose straight up from the crown of his head, explained that his life had been ruined by an inordinate sensitivity to odors. "I can identify a person by smell alone," he told Bibi. "I can identify their shoes. I can tell you what they had for lunch and how long ago. I can tell you how many cigarettes they've smoked in a day, and what brand. How can I carry on a conversation with someone when I sense a universe of information they're unaware of? How can I kiss a woman when all I can smell is her toothpaste? It's destroyed my life!"

Bibi met everyone. In addition to the Gravity Man, and the other fellow, whom Bibi privately dubbed The Pineapple, there was a woman with a great round head, known as Ms. Pumpkin, and a fellow called the Bunny Man, because of his exceptionally long, tapered ears. There was a man with no nose, a woman with no ears, and another with a missing chin. There were several families, one of whom had four children named after household products—"Wife just up and named 'em after whatever washed up on shore that day," the father told Bibi—including a girl of four named Kleenex, a toddler called Rayovac, and twin five-year-old boys known as Ajax and Comet.

The family had built a platform of driftwood and salvaged planks amidst the girders of the bridge, and at night they slept while the sounds of cars and trucks hurtled just a few feet above their heads.

"But can't you find work?" Bibi asked the man, whose story had caused an odd feeling, like an old piece of timber, to lodge at the center of his chest. "What about The Boom?"

"It may be booming for them," the fellow said, nodding toward the tall buildings on the other side of the river, "but it sure ain't booming for us."

The moon sank toward the horizon and the night deepened. Kleenex's mother made up a broth of scavenged shoe leather and a few wrinkled carrots she'd managed to grow along the riverbank, and with little Rayovac sitting on his lap, Bibi took great gulps of the steaming brew from an old tin can. He watched as the fire heaved its red and yellow glow against the sky, and when the moon set the dome filled with new stars, as though some of the embers had stuck in place.

In an attempt to be helpful, The Pineapple gave Bibi directions to a place known as Soap Valley, which was the center of the nation's detergent industry, while the Bunny Man explained how to find Rope Basin, a region of hemp plantations at the edge of the desert. The Gravity Man gave him the address of the Lumber Relations Board, of which he had once been a member, and Ms. Pumpkin told Bibi how to contact a company that made shoes for people with oversized feet, in case he ever did manage to locate his enormous cousin.

As the night wore on things got wilder. Bibi danced an impromptu mambo with the woman with no chin, and taught the bridge dwellers the limbo, which they performed with abandon in the firelight while Nubbin pounded out a rhythm on an upturned paint tin. The Potato Man delivered speech after speech, the Gravity Man did backflips, and The Pineapple repeated the story of his olfactory misfortunes thirteen times. Toward dawn the talk grew more random. Ms. Pumpkin, whose manner had grown strange after she downed several bottles of vinyl cleaner mixed with No-Doz, postulated the existence of a place called Nope Valley, which must by definition exist in counterbalance to one called Hope; and as the first light of morning streaked the sky, the Potato Man realized that the memory kicking about his mind all night did not have to do with Hope Valley at all, but rather Dope Hollow, an area inhabited by a population far too moronic to bother seeking out.

All in all, Bibi thought, he had never spent a more enjoyable evening.

In the next weeks Bibi found himself leading a strange dual existence. *I feel more at home with these people,* he noted in his journal, *than anyone I've ever met.* He still spent much of his time, when he wasn't working on his research, at the estate; but several times a week he traveled across the wilderness of the city to meet his friends beneath the bridge. Bibi's arrival was always cause for celebration, for he'd bribed Peter's cook into providing him with leftovers from the family's expansive meals. Slipping beneath the underpass, he'd slide down the embankment to the riverside, open his rucksack, and produce for the wide-eyed bridge dwellers one Tupperware container after another, stuffed with beef Wellington, lobster Newburg, or coquilles Saint-Jacques. He brought gumbo and jambalaya, croquettes and fondue, pâté de foie gras, stroganoff and succotash. They'd build a fire and feast beneath the roaring span, with all the wheels of the city spinning above their heads, and talk and laugh till the small hours of morning, while the river wound its endless way southward.

"How can you do it?" a worried Cilantro asked Bibi when he confided how he'd been spending his evenings. "You could get yourself killed!"

And she proved entirely accurate in her estimation of the danger involved. In a little over a month, as Bibi made his way with food-laden rucksack through the war zones of the city, he was robbed seven times. He learned to prowl like a cat through the darkened streets of the metropolis, to hide in abandoned cars, to huddle in trash bins and bury himself beneath heaps of slag. Once he outraced a gang of Manitoban youths through a landfill composed entirely of disposable diapers. On another occasion he eluded a band of Andalusian thugs by curling inside an abandoned tractor tire, breath held and heart pounding, as they thundered past him in the night.

He learned to love the monologues of the Potato Man, which varied endlessly from visit to visit; and he hung on every word in hopes that he might uncover a clue to aid in his search. He became like family to Kleenex and her brothers, as well as another group whose children had simply been named One, Two, Three, and Four, in order of appearance. They took to calling him Uncle Bibi, and gathered around breathlessly when he arrived, his pockets filled with bonbons. Bibi brought books and clothes and blankets and anything else he thought his friends might need; and he learned to keep silent when the estate housekeeper passed him in the hallway, muttering to herself about cases of missing shoe polish and aftershave. But despite the friendship he'd found in his new life, as the weeks went by and autumn settled deeply on the land Bibi was possessed by the feeling that he was getting nowhere in his search for the Hubcap King.

One twilit evening, after carrying twenty-three servings of chicken marengo across the nightmare wastes of the city, Bibi left his friends to their meal and strode out alone onto the bridge. In the dusky light, beside the whistling roar of the traffic, he stood on the walkway at the center of the span and watched the river, like a fat brown snake, coil and uncoil itself beneath him. He watched as darkness settled over rooftops and soaked between skyscrapers, buildings lit up and headlights made their way through the veiny labyrinth of the streets. The city was an animal, burgeoning and muscular, with a thousand glittering eyes. Bibi felt all the joy and the ugliness, the wonder and desperation of it wash over him. His soul burned with yearning and confusion. He wanted more than ever to reach past the chaotic spin of events and touch the very heart of the world, its still yet pulsing center.

"Well, River," he called to the great beast below him, as he teetered over the rail, relishing the pull of its whirling depths. "What next?"

The time had come to move on.

Serena decreed that the grandest bash ever was to be thrown in honor of Bibi's departure: a masquerade ball, featuring foods from around the world, a fifty-three-piece orchestra, and a company of Bolivian tightrope walkers. Just before dusk on the evening of the event, Bibi slipped away and, with a team of chauffeurs recruited from around the neighborhood, drove out with a fleet of Bentleys and Rolls Royces to pick up his friends from beneath the bridge.

"Home, James," intoned the Potato Man as he stepped past the chauffeur-held door into a silver Rolls—looking quite natty, Bibi thought, in a tattered blazer and a pair of sunglasses salvaged from a dustbin.

"Care for some caviar?" inquired Ms. Pumpkin, as the Gravity Man bounded into a snow-white Bentley beside her. "Tell me, how *are* Maxine and the boys?"

In honor of the occasion, the bridge folk had scavenged through trash piles all across the city; and before they left the riverside they'd dressed Bibi in the most outlandish getup he'd ever worn. On his feet were a pair of orange basketball shoes, topped by a set of argyle socks; for pants he wore silver jodhpurs, a bit too loose at the waist and held up with a length of rope; his shirt was a yellow turtleneck several sizes too big, accented by a pink ascot; and to top it off was a captain's jacket, unraveling slightly at the cuffs, with epaulets on the shoulders and tiny ships embossed on the buttons. Nubbin completed the outfit by smoothing out a crumpled red beret and, standing on the shoulders of Kleenex's father, placing it atop Bibi's unruly mass of hair.

"I hereby dub thee," he announced, "King of the Tramps!"

As the fleet of limousines pulled up to the door they were met by Serena, who cut a stunning figure in the garb of Cleopatra. She greeted them with a warm but disconcerted smile; for between the darkness of evening and the unfamiliar costumes, the Queen of the Nile didn't recognize a single one of the guests who disembarked from the row of fine automobiles.

"Why, you've all come as hoboes," their hostess exclaimed, peering at the Potato Man and the others in the darkness. "How marvelous! Where did you ever manage to find such delightfully hideous masks?"

It was a grand night. The food was superb, the tightrope walkers superlative; and the costumes surpassed everyone's wildest expectations. In addition to the legion of hoboes, Bibi consorted with trolls and gargoyles; sultans, sheiks, and all manner of royalty; knights, chimney sweeps, and mass murderers; vampires, executioners, and trollops. Cilantro, in a moment of inspiration, had concocted the most unusual costume of the evening, arriving in the guise of an enormous hourglass ("Well, she's certainly got the figure for it!" remarked one onlooker). She'd arranged to have Bambi Poorhall hang his latest silkscreen series in commemoration of the evening, and although none present could yet know it, this group of abstract yet oddly familiar forms—each shaped a bit like the continent of Australia—was to change the direction of American art for years to come.

Bibi watched in admiration as Serena worked the crowd, pausing here to chat, laying a hand on a shoulder there, collecting and dispensing compliments with infallible elegance. "She doesn't need to break the ice," remarked the Professor, whom Bibi scarcely recognized in his role of Sir Isaac Newton, "—at one glimpse of her, it melts!"

In a matter of no time Serena had the Potato Man engaged in spirited conversation with Congressman Glib O'Reilly, who'd come as Smokey the Bear, and she'd hooked The Pineapple up with Lester Proboscis, the famous nose and throat specialist, disguised as Cyrano de Bergerac. The Bunny Man confessed his deepest secrets to best-selling author Susie Jacqueline, who was impersonating the Easter Rabbit; while Nubbin hobnobbed with industrialist Ransom Stonefellow, who'd arrived dressed as Father Time himself—complete with sickle, robe, and floor-length grey beard.

Toward midnight, Bibi and Peter finally managed to track each other down amidst the commotion.

"Sure you don't want to just forget this whole hubcap thing and stay on here?" offered Peter, who with his red beard appeared exceptionally convincing in the role of an Alsatian pirate. "You could marry Cilantro, you know she's crazy about you, we'd take you into business as a full partner—"

"What about you?" Bibi countered. "Why not come with me? No one ever said the search for meaning has to be a solo effort."

"What?" responded his friend. "And leave without ever checking out my new investment scheme?"

The two looked at each other, then burst out in laughter.

"Ah," Peter said, laying his arm across Bibi's shoulder. "I'm a cynic, remember? I guess money's going to have to be meaning enough for me."

Bibi had arranged to have a punch bowl loaded with unique libations for the bridge dwellers; and in the wee hours of morning the celebration really got under way. The Bunny Man danced the craziest samba with Serena she'd ever known, while The Pineapple watusied with Cilantro. Ms. Pumpkin polkaed with Leonard, and the woman with no chin tangoed the Professor to exhaustion. The General, who'd dressed for the occasion in full battle regalia, led a lineup of pirates, minutemen, and sumo wrestlers in a cakewalk, while Nubbin danced a solo tarantella. The orchestra, booked at the union maximum of 95 minutes' playing time, voted to renounce their contracts and play till dawn, abandoning their classical repertoire in favor of honky-tonk and smoldering rhythm and blues, while the Potato Man leapt onto a table and shouted over the crowd: "The hokey-pokey! The funky chicken. Surely if we all danced together, the world would be free of strife!"

Finally the entire group, servants and chauffeurs included, ended in a grand circle on the lawn, dancing hand in hand beneath the stars. They danced in, they danced out; the circle bubbled to a huge orb, then folded in on itself in a chaos of delight.

"If only old Sphere could see us now!" cried the Professor as Bibi, hand in hand with Cilantro, pranced madly past him; and when the circle next closed in, Serena gasped in Bibi's ear, "What a wonderful group of guests you've brought. I do believe everybody's actually having as good a time as they all say they are!"

. . .

At last, as the eastern edge of the sky turned violet, then golden, and the sun crept wearily over the horizon as though it, too, had been up all night, the guests returned to their cars to take up where they'd left off the day before. As they waved good-bye Serena took Bibi's hand in hers. "It really was the ultimate party," she said, her features shining with a new and profound tranquillity. "I don't know how to thank you enough."

Bibi doffed his beret and bowed deeply. "Your happiness, madam," he replied, "is the only thanks I need."

With that, Bibi slipped away to the kitchen pantry, where he spent the next few minutes in a painstaking selection process. Afterward he made his way up the back stairs, to a room that was not the one in which he customarily slept.

"Bibi?" a voice murmured on hearing him enter. "Is that you?" Eyelids fluttered in the semidarkness of the room. "Did you bring the—" Bibi rubbed a smooth green oval across her lips. "Olives?!" At that Cilantro opened her eyes wide.

"And sun-dried tomatoes," said Bibi, laying his riches on the bedspread. "Artichoke hearts drenched in olive oil. Stuffed grape leaves. Feta cheese. Fresh rosemary sprigs—"

"Bibi," Cilantro exclaimed. "Bibi, oh Bibi—oh, baby!" With that she stretched out her arms and drew him close; and the two commenced their final, finest dance of all.

But if truth be known, his lover must have found it a trifle odd when afterward, as they rested together side by side, Bibi took her hand in his and, gently folding her ring finger over against her left palm, held it that way in the darkness for a long, long time.

Later that morning Bibi dreamed he was flying above the city. At first the experience was pleasant enough, but as he coasted along between the buildings, an uneasy feeling began to grow in him. He couldn't tell what it was at first, but gradually the conviction developed that something here was dreadfully, terribly wrong. He swooped down for a closer look, noting the steady, plodding gait of passersby, the fixed intensity of their gazes. He watched traffic cops, arms moving in fixed, machine-like rhythms; street vendors, mouths opening and closing mechanically as they hawked their wares. And all at once, Bibi realized what the problem was. Everybody was asleep. Businessmen, taxi drivers, shopkeepers, laborers—all of them, everyone—a legion of sleepwalkers, dozing their lives away in the dreamy hubbub of the streets. As Bibi watched, the cars below him transformed into beds, spinning through intersections with sleepers twined in sheets upon them; and he was filled with the vast and inescapable realization that he was finally, irrevocably alone.

Bibi awoke shouting, with Cilantro holding him. "Wake up! Everybody. Wake up!"

"It's O.K.," Cilantro told him, stroking the hair back from his oversized brow. "Everything's going to be O.K." At that Bibi stopped shouting and lay there quivering. "It was just a dream. Really."

They lay quiet for a long while, holding one another in the shuttered, twilit room.

It was Bibi who broke the silence finally, using his lover's given name for the first time. "Faith," he asked her, "what's your deepest sorrow?"

Cilantro smiled, a bit sadly. "When all is said and done," she answered, "I'm just like everybody else."

It seemed to Bibi he'd heard those words before, but at the moment, he couldn't remember where.

It took a dozen limousines to carry everyone who wanted to see Bibi off to the station. In addition to Peter's family and the Professor and General, there were the bridge folk, for whom Bibi had wrangled an invitation to stay on at the estate as long as they liked ("You can't tell me," Serena exclaimed, "that such lovely people have been sleeping under a bridge all this time. My word!") as well as Cilantro's artist friends and a host of servants and chauffeurs from the neighborhood, all of whom had grown exceptionally fond of Bibi during his visit.

Peter, it had been decided, was to remain behind and take the reins of his family's empire while his father made the gradual transition to retirement. The General was to stay on as a permanent and honored guest. The Professor, for his part, had so impressed Peter's father with his erudition that Leonard planned to set him up with a fully equipped research facility to continue his work. "And don't you worry about your friends from the bridge," the scholar assured Bibi. "We'll find well-paid research positions for each of them. They're unpopped kernels if ever I've seen any!"

The Gravity Man was the only one missing from the group, for he'd said his good-byes early and left to seek his fortune with the Bolivian acrobat troupe. The Pineapple had negotiated a lucrative contract with cosmetics magnate Fax Proctor, whom he'd met the night of the party, for use of his ultrasensitive nasal apparatus; and ever since that evening there'd been whispers in the political community that Glib O'Reilly, impressed by the Potato Man's gift for oratory, was planning on sponsoring him for a seat in Congress.

Serena was in tears by the time the train was ready to board, and the others seemed scarcely better. Cilantro sat on a bench at the edge of the platform, clutching little Kleenex to her breast and dabbing at her eyes with a handkerchief, as Peter approached Bibi and embraced him. "Hang in there, Birdman," he said. "Keep your head in the clouds and never stop flying."

"Onward," cried the General. "Never give up your flag!"

"Think and dream," said the Professor, shaking his hand. "Adventure on for all of us."

"Take care of yourself, old man," said Leonard, with a hearty clap on the shoulder. "And, er—do try to get into something practical."

The bridge dwellers gathered around Bibi for a massive group embrace at the edge of the platform, the children squealing and tugging at his legs, while the Potato Man leapt onto a ticket counter and delivered a passionate address on the nature of friendship and destiny.

At last there was no one to say good-bye to except Cilantro.

"Faith," said Bibi, taking her into his arms, feeling an odd sort of hollowness beneath his rib cage that he'd never experienced before. The two stood holding one another in silence for a long time, tears rolling down both sets of cheeks, until Cilantro said simply, "You have such blue, blue eyes," and, finally, turned away.

Then it was time to board, and all the bothersome business of tickets and conductors and finding his seat. As the train pulled away and the figures on the platform fell behind, Serena's handkerchief fluttering in the wind, Bibi realized that he was leaving behind the only real friends he'd ever known.

6.
THE SHAPE
OF TUESDAY

Over the next several years Bibi crossed America seven times. He journeyed through three booms and two recessions. These years saw the suicide of the new president, the mental collapse of his successor, and the resignation of the next after the failure of his "Good Deal" program for economic development. During the same period the government weathered five assassination attempts, eleven sex scandals, and a failed attempt to put down an insurrection in Tierra del Fuego.

On his fifth sojourn Bibi finally located his cousin and her lumberjack husband, living in a hovel at the edge of one of the industrial cities that had sprung up along the borders of the desert. But the man, whose name actually turned out to be McPhee, had been laid low by an accident in which he'd somehow come between a 220-volt current and its rightful ground, and had subsequently lost all power of speech. Confined to bed, his massive frame had dwindled till he looked like nothing so much as an enormous heron, all legs and bones, huddled beneath the covers in a vain attempt to stay warm.

Bibi tried to get the pair to reveal the whereabouts of the elusive Otto, but the woman, whose mind had cracked beneath the strain, merely eyed him suspiciously and replied: "Ottoman? Umpires! Alas, Ahoy, all hope has flown!"; while her stricken husband, breathing heavily as though struggling to communicate something of great importance, pointed mutely to a towel rack against the wall, then scratched onto a scrap of paper a message Bibi found entirely obscure:

Beware the Sallow Man!

At last, after splitting the unfortunate couple enough firewood to last the winter, Bibi gave them what little money he had and moved on.

He revisited what had once been the limitless reaches of the Frontier, now reduced to bits of parkland sandwiched between shopping centers and housing developments. He traveled to all the great cities of the continent, and several times made the trip back home to see his aging mother at Christmas.

"How you've changed, my son," the good woman exclaimed, on seeing the tanned, muscular stranger who stood on her doorstep. "But at least you're not dead!"

Bibi recrossed the Great Divide, now populated with villages and ski chateaus with names like "L'Alps Amerique" and "Matterhorn Villas." He even paid a visit to what was now called Middlemont Valley, having heard it had changed considerably—and indeed it had. The insurmountable cliff where Bibi nearly lost his life was now traversed in twelve minutes by gondola. Rival tour guides in restored horse carts thronged the streets, calling out:

DISCOVER THE TRUE STORY OF:
LARGEMONT!   SMALLVILLE!

Both reverends had retired, as had the trash collector, having all become wealthy through real estate investments; and Nurse

Baker had opened a boutique known as Magic Wanda's, which specialized in paisley prints and other protozoic designs. Indeed, the entire community had mended its differences, and was now united under a new doctrine, engraved on the stone archway at the entrance to town:

GOD IS COMMERCE

As the outside world changed, Bibi felt himself changing too. He felt weightier, was the only way he knew how to express it— as though the gravity of life were increasing with each new highway or housing development he encountered. Even his dreams of the Nine-fingered Woman, and his hopes of one day coming to understand love, could do little to compensate. He grew from lankiness into solidity and his elongated features became ever more forward-reaching, while his desire to find the Hubcap King grew first to yearning, then to hunger, and finally, near obsession.

Bibi's journals, the repository of his inquiries into the nature of existence, grew over time to fill seventeen volumes. At one point he devoted several weeks to recopying them in a smaller hand, reducing their number briefly to thirteen, but like a gas expanding to fill available space, his thoughts soon swelled to seventeen volumes once more. Unwilling to separate himself from any portion of his collected understanding, Bibi struggled on beneath its weight, hauling the tattered notebooks in his bulging, disintegrating rucksack wherever he went.

With few alternatives remaining, Bibi focused his search on the final frontier of the continent: the Great Desert. Here, in the transparent air, Bibi renewed his studies of the celestial bodies. He learned to sleep by day and haunt arroyos and mesa tops by night, and in time grew able to see the invisible tracks left by the stars and moon as they made their way across the sky. He became conversant with the spirits of the land—ghosts of prospectors and native shamans; and although he asked for help in his search, their reply was always the same: "In your heart you already know the way. Why bother us?"

It was on just such an evening, when the face in the moon bore an uncanny resemblance to his own, that Bibi stumbled upon the Institute of Living Time.

There seemed at first to be nothing unusual about the building at the foot of the rise below him. Tilted and tumbledown, silhouetted against the sky in the rumble and flash of an impending storm, it appeared at first as though it might even be abandoned. Bibi edged along the rim of a butte in the cool blue moonlight, then slipped into a wash that dropped steeply to the desert floor below. Having been without human contact for weeks, he'd decided it was worth a closer look.

His first hint that there might be something odd about the place was how long it took him to get there; for through some quirk of lighting or perspective, the structure proved to be both larger and further away than he'd anticipated. Not only that, but its shape, which he'd taken from above to be a rectangle, proved actually to be a somewhat twisted rhomboid, which teetered dangerously against its desert backdrop as though it might fall over at any moment. And at its apex was the most peculiar weather vane Bibi had seen anywhere. It consisted of an assemblage of spheres that might have represented celestial bodies or atomic particles—but the arrows which ought to have indicated wind direction were marked instead with the initials A.M., P.M., B.C., and A.D.

Thunder groaned and rattled as Bibi mounted the stairs to the sagging front porch; as he rapped at the door the bottom fell out of the sky and rain whooshed down over the desert. Lightning flashed and thunder roared; the building trembled but did not fall. A second flash lit up a sign beside the doorjamb:

INSTITUTE OF LIVING TIME
SERIOUS INQUIRIES ONLY!

Bibi knocked again. He could hear echoes receding on the other side, as though through a maze of passages, but that was all. He jiggled the knob, and was just on the point of investigating the latch with his penknife when the door creaked open a little and a single eye appeared through the crack, lit by the flickering glow of a candle.

"You from Chrontec?" came the voice that went with the eye. It was hoarse and suspicious, dry as a bit of shoe leather left in the sun.

"Chrontec?" replied Bibi. "Actually, you might say I'm a sort of pilgrim. I'm looking for my Uncle Otto, you see, and I—"

"Otto?" The voice oozed distrust. "Well, he's not here!"

There was a pause, as though a decision were taking place on the other side; then the door opened further and a second eye came into view beside the first. The face they inhabited was exceptionally round and smooth, devoid of wrinkles or other signs of age, and hairless but for a single odd forelock that drooped low over the forehead. It would be too simple, Bibi thought, to say the fellow had the face of a clock, though it had all the roundness and precision of a clockface; and his nose jutted up from its center like the pointer on a sundial. The man stared with round dark eyes which were also like clocks; and looking into them Bibi imagined he could hear his thoughts ticking away.

"Listen," Bibi began, "if this is a bad time for you—"

"Bad . . . time?" croaked the man. He laughed, the hoarse peals echoing along the corridor behind him before cutting off abruptly. "What a notion!" The door creaked open further and the fellow looked him over.

He has cold eyes, Bibi thought. *Round and hard as marbles. Eyes that do not believe in blinking.* And there was something about his presence that reminded him uneasily of the Man with the Terry Cloth Face.

"Well," the fellow said finally, "at least you seem to have a sense of humor. If you're really not from Chrontec, I suppose you might as well come in."

Bibi followed as the man produced a lantern from a shelf behind the door and hustled away down a linoleum corridor, cloaked in darkness and set about with half-invisible objects—*was that a grandfather clock?* Bibi wondered—*and over there, an hourglass?*

"Come along," his guide hissed. "We've no time to lose!" Bibi stumbled after as best he could, while peals of thunder rocked the building and chimes went off in the shadows, and cuckoos called at random from nowhere in particular.

"Damned storm's killed our power," croaked his host as he scuttled troll-like down the corridor. "Lucky so many of our pieces are wind-ups, or we'd never know what time it was, eh? Heh heh! Eh?" His laugh cackled through the gloom, then cut off as abruptly as it had begun.

Bibi followed as the man led the way up rickety staircases, through cobwebby doorways, over mounds of cogs and gears. The place, which hadn't seemed overly large from the outside, seemed to have swelled since he'd entered it to near infinity. Lightning flickered through windows set high in the walls, lighting up shapes around them for a dreamlike instant before plunging them back to obscurity: suits of armor, Egyptian sarcophagi, skeletons of extinct animals—and clocks, clocks, clocks, clocks, clocks. They looped and twisted, swiveled and turned, till at last Bibi lost all sense of direction or dimension. He reached out to touch a doorjamb, but found it several feet from his fingertips. He stooped to clear a rafter, but it slammed into his nose. He felt at once large and small, finite and immense; he could no longer tell if they had been going on this way for hours or eons. In the black and tangled corridors time itself seemed to have run down, like an unwound watch; the minutes had turned to snails, gliding their slow trail of mucousy moments across the firmament of infinity.

. . .

At last the man led the way down a ramp and through a set of double doors, and the two emerged into a spacious workshop lit with candles and kerosene lamps, and overflowing with temporal paraphernalia. A pendulum hung from the ceiling; below it was a mound of metronomes. In one corner Bibi saw a pile of tortoise shells; in another a clutter of tree trunk cross sections—and the far end of the room held an unsettling array of scythes and gravestones.

Bent over a desk at the center was a man in a wheelchair. He spoke without looking up: "Gnomon, would you mind checking this afternoon's telechron reading? The horologic count is much lower than expected, and given the sidereal nature of the data—" He wheeled about and stopped in mid-sentence.

"Well," he continued after a moment, glancing over Bibi's desert-worn exterior. "Who have we here—Attila the Hun?"

"Found him banging on the door at nineteen hundred hours, eleven minutes, fifty-three seconds, Chief," explained his assistant. "Claims he's not from Chrontec."

"Never heard of our distinguished competitors, I suppose?" The man's eyebrows lifted skeptically; and as they squinted at one another in the candlelight, it occurred to Bibi that this must be the saddest-looking being he had ever encountered. Rheumy, melancholic eyes, magnified by thick-lensed glasses, brooded beneath his dark, overhanging brows. His cheeks sagged in abject surrender to gravity. His mouth drooped earthward at the edges, as though it no longer had the will to hold itself up. Even his nose seemed sad, thought Bibi, with long, sorrowful nostrils that quivered when he spoke. And his legs, resting hopelessly against the seat of his wheelchair, were as withered and shrunken as old bones.

He looks, Bibi thought, *like someone who's seen it all.*

"But come now," the man's lips flexed in what might have

been an attempt at a smile. "We're forgetting our manners. Gnomon, aren't you going to introduce me?"

The assistant's eyes glittered in the lamplight like ball bearings. "Mr., ah . . ."

"Brown," interjected Bibi. "Bibi Brown."

"Bibi Brown," announced Gnomon, "I hereby present the honorable Dr. Diem S. Clook."

"Clook?" repeated Bibi, involuntarily.

The doctor extended his hand. "Allow me to be the first to welcome you," he said, "to the Institute of Living Time!"

While Gnomon went off to check on the electrical system, Dr. Clook spent the next one hour, twenty-three minutes, and forty-seven seconds leading his guest on a tour of the institute, while delivering a ceaseless monologue on his life and work.

"I began my career," he informed his visitor, rolling his chair down yet another endless corridor as Bibi strode alongside, carrying a lantern to guide their way, "by initiating the scholarly world's first investigation into the Metaphysics of Pointlessness. Unfortunately, the immediate outcome was that I could no longer find any reason to pursue my work. And this"—here the doctor stopped and mopped moodily at his glasses with a bit of tissue paper—"was the first great disappointment of my life.

"Recovering however from this early setback, I pushed boldly forward into a new arena: the History of Melancholy. How far back did it go? To the first humans? Beyond? Were the dinosaurs depressed?"

Holding the lantern high so the doctor could see what he was doing, Bibi revealed a pile of what appeared to be mastodon tusks piled up along one side of the passage—rather untidily, he thought. The storm appeared to be abating, sending only an occasional bluish tremor against the windows, to illuminate his host's features with a melancholic light. Clook checked his lenses against the lantern, shadow looming and flickering against the wall, then put them back in position and resumed his gradual, rolling progress.

"But this line of inquiry soon gave out, and I was brought at last to the study of time itself. I first explored the notion that time might be a form of gravity, having noticed how heavily the moments sometimes weighed upon me. And this led to my well-known research into the Geometry of Duration. 'What are the dimensions of a second?' I asked myself. 'Are there, in fact, "wee hours"? What is the shape of Tuesday?'"

The doctor paused, as though reaching into some hidden vault of memory—and whatever he found there, it seemed to Bibi, must have saddened him immensely, for his eyes welled up with moisture, and he heaved an enormous sigh.

"Having exhausted these avenues, I moved my operations out to the desert, where I commenced my investigations into the geographical nature of time. No longer was I concerned with *what* time was—I wanted to know *where* it was. And it was here that I struck, as they say, pay dirt. It seemed all my efforts were about to come to fruition. That is, until the accident—the terrible, terrible accident . . ."

"Accident?" prompted Bibi, for Clook had stopped in - mid-roll and now sat motionless, staring down the hall into the shadows. But the lights chose that moment to flicker a few times, then come back to full brightness. With a visible effort the doctor pulled himself erect and attempted what might have been intended as a smile. "Let there be light!" he quipped, blinking against the renewed glare. "But come—I must show you the collection."

With that he rolled to a door at the opposite side of the hallway, where a sign read:

DR. JULIAN CALENDAR MEMORIAL COLLECTION

"In honor of my late teacher—Jules, as we called him. I am glad he did not live to see me like this." With that Clook pulled a ring of keys from his coat pocket and, lofting them ceremoniously in the air, opened several latches. Stepping through the door behind him, Bibi found himself entering a new world, the likes of which he'd never imagined. He stood there for a long moment while a complex, interlocking symphony of ticks and tocks swelled in the silence like a thousand beating hearts. Here were water clocks, atomic clocks, Mickey Mouse watches; clocks that ran clockwise and clocks that ran counterclockwise—even experimental units in which the hands ran in opposing directions. There were models with thirteen hours instead of twelve, others with letters in place of the numbers, and finally, an attempted hybridization of an alarm clock with a times table, in which twelve o'clock was represented by the number 144.

"But everything's all out of sequence!" exclaimed Bibi.

"Oh yes, we don't always go in order here," his host nodded. "We like to skip around!"

"But how," protested Bibi, "is anyone ever able to really know what . . . time it is?"

"You haven't seen anything yet." With that his guide rolled to the far end of the room, where a group of movable partitions stood covered in calendars of every description. "We have here one of the finest collections of experimental prototypes in existence!"

Bibi's head was spinning. First he examined a series having all the usual months, but in alternate orders: January, following July, preceded by November. Then there was a set in which the months went forward as usual, but the day of the week always stayed the same.

"Yes," confirmed Dr. Clook. "Under this system, it is entirely possible to have a month of Sundays!"

Finally Bibi halted before an attempted integration of the months of the year, the days of the week, and the twenty-four hours of the day.

"So by this approach," he began, "today would be—"

"February, the Eleven O'clock of Thursday," replied the doctor. At this Bibi had to sit down.

• • •

At the insistence of Clook and Gnomon, both of whom seemed to have grown increasingly fond of him since their first meeting, Bibi stayed on at the institute for over a week—if such measurements could be said to have meaning any longer. Indeed, the more he got to know them, the more Bibi found his hosts utterly transformed; and his initial trepidation soon faded away beneath their constant attentiveness. Gnomon toured him daily through some new aspect of the place's temporal infrastructure, while Clook involved Bibi in the assembly and testing of various timepieces, even going so far as to attempt an occasional joke. Bibi often noticed the two whispering between themselves, and casting occasional glances in his direction—no doubt deciding which new discovery they might share with him next. Once they'd grown used to his presence, in fact, the two appeared to revel in the unaccustomed companionship; sometimes it seemed to Bibi that they did not want him to leave at all.

One morning as Bibi was sitting in the institute library leafing through a volume titled *Memories of Things Forgotten*, his attention was taken by an odd, faint noise that sounded as though it were coming from very far away. Sometimes like laughter, and again like sobbing, it would stop, then start, then break off again, seeming to issue from a maze of dimly-lit corridors that branched off from the rear of the place, which he'd not yet explored. The sound brought back his unease, like the scratching of fingernails on an infinity of blackboards. Finding it impossible to carry on with his reading, Bibi crossed to the back entry. Here he heard it again, more loudly: a series of gasping or chortling sounds that reverberated from some hidden point in the building's interior.

"Hello?" Bibi called into the shadows. "Dr. Clook? Gnomon? Is everything O.K.?"

Although the echoing vibrato of his voice along the dark tangle of corridors did little to restore his confidence, Bibi was concerned that someone might be in need of assistance; and so, moving toward what appeared to be the sound's source, he found himself stepping reluctantly into the linoleum-clad dimness. At first Bibi tried to keep track of every turn and junction in the passage so that he would not become disoriented, but amidst the infinitely branching tributaries this quickly proved impossible; and after he'd passed the same stuffed triceratops for the third time, he knew he was again utterly lost. Just when he'd given up all hope of ever finding his way back out of the labyrinth, Bibi rounded a bend to come suddenly upon Dr. Clook, seated in his wheelchair before a door that looked, in the faint light, as though it must have a dozen or more locks on it.

The doctor was crying.

"Thirteen years," he choked between tears, scarcely seeming to notice Bibi's arrival. "Thirteen years to the day!"

"Dr. Clook?" Bibi stepped to his side. "Are you all right?"

His host blinked up at him through moisture-smeared spectacles. "I'm terribly sorry," he sniffed, wiping his cheek on his sleeve, "for this dreadful display of emotion. It's just that today's the thirteen-year anniversary since the . . . the . . ." He drew a handkerchief from his pocket and blew his nose noisily.

"The accident?" Bibi finished quietly.

Clook nodded. He folded his handkerchief and replaced it in his pocket. "I was working late in the lab one evening," he said, staring moodily down the hall, as though his past still lay somewhere among those twisted corridors; as though it might even be recoverable, if only he could discover where he'd left it. "I was absorbed in a series of exceedingly delicate measurements on the relation between simultaneity and duration. All at once, while carrying a sample across a catwalk some fifteen feet above the floor, I was stricken by one of those spells of vertigo which, as you've no doubt noticed, are an unavoidable by-product of tinkering with one's basic reference systems." With this, Clook glanced toward his listener; and indeed, it seemed to Bibi that he could feel the vertigo rising in him as well—as though his feet, if he'd dared look down, would have been hovering visibly several inches above the floor.

"I tried to fight it off," the doctor went on, "but it was no use. Senses fading, I grabbed for a handrail, but it broke through—and in the pivot of an instant I'd tumbled over the edge, straight into a vat of forward-moving time."

"A vat of time?" repeated Bibi. "But . . . can it be that such things exist?"

"I myself am the proof," replied the doctor, bitterly. "Although I was only submerged from the waist down, and only for a matter of moments, the bottom half of my body was aged by decades. And I, in the prime of my youth, was left with the legs of a one-hundred-and-twenty-three-year-old man!"

"How dreadful!" exclaimed Bibi. In the dim light of the hall, as he looked upon Clook's strange, sad face, he was hard put to convince himself he was not dreaming.

"To have the rest of me hale as a spring chicken, while my legs have passed into their golden years—ah, time is a form of pain!" The doctor paused for a long moment, staring along the twilit corridor. "But then, there's many a man who's died at the hands of time. In a way, I suppose, I was lucky." As though emerging from a trance, Clook looked up at his listener. He blinked several times behind his thick lenses, then swiveled his chair abruptly to a halt before the door with the locks on it. "But things being what they are, I suppose there's no harm in letting you have a look for yourself. Come along and you'll see a marvel the likes of which few people have even dreamed!"

Fumbling with his key ring, the doctor turned the latches one by one and wheeled through the door, gesturing for his visitor to follow. Bibi stepped past an array of pipes and bubbling basins, to stop before an instrument that looked like a cross between a microscope and an hourglass. His host dripped a bit of vaguely luminous fluid from a flask onto a slide, then placed it beneath the lens and motioned him over.

"Take a look for yourself," Clook whispered hoarsely. "Raw, unadulterated time—ninety-nine percent pure."

Bibi's head was pounding. He bent and looked into the eyepiece. What he saw there were not, as he'd half imagined, miniature clock faces, but tiny spinning whorls of light.

"Yes," confirmed the doctor. "Time is circular."

Bibi stared. The disks spun, each like a tiny moon, or—what else?—a hubcap.

"Our research indicates," said Clook, "that much of this stuff may have been left over from before the age of the dinosaurs. We've discovered vast deposits of it, trapped in strata far below the desert floor. Why, it's so pure, and there's so much of it, you could quarry and sell it. Make millions." His voice trembled, and his eyes burned. "They've sold off practically all the space in the world already. Time is the last frontier!"

"But selling time . . ." stammered Bibi, "couldn't that have unpredictable consequences?"

"It's a dangerous notion, I'll admit," agreed the doctor, whose reason had clearly been sprung by having too much time on his hands. "After all, no one's certain how infinite the supply really is. All we can be sure of is that nobody ever seems to have as much of it as they'd like. But the secret's bound to leak out, and mark my words, when people hear of this there's going to be a time rush the likes of which this world's never seen!"

That evening, in response to Bibi's announcement that he really ought to be moving on, his hosts staged an extravagant farewell dinner. Both Gnomon and Clook seemed in exceptionally high spirits as they laid out a spread of instant potatoes and minute rice, flavored with parsley, sage, and rosemary. Indeed, the doctor's marble-eyed assistant exhibited an almost affectionate attentiveness as he dished out his delicacies, topping off Bibi's glass again and again with vintage wine from their private stock ("Aged years in a matter of moments!" boasted Clook), and prattling on all the while about the work of the institute.

Dr. Clook, for his part, was particularly solicitous in clarifying Bibi's questions on fine points of temporal theory, including the particulate versus wave models of time, the politics of velocity, and obscure concurrences between such diverse phenomena as menstrual cycles and church bells. He offered frequent, spirited toasts—"To the Upper Mesozoic! To the Big Bang!"—topping off Bibi's glass enthusiastically after each round. Swept away by the unaccustomed hospitality, Bibi shared with his hosts his most intimate points of temporal conjecture, and even went so far as to read several passages from his journal aloud.

"Time," he intoned, "is an express train, hurtling at breakneck speed toward a destination from which it can never return."

"Indeed," countered Gnomon, whose manner had become visibly inspired in direct proportion to his wine intake, "—but could it not be equally posited that *we* are the train, able to travel in only one direction, while time, the track, extends infinitely in both?"

"There's no time like the present," interjected Dr. Clook, refilling Bibi's glass, "and what is the present but the collision point between two trains marked 'past' and 'future'—with we ourselves being the casualties?"

"Have you ever considered the notion," Bibi conjectured, "that time might be a sort of U-turn, with the starting and ending points identical?"

"I," put in Gnomon, "have long been possessed by the certainty that all events are actually simultaneous."

"But can we not agree," asserted Clook, "that the most fundamental question is what *time* the universe began? Was it midnight? Six A.M.? I, for my part, have always been certain it happened at four in the afternoon. Yes, the universe must have begun at tea time!"

The rest of the evening dissolved into a blur from which Bibi could later retrieve only fragments. Over dessert, which consisted of a potpourri of dates and currants, there was a debate on the interchangeability of the space–time continuum, ending in the conclusion that next year's events might theoretically be predicted using nothing more than an ordinary ruler. Then there was a discussion of chromatic theories of time, which resulted in the development of a system correlating the colors of the spectrum to the days, weeks, and months of the year—though no one present, unfortunately, could ever remember the details afterward.

Thoughts reeled and staggered through Bibi's head. What had brought them together on this day, at this place, on this tiny lump of rock spinning in the vast emptiness of infinity? The chances of such an event taking place seemed impossibly remote. Bibi watched Gnomon and Clook argue and gesticulate, but as the evening wound down everything began to seem increasingly far away and enormously strange, as though he were driving a car backward down an unfamiliar highway, using only the mirrors.

Bibi's final recollection of the evening was of a stricken-looking Clook struggling momentarily to his feet, only to collapse back in his chair crying: "I have just realized that three o'clock is a complete illusion!"

That night Bibi dreamed. He dreamed of trees going bare, of beards turning white, of cemeteries and skeletons, of endless successions of events draped over limitless reaches of eternity. He dreamed of flying clocks and burning clocks, of men and women dashing about some sort of a factory shouting: "Allegro! Adagio!" He dreamed of an assembly line where seconds were joined to make minutes, minutes to make hours, hours bonded into days, years, eons . . . He dreamed, finally, of being imprisoned in an enormous clock. Every time the chimes sounded he was compelled to run down a set of stairs and out a door at its base, where he bobbed up and down, emitting a chorus of cries and shrieks. Bibi repeated these actions many times before he realized: he was the cuckoo.

When he finally awoke, sunlight streaming through an open window and the ticktock of an immense hangover pounding in his brain, Bibi found himself unable to move. It gradually became clear to him that he was lying on a bed, arms and legs manacled to the frame; and as the fog in his head began to lift, he realized that Dr. Clook was seated beside him.

"I'm terribly sorry," the doctor greeted him, "but Gnomon has convinced me that knowing all you do, it would be a terrible error of judgment to allow you to escape. We can't allow news of our discovery to leak out just yet, you see. We wouldn't want it to appear in *The Times*!" He peered at his captive closely, as though to see whether he'd appreciated his little joke; and Bibi thought that just for an instant he saw the faintest flicker of a smile pass across his lips. "But seeing as how we've enjoyed your company so thoroughly," Clook went on, "we've decided to offer you a choice. You can languish here for the rest of your natural life—or wander the Canyons of Time for all eternity."

"If it's all the same to you," Bibi answered, "I'd rather be outdoors."

Bibi's bed rocked back and forth as a crane, with a grim, gloating Gnomon at the controls, swung him out over the edge of the canyon. As he dropped slowly into the abyss, Bibi could see the silhouetted figure of Dr. Clook in his wheelchair on the rim, waving good-bye—rather sadly, he thought. But as his limbs were still fastened in place, Bibi was in no position to return the farewell. Having little choice, he surrendered to his descent, rocking like an infant in his airborne cradle while the varicolored walls of the canyon slid past. He glimpsed imprints of fossilized plants, of skulls and vertebrae, the footsteps of huge, unidentifiable animals embedded in the sandstone surface. Veins of bright metal and crystal-laden alcoves coasted past his eyes—and despite a mild case of airsickness from his overindulgence the night before, Bibi had to admit that all in all this was the most relaxing descent of a sheer cliff he'd ever experienced. In fact, since his head was still pounding and it seemed such a long way to the bottom, he thought he'd allow himself the luxury of closing his eyes for a moment.

Bibi had just drifted into a pleasant, confused dream of interlocking mirrors, with Druids and pyramids receding into them, when his arrival at the canyon floor jolted him from his reverie. He'd scarcely had time to collect his wits before his bed tilted, the shackles released, and he slid unceremoniously to the ground, his rucksack plunking to the earth beside him.

The least they could have done, Bibi thought, watching his slumberous vehicle sail back the way it came, *was to leave me a place to sleep.*

But there was something odd about the notion—it rose from his mind with an unaccustomed torpor, like some enormous animal heaving itself from a mudhole. Unsettled by the sensation, Bibi experimented with assigning names to the rainbow colors of the cliffs that surrounded him; but he found himself able to generate the single concept *Orange* only after a strenuous effort and an exceedingly long wait. Gingerly, he attempted to raise his left hand; the quickest movement he could manage was scarcely equivalent to a slow-motion scene in a movie. Not only that, but his heart, which up to this point had always been reliable, had begun to hesitate between beats, as though wondering whether it was worth the trouble to go on.

A surge of panic went through him—if one can describe an emotion that slid past with all the velocity of a fleeing slug in such terms—and Bibi scrambled to standing position. Or tried to: the result was more like extricating himself from a pool of molasses. Eons seemed to pass while he lifted one foot, placed it beneath him, shifted the other, flexed his muscles to push upward against the overwhelming force of gravity—which, as Clook had predicted, did appear to have increased in direct proportion to the slowing of time. On his feet at last, Bibi attempted to gather his thoughts, but he found the effort impossible: his ideas were sleepwalkers, each plodding off in its own somnambulant direction.

At length, summoning all his powers of concentration, Bibi managed to focus the concept *Move!* in his mind long enough to thrust himself from his resting place and stagger vaguely off along the twisting, rocky corridor. After an immeasurable duration, he reached a point where a cluster of narrow ravines split off from the main canyon. In the hope of finding some improvement to his condition, he chose one of the passages at random and stepped into it.

Here, to his surprise, Bibi found a lightness rapidly coming into his spirits, and his oppression immediately began to lift. Notions fluttered about his mind like trapped birds. His thoughts started to ramble, then to canter, and finally to race— till before long they were bounding ahead of him like a legion of kangaroos, while Bibi hurtled along in their wake, lungs filling and emptying like a bellows gone mad. The sun spun so quickly across the sky his eyes scarcely had time to adapt; the moon sped through its phases in a matter of moments—and Bibi was only saved from a premature end by a series of extraordinary leaps which carried him to the end of the passage and back out to his starting point again.

More cautiously, he investigated the canyon's other offshoots. He finally selected a particularly inviting one, marked by a series of pools and rivulets that trickled along its sandstone floor. Here he paused to drink from a puddle, and was shocked to see the reflection of his own face—which having not yet shed the years accumulated in the other passage, was patterned with creases and framed by an unruly mass of white hair. But even as he stood there, Bibi saw time beginning to reel back. He watched his hair change to grey, then back to brown, while his wrinkles smoothed out and vanished. His features became youthful, then childlike—and in sudden realization, he wrenched himself away just in time to avoid undoing his own birth.

Tentatively, Bibi explored the rest of the passage, taking on years and sloughing them off in a rhythm he gradually came to enjoy. Deep in the canyon's interior, he came upon a series of sandstone basins, each of which held its own self-contained universe. Reflected therein, Bibi glimpsed the birth and death of the solar system, the fates of his unfortunate ancestors (who even hundreds of generations back, armed with clubs and crude stone implements, had carried on their unbroken chain of self-annihilation), and forty-seven different conclusions of his search for the Hubcap King. He saw streams of discarded destinies, of uncertain outcomes waiting to be fixed; seething cauldrons of causes and effects that joined and unjoined at random. There were realms where time was relative and realms where it was absolute; universes ruled by fate and universes of free will; dimensions that were outside time itself and impossible to contemplate without risk of insanity. At one pool he lifted a handful of water to his lips, but several drops spilled from his palm—and before they reached the ground he felt he'd lived a thousand years.

At last, exhausted, Bibi made his way back out to the main passage, where he sat down upon a boulder with the intention of figuring out a way to escape. But here, to his surprise, Bibi found himself unable to figure anything at all; for he had come at last to that zone of the labyrinth where time ceased altogether—and without time to carry them along, his thoughts ceased as well.

And in that clarity of a mind that was, for the first moment in his life, free of thought and therefore utterly still, Bibi saw time for what it was.

He'd always believed that thoughts required time in which to unfold themselves—but he now saw that, without thought to hold it in place, time could scarcely be said to exist at all.

Having seen through the illusion of time, Bibi realized he was essentially unbound by it.

So he decided to step outside it.

All at once, Bibi found himself standing on the porch of the Institute of Living Time again, in the instant just before he'd first knocked at the door. Thunder, as before, rolled and rumbled across the desert; as before, the sagging boards shook beneath his feet.

Bibi looked about at the shapes of the surrounding hills. The desert receded to nothingness on every side; the moon hung in the sky like a pendulum. He saw his fist, poised to knock in the air before the door. Slowly, he let it fall to his side.

My God, thought Bibi. *There's no way I'm going through that again.*

With that he turned on his heel, descended the porch steps, and set off into the wilderness once more.

7.
GRAVITY

Time remained stretched out of shape, like a deflated balloon, for weeks after Bibi's insight into its nature. The minutes were like hours, the hours were like days, and the days lollygagged forward like prehistoric beasts headed nowhere in no particular hurry. The world, which had always seemed unreal to him, took on a renewed air of insubstantiality, as though he were wandering a landscape of pure imagination.

The wonder and beauty of existence swept over him in great, fierce waves: the universe was full of bright, shining things, punched out of nothingness and into being, created anew each moment.

He felt like a sleeper awakened from a lifelong dream.

In the light of his new understanding, Bibi reexamined the nature of perception. He watched as his mind wrapped sense around raw information: labeling that object *bush*, bending that mound into *mountain,* passing the light that was the universe through the prism of time, space, and consciousness, splitting it into form.

He understood, or thought he understood, the purpose of existence: he, like every human being, was a window through which awareness might shine into the universe—a window that, till now, had had its shade drawn against the light.

We are, he wrote in his journal, *bits of God in skins.*

And later he scribbled: *We are time!*

He'd let go of everything, it seemed. He felt not even gravity could hold him any longer.

Driven by a renewed and purified impulse to find the Hubcap King, Bibi pushed deeper than ever before into the desert, to the howling wastes at the center of the continent where the wind blew all the time. Here there was not a single stream or spring for miles. Shrubs struggled to hold themselves to the earth; battered trees clawed at one another in the ceaseless tempests. Bibi learned to live on cacti and the flesh of scorpions; his skin turned as dark as shoe leather, his beard grew thick and untamed, and his eyes became as clear as the night sky. Finally, days passed without a glimpse of a single green or growing thing, and the wind blew every thought out of his mind until he felt as vast and empty and wild as the land itself.

Having traveled in this manner for some time, Bibi glimpsed one afternoon, in the haze of a salt flat ahead, an object that did not seem to belong there. As he drew nearer, dust rising and swirling about his boots, he could just barely make out what appeared to be an upright post with a shiny rectangular surface mounted atop it. This materialized, with his approach, into a sign bearing the message:

**GOVERNMENT TESTING AREA
WARNING!**

WATCH OUT!!
DANGER!!!

So, what isn't dangerous? shrugged Bibi, who, having escaped the Canyons of Time, now believed he could conquer anything. The sign, backed by a high, wire mesh fence that seemed to extend indefinitely in either direction, was discolored, tilted and peeling, as though no one had attended to it in a long while. After a few minutes of contemplation, Bibi found a place where an animal had dug beneath the barrier, and wriggled through. On the other side he found exactly what he'd seen on the first: salt, dust, and desolation. But as he pushed on, Bibi noticed a peculiar sense of buoyancy beginning to overtake him, as though his rucksack were filled with feathers, and his feet inflated with helium. Despite the heat, he felt such a renewed energy that he began to skip along like a child, and even took an occasional leap into the air.

After several miles there appeared in the distance what Bibi took to be a tornado or dust storm. But as he drew nearer he realized this was like no storm he'd ever encountered. A great swirling mass, similar to a funnel cloud, it spiraled from a point on the ground to a wide, dark wedge against the sky. But unlike other desert whirlwinds, this one revolved in an absolutely stationary position above a single patch of earth. Not only that, but where it met the soil there appeared to be a sort of crater, from which debris swept up in a continuous whirl of motion. There was something ominous about the thing, as though it were an enormous bird of prey hovering over the planet; and a tremor ran through Bibi's bones as he looked upon it, unsettling him to his marrow.

Bibi's sense of oppression only increased as he neared the place. A roaring and a rumbling filled the air, and the ground began to tremble; the sky grew steadily darker, while gusts of wind swept unceasingly about him; until, after some hours of walking, Bibi found himself at the base of the black, seething mass, staring into its heart, still unable to comprehend what he was seeing.

The crater was enormous, extending as far as he could see in every direction. Reeling, vertiginous, Bibi stood at its edge, peering into the boiling sea of chaos that rose with a howl like a thousand freight trains into the sky. He watched as boulders, dust, even streams of what appeared to be lava, swept upward into the atmosphere—and as he looked on he felt the updraft beginning to affect him as well; for his head seemed as though it might lift from his shoulders, and his feet threatened to leave the ground at any moment. On a hunch Bibi picked up a stone and hurled it over the pit; at first the projectile arced down as expected, but then it jiggled and jarred as though in hesitation, until finally its path leveled out and it mounted rapidly toward the sky.

Bibi circled the site for several days. *There is*, he wrote in his journal, *an undeniable alteration in the effects of gravity in the region, whether through natural or man-made activity I can't tell. Reversing Galileo's experiments, I have hurled both rocks and feathers into the crater, and found that they ascend at roughly the same rate. I have spent hours examining it in hopes of finding a source, but it appears to have no bottom.*

The strangest effect, however, is the influence it has had on my dreams, for I now find them populated by ravens and dirigibles, and clouds of moths streaming up in darkness toward the light of the moon.

On the afternoon of the third day Bibi glimpsed in the distance a makeshift hut from which rose, like an echo of the cloud above it, the smoke of a cookfire. As he approached he found the structure even more ramshackle than it first appeared: a collection of branches and debris held together by fence wire and bits of string. Bibi peered into a window, stuck his head through the door, and found no one about; but on rounding the front of the place he was surprised to come upon an old woman, seated on a stump before the brink, white hair hovering weightlessly about her head like a halo. There was an upright surface in front of her, against which she performed a series of graceful, delicate movements with a device held in one hand. Perhaps it was the incongruity of action and environment, or that his mind was beginning to release its hold on such identifications, but it took Bibi several moments to recognize the surface in front of her as an easel, and the object in her hand as a brush.

The old woman was painting!

"Hello," Bibi called out—or tried to, for his voice, which had not been used in weeks, emitted a horrendous croak in place of the intended greeting.

The woman did not respond.

Assuming she was unable to hear him over the roar of the updraft, Bibi stepped across the clearing to stand beside her; but the artist kept her eyes on her work. Dipping her brush in a collection of daubs on a makeshift palette, she applied a stroke or two to the paper, then fixed her gaze on the crater, then dabbed again.

"Greetings!" Bibi tried again from his new vantage point. But he still got no response. He moved closer, and finally went so far as to pass a hand in front of the artist's eyes; at this she merely waved him away like a bothersome insect.

At a loss for what to do, Bibi stood aside and watched. The woman's face was remarkable, he thought. Wrinkles radiated from her eyes, and her cheeks were as sunken as dry water holes; yet there was a lightness and a brightness to her that Bibi had never seen in a person of her age. Her skin, despite its furrowed surface, was unusually luminous, and her blue eyes gleamed from their settings like twin stars.

As the artist showed no signs of objecting, Bibi circled behind to examine her work. From over her shoulder he glimpsed a maelstrom of color which rose like a living thing from the page; as he looked more closely he found she had reproduced the depths of the great crater almost exactly. A tangle of shape and shadow, shot through with rising darkness, the image was almost more terrifying than the thing itself.

Bibi watched as the woman added a bit of black, a hint of white, and a rub of red, then put down her brush and studied the result for a long moment. Slowly, almost ceremoniously, she lifted one hand into the air and unclipped the clothespins that held the page to the easel. Then, in a motion so swift as to seem instantaneous, she swept it from its surface and into the abyss.

Instinctively, Bibi lunged after it; but he was too late. He watched as the painting drifted for a short distance with its surface upturned, hanging against its subject like a universe in miniature. Then it began to float upward, and finally to accelerate, till at last it dwindled to a dot against the sky and was lost.

Astonished, Bibi turned back, but the artist had already taken up the brush again. Now she studied the cloud which mounted above them, all but blotting out the sky. The boiling mass rose in duplicate from the page; the sun struggled to shine through its center, while blackness faded to blue around the edges and the parched landscape groaned beneath it. Looking on, Bibi discovered things about the world he'd never noticed before; how the color of the sky paled by infinitesimal degrees as it neared the horizon, and shadows thickened or lightened at different points around their perimeters. The woman worked quickly and precisely; when she had finished she again studied the result for a long moment before sweeping it without hesitation into the void. Then she began once more.

At last, as the sun began to fade and dusk edged across the land, the painter put down her brush and turned for the first time to regard her visitor. Her eyes were so clear that a shudder ran through Bibi as they met his; for it seemed he could see straight through them and out the other side.

"I have no words left for what happened here," the woman spoke, in a voice as ancient, cracked, and broken as the desert itself. "All that remains are pictures." She looked over Bibi's battered, desert-worn exterior from his head to his feet, then from his feet back up again, and nodded in a way that seemed somehow definitive. "I suppose," she chuckled, "you fancy yourself some sort of mystic."

"Well, I . . ." Bibi began. But he could find no words with which to continue. With that the artist rose, started a fire and washed herself from a bucket, then began heating up a pot of beans in a ring of stones; and although she said not a word more, when she dished out the food she placed a can of condensed milk and a second bowl of beans on a stump at the edge of the fire. Gaunt and ravenous from his passage across the wastes, Bibi drank and ate hungrily. Then, somehow feeling oddly at home, he spread his bedroll at the edge of the firelight and sat silently upon it for a long while, watching the embers burn themselves out, before settling into sleep.

Days went by. Bibi busied himself with repairs around the shack, hauling water from a tiny spring in a cluster of rocks, writing in his journal, and watching the endless creation and destruction of the old woman's work.

She painted the crater, and painted the cloud that rose above it. She painted at dawn and painted at sunset, beneath clear skies and in howling storms. One work reproduced her subject almost exactly; the next in swirls of color so abstract Bibi could scarcely recognize it. But each time she finished the result was the same: she swept the product without hesitation into the crater. After the first day Bibi put aside his attempts to communicate and simply watched; and before long he became as absorbed in the woman's activity as she was herself.

She appears, he wrote in his journal, *both fierce and kind, dragon and grandmother—and her eyes, like the crater, have no bottom.*

It was the eyes, he later reflected, that kept him there.

. . .

The two stayed up late one night, watching the moon rise while the great cloud roared above them and the fire hissed its sparks against the darkness; and at last the old hermit told Bibi her story. She had lived here as a solitary witness for years, she said—how many, she could no longer remember.

"At first there were others," she told him. "But after a while they lost interest and drifted away."

"But what exactly was it that happened here?"

"A government research project."

"Some kind of anti-gravity device?"

The old woman nodded. "Ultimate weapon. Supposed to lift your enemies right off the planet." She gestured skyward, white hair drifting about her head, and emitted an ironic laugh. "As you can see, they've still got a few bugs to work out of the system."

They sat and watched while the gigantic cloud whooshed above them. In the distance Bibi could see the lights of what the Anti-gravity Hermit had identified as the government research facility, twinkling like a fallen star along the rim.

"And you?" the woman asked at length. "How have you been spending your days until now?"

"I've crossed America seven times trying to find my Uncle Otto," answered Bibi, "the Hope Valley Hubcap King."

"I gather"—she squinted at the old photo Bibi handed her in the firelight—"that so far you've not been successful?"

"Well, let's just say I've managed to figure out where he *isn't*."

The old woman listened as Bibi related the story of his search, the fates of his father and other ancestors, and all of his adventures. "But surely you realize," she said once he'd finished, "that it's not *where* or how hard you look that's the point. Once you're really ready to find your uncle, you'll find him just like that." She lifted her fingers into the air and snapped them.

They sat for a long time after that, while Bibi peered silently into the depths of the crater. "Do you have any idea how far down it goes?" he asked finally.

"Maybe to the center of the Earth," replied the Anti-gravity Hermit. "Maybe beyond. Perhaps even through time. Could be this is what happened to the lost continent of Atlantis."

They were quiet for a while. At length Bibi screwed up enough courage to raise the question that had been nagging at him ever since his arrival.

"Why," he asked her, "do you destroy your work?"

The artist looked at him in the firelight. "It won't last anyway." She shrugged. "We can hold on to nothing in life. Don't you know that?"

"But—" sputtered Bibi, "don't you believe in the power of creation?"

"Of course. Why else would I go on doing it?"

"But with these paintings you could let the country know what's going on here. Change the world!"

"Your head's in the clouds, son."

"But my feet are on the ground."

The old hermit shook her head sadly. "You can't trust gravity," she told him. "Not anymore."

Over breakfast the next morning, Bibi tried to share his insights into the nature of time with the old woman, but she seemed more interested in her oatmeal than in his conversation.

"Words," she responded, waving her hand in the air as though shooing away a fly. "Mere words. There's no weight to them. Can a hen sit on the word 'egg' and produce a chick? Can you put two 'B's' and a couple of 'I's' together and create a life? You could hurl all the words you wanted at what happened here, and still be no closer to comprehending it."

She seemed even less interested in his quest to understand the universe and America.

"You'd settle," she responded, "for mere understanding?"

A new sort of aperture appeared in their relationship after that. Later that afternoon, as Bibi sat scribbling in his journal, the Anti-gravity Hermit turned away from the painting she was working on and suddenly demanded: "What does a TREE mean? What is the Significance of Dirt?" Her eyes burned into him. "Do you feel the wind on your face? No. Only the letters W.I.N.D." She pointed her brush at him. "The truth is not something you can pin down, son—it's a living, growing thing!" She indicated the stack of notebooks by Bibi's side. "You'd be better off throwing your whole pile of mental meanderings over the edge!"

On another occasion, as they passed each other at the center of the compound, the woman stopped and drew a circle in the dust with a stick.

"This much," she said, "you and I—any individual human being—can know."

She drew a larger circle around the first.

"This much scientists, government, religious leaders—the entire human race put together knows."

Pointing her stick to the horizon, she wheeled around, indicating a boundless circumference. "This much no one knows."

She stared at him.

"In which ring do you wish to stand?"

Later, she handed Bibi a sheet of paper. On it she had drawn various figures. Some were letters of the alphabet; others were numbers; some Bibi had never imagined before. Strangely, even the familiar ones no longer seemed to refer to anything. They were simply scrawls, devoid of meaning, like ants that had crawled onto the page and gotten squashed there, entirely at random, for no reason at all.

"The brain is such a dull organ, isn't it?" The woman remarked, looking over his shoulder. "Grey matter, merely grey—not a drop of color to it!"

That evening, far beyond midnight, Bibi was awakened as he slept beside the fire by the crunch of feet on gravel. He opened his eyes to see the Anti-gravity Hermit standing like a vision at the very edge of the pit, tilting out into the updraft, toward the faraway lights of the government station.

"They've broken the law of gravity," she cried into the darkness. "And by God, there'll be hell to pay!"

What a curmudgeon, Bibi sometimes thought. What a crank the old woman was! And yet . . . Despite all her admonitions, there was no way he was going to give up writing in his journals.

Weeks passed. In the mornings, as day broke amidst the terrible beauty of destruction, Bibi walked the crater's rim. Pillars of blackness rose from the tumult, while shafts of light from the new, red sun glinted through the gloom. It was like the dawn of time, the beginning of creation—a new creation, begun in chaos, born out of destruction. He felt like a speck, a bit of dust against it.

What faint glory it was, Bibi thought, to be anything human—even the leader of an empire. King of the Specks; that was the best one could hope for. It was increasingly clear to him that the only satisfaction lay in living for something greater than oneself. But what *was* that something?

When Bibi dropped backward into his own mind, when he merged again with that perfect point of stillness he'd found in the canyons, he sensed beyond doubt that his true self extended indefinitely, without limits. *To be a speck,* he thought, *and to be the universe. That's what it is to be human.*

Still, human beings should not have created what had been created here. If the universe wanted to wipe the slate clean and start all over again, thought Bibi, she ought to leave humans out of it.

Let her do it herself!

·   ·   ·

Late one afternoon, as day crept toward dusk and the air was filled with the wailing roar of debris, the Anti-gravity Hermit was putting the finishing touches on another painting, which she'd refused to let Bibi look at until it was complete. Having labored for some time, she leaned back on her tree stump and, as was her custom, regarded the result for a long moment. She seemed just about to sweep the product over the edge as usual when she turned to regard her onlooker, who was seated on a nearby stone scribbling away again in his latest journal.

"I've just completed," she announced, "the only work I've ever produced that I'm not going to throw away—at least, I *hope* I'm not throwing it away." With that, she rose to her feet and presented it to Bibi.

"Study it well," she told him. "It explains everything in the universe."

Bibi looked down at the paper, then up again at the artist. The page was blank.

The old woman was laughing.

"You've crossed this country seven times"—the Anti-gravity Hermit shook her head as though in astonishment—"without seeing anything but the inside of your own skull. Why, you've crossed the wrong America. When you've reached the farthest shore you'll find there's a whole new continent to cross!"

Bibi looked at the ground, felt some inner edifice crack inside him.

"But be that as it may," the woman went on, "I hope you will give me the honor of your presence as I offer up my latest and greatest work of all."

Bibi glanced toward the easel, but the page in his hand was the only one in sight.

"You see clearly enough the gravity of the situation—" the old hermit continued. For the first time Bibi realized she'd been backing slowly away as she spoke, and was now standing uncomfortably near to the edge of the crater. "But what you do not yet see"—she had to shout to be heard above the roar—"is the situation of the gravity!" The uplift took the old woman's hair and stood it on end. "Hold on to nothing in this world," she howled above the din. "Not even *me!*" With that she wheeled and leapt into the void.

"No!" Bibi cried, lurching heavily forward to stop her. But he was too late.

The artist dropped a short way, arcing spread-eagled toward the center of the crater. Bibi watched as she spun in place, the flowers of her dress a blur of brightness. Then she began to rise—at first slowly, then more rapidly, a whirling wash of white hair and color patches. As she ascended, she was sucked toward the center of the cloud, where she mixed with rocks and dust and flying sticks, disappearing and reappearing like a phantom. Finally she shrank to almost nothing against the looming sky. Bibi could never be sure afterward, since her form was mingled with debris and she seemed so very small and far away, but it seemed that in his last glimpse of her he saw the old hermit separating into pieces: arms splitting off from shoulders, shoulders from torso, legs separating from feet—until, the forces which held her together having dissolved, there was nothing left to her at all.

Bibi stayed on at the encampment for several days, feeling a loneliness that, for all his time in the wilderness, he'd never known before. He drew shapes in the dust with sticks, threw stone after stone out into the void, traced the outlines of his Australoid scar again and again. Finally he just sat at the rim of the crater, staring into its depths for hours on end.

The Anti-gravity Hermit had been right, thought Bibi. Not only hadn't he understood the situation of the gravity—he hadn't understood the universe, America, or much of anything else, either. His insight into time, he now realized, had belonged to a particular moment; when it was over he'd failed to let it pass.

At this point he'd been carrying it around with him for so long that, like a corpse, it was beginning to stink.

His sense of exaltation left him. Everywhere Bibi looked he saw only the contents of his own mind. Was that a rock on the ground, or just a concept with the word ROCK wrapped around it? With tremendous effort he tried to divest it of its ROCK-ness, to see it for what it was, as a child might see before know-ing the names of things, but stubborn, rocklike, it remained a rock—and as far as Bibi could see, the same rocks extended in every direction, an infinite number of rocks in an infinite array of universes, and he could see none of them as they truly were.

Bibi sensed there was a brand of knowing that went deeper than any of his attempts at understanding: but whatever that was, it seemed infinitely out of reach. He'd thought he'd been moving forward, always progressing—but he now realized that, like the hands of a clock, he'd been traveling in circles.

On the third day he rose, possessed by a new sense of certainty. First Bibi washed at the spring and repacked his belongings. Then he piled up the Anti-gravity Hermit's few remaining pos-sessions—easel, paints, brushes, paper—and set fire to them, along with her tiny shack. This was an action she would have approved of, he thought. He stood watching until all had burned to cinders. Then, hoisting his pack onto his shoulders, aware of every movement in his body, Bibi placed one foot be-fore the other until he arrived at the very edge of the crater.

There he teetered for a long time, leaning out into the up-draft, arms spread wide against the upsurge, a strange exhilara-tion coursing through his flesh. The old woman had said to hold on to nothing, hadn't she? Bibi tilted above the chaos, felt his scalp lift as his hair pulled skyward; his very bones seemed filled with light. How easy it all now seemed! Taking a deep breath, Bibi readied himself. Then, stepping backward, he slipped his rucksack from his shoulders. Slowly, he unbuckled the straps.

Reaching into it, he extracted the first of his journals; it held musings from his first days in the wilderness—a time long past, in a life that was no longer his own. Bibi lifted the volume high, as a priest might raise a ceremonial vessel, and stretched his arms out over the void. Then all at once, he let go. He watched, a peculiar sensation twitching about his abdomen, while the thin flat rectangle flapped, fluttered open, and ascended into the sky. One by one, he released the next, and the next, staring after them as they rose, lifting into the air like birds uncaged, and were gone.

Bibi stood for a long moment after that, leaning out over the abyss, savoring the sweet emptiness of the void, feeling as though his existence had finally shed all of its weight.

Then all at once, his mission at last clear, he turned and set off walking.

After a day's travel Bibi glimpsed the smoke and lights of the government facility, just a few miles further along the rim. That night, after the moon had set, he slid on his belly up to the electric fence and studied every inch of the compound within. At its center was a building, lit with greenish lights, that sent out a constant hum, along with endless streams of smoke: this, Bibi guessed, was the power station for the operation. He saw others that might have been laboratories, meeting areas, or barracks. Numerous outbuildings trailed away into the darkness. But the most striking thing was that the high fence that protected the compound was continuous on three sides only; the fourth, which fronted onto the crater, was apparently considered impervious to entry.

Bibi spent the next several days out of sight of the station, investigating the gravitational properties of the crater. He found that, far from being continuous, the force varied widely from one region to the next. In some areas a rock dropped over the side floated slowly downward before beginning to rise; in others it did not fall at all, but floated in position; in still others it began to ascend the moment it crossed the edge.

Bibi experimented with the more neutral zones of the rim, where an object might float for hours before deciding whether to rise or fall. Holding to roots and branches of shrubs, he lowered himself over the side to test what effect this might have on his body. He found that in some places it was possible to hover weightlessly for long periods of time—moreover, he rather liked the sensation.

For the next several nights, summoning every quality of silence and invisibility he'd learned from his time in the desert, Bibi crept to the edge of the compound. He observed the movements of security personnel, and came to know every detail of their rounds. He placed spoonfuls of canned goods he'd salvaged from the Anti-gravity Hermit's supply at regular intervals through the fence; before long he'd confirmed that the guard dogs found a variety known as "Stu's Beef Stew" entirely irresistible. By the end of the week he was able, through careful application of the stuff, to control their movements almost entirely.

He pronounced himself ready to proceed.

The following evening, several hours before moonrise, Bibi slithered to the edge of the compound and spooned liberal portions of "Stu's" through the mesh at calculated points around the perimeter. Then he crept back along the fence line to the place where it met the rim. Fishing a coil of rope from his rucksack, he felt around in the darkness until he found an exposed root as far under the wire as he could reach. He fastened one end of the rope to this holdfast and the other to his waist. Then, having no idea what properties to expect from this particular region, he leapt into space.

The first and most striking result of Bibi's action was that nothing appeared to happen at all. He felt a vague coasting sensation, as though he were a hockey puck shoved frictionless into the blackness. He seemed to float interminably in this way before a distant tug signaled the end of his tether. Recoiling now, Bibi felt himself tumble back, the lights of the station spinning in his eyes, until he intersected with some new zone of gravity refraction and was swept up in a long, looping spiral which brought him with a jerk to the end of his rope. Pulling himself hand over hand toward the rim, Bibi came to earth just inside the fence.

Crouched low amidst mesquite and creosote, clinging to rocks and shrubs against the upward pull, Bibi worked his way toward the cluster of buildings at the center of the compound. At this moment, according to his calculations, the guards and dogs would be precisely on the other side of the enclosure. Having reached the last available cover, he loaded some stones into his rucksack for ballast, then scurried across an open field to the power station.

Gaining the relative safety of the building's shadow, Bibi circled the structure in the ghostly glow of the lamps that stood like sentries about the perimeter, without knowing exactly what he was looking for. As he rounded the south edge there came to his ears a sudden sound as though of snuffling or grunting, followed by the rapid patter of footsteps. Bibi pressed himself into a doorway, every muscle quivering with tension; he peered cautiously around the corner to see the approaching silhouette of a guard with leashed dog tilt abruptly and stagger—and the poor fellow's arm was nearly yanked from its socket as the beast veered hungrily off toward the nearest cache of "Stu's." Amidst the shouting and cursing of the guard, Bibi slid out of his hideaway and continued around the building, until he spotted a second-floor window that was slightly ajar. Unloading the stones from his pack, he gained the sill in a single leap. Clinging to the ledge, he carefully studied the scene inside. Below sat a lone guard before an array of video monitors, bobbing gently up and down several inches above his chair, emitting a cacophony of grunts and snores.

The gravitational properties inside the structure were such

that Bibi had to haul himself hand over hand along a series of pipes to reach the floor. Here he stopped in place, heart ricocheting about his chest, as the guard snorted a few times and mumbled, then recrossed his arms and settled back down. Having reached the ground, Bibi sprang lightly over the head of the unconscious sentry and entered a long hallway lit with fluorescent lights.

He edged along one wall until he came abreast of a door that sent forth a rumbling sound, as though of engines or turbines. The entry was locked, but Bibi found a ventilation window above it open; and in his near-weightless state he was able to wriggle through it easily. Inside he found a dark, massive chamber laced with catwalks; a churning inferno of machinery puffed away in the dimness, emitting occasional bursts of steam. Sensing that he was close to the object of his mission, Bibi began to work his way toward the engines, hauling himself along the inner wall by a network of conduits. He'd only gone a short distance, however, when he happened upon an electrical outlet, with a tangle of plugs and wires sprouting from a single three-way adapter.

Hmm, Bibi thought, *I wonder what this is for?*

On impulse, he grasped the adapter and yanked it from its socket.

The next thing Bibi knew there was a great crash, and he felt himself crushed against the ground as though by an enormous weight. He felt so heavy he could scarcely lift his head. Sirens were going off and emergency lights flashing everywhere. Turning with difficulty, Bibi dragged himself toward the door like some immense, stricken animal, while gravity yanked chunks of plaster off the ceiling and rained them down around him. After a lengthy struggle, he managed to raise one arm high enough to turn the knob; the door creaked open and he pulled himself into the hallway, face squeezed against the linoleum as though a gargantuan foot were planted on the back of his neck.

From the corner of one eye Bibi saw the formerly sleeping guard drag himself around a corner and into the hallway behind him.

"Sshhhtoppp . . . ooorrrIIllsssshhhhoooooott!" his pursuer shouted—or tried to—for, as Dr. Clook might have predicted, the increase in gravity was affecting time as well; and the man's words emerged as flaccidly as a tape played at half speed. While Bibi rapidly rediscovered his childhood knack for crawling, the guard, with a mighty effort, managed to pull his revolver from his holster, and shoved it along the floor in an attempt to take aim. But the barrel refused to stay upright, and the bullet, when it emerged, traveled scarcely a yard down the corridor before plunking to a weighty halt against the linoleum, throwing up a puff of dust only a few feet in front of the man's face.

Bibi redoubled his efforts, but was able to pull himself forward by mere inches at a time. A chorus of barks and shouts broke out behind him; he craned his neck around to see a company of guards and dogs burst into the hall, only to collapse in a chaos of fur and uniforms against the gravity-laden floor. The impact knocked several of Bibi's pursuers senseless; but the others soon gathered their wits and joined the first guard in relentless horizontal pursuit, dragging their helpless, scrabbling canines by their leashes behind them.

At this point an explosion and a billow of smoke came from the room he'd just exited; at the same instant a terrific impact smote Bibi on the back of his head. Gulping for breath, he rolled over to find himself mashed against a new surface—which, after some investigation, he determined to be the ceiling. With an effort, Bibi turned to look behind him, half expecting to find himself surrounded. But his pursuers were pinned to the new surface as well, flopping against it as ineffectually as a school of beached fish. Several guards struggled to aim their weapons, and some even succeeded in firing; but this time their bullets plunged upward, to embed themselves in the ceiling.

The reversed force proved to be every bit as intense as the

first, and again Bibi found himself able to move along by mere centimeters—although the presence of lighting fixtures did provide better leverage for his hands and feet. Only a few minutes passed, however, before another bang slammed him to the floor. The shifts appeared to be increasing in frequency; before long Bibi and his pursuers were enduring impact after impact, scarcely able to scramble a few feet forward before being crushed to the opposite surface again. Under the repeated pummeling, the hall filled with dislodged tiles, fragments of plaster, and a haze of dust through which Bibi and his pursuers made their way at a snail-like pace. The situation, however, did have its benefits, as more guards and dogs were knocked unconscious with each reversal.

After an hour or more of such gradual fleeing, Bibi dragged himself around a bend in the hallway and came to rest beneath a low window, set into the wall no more than eighteen inches above his head. Battered to exhaustion by the endless gravity reversals, he found himself utterly unable to reach it. Focusing all his attention onto one hand, he'd manage to raise it no more than an inch before, as though made of granite, it plunged to the floor again. Finally Bibi discovered that by pressing the fingertips of one hand against the base of the wall and shoving the elbow of that arm with his other, he was gradually able to lever his fingers upward. First his fingertips went vertical, then the palm, until finally his whole forearm was pressed against the wall. After a tense struggle, Bibi managed to push one hand over the sill; and using every muscle of his desert-hardened body, he hauled himself through the aperture, just as the first guard clawed his way around the bend behind him.

Bibi half expected this to be the last action of his life; for had the gravity on the outside of the building been equal to that on the inside, even a twelve-foot drop might have proved fatal. But here he must have entered some fresh zone of gravitational disturbance; for on clearing the sill he found himself drifting toward earth as slowly as a feather—to come to a dead stop mere inches above the ground, utterly unable to touch his feet to the surface. Bibi flailed frantically in place, hearing the groaning, stretched-out shouts and barks of his enemies as they neared the window. Finally he discovered a sort of swimming technique by which he could flounder his way forward; and he began, as rapidly as he could, to make his way toward the edge of the compound.

Meanwhile, all around him, gravity was coming to pieces. A radio tower toppled to the ground, while enormous boulders rose into the sky; lengths of fence snaked into the air, as buildings folded in on themselves like cardhouses; and everywhere was the rise and rain of debris.

Bibi heard the shouts and barks break out anew, and revolved in place to see a swarm of men and dogs shove themselves out the window after him. Luckily his pursuers, despite their wildest flailings, were unable to move forward any more quickly than he. Now they raised their guns, but the barrels were pulled skyward; and the bullets, when they emerged, were sucked straight into the heavens. The entire group must have been drifting into some vortex of upward motion, for the next time he glanced down the ground was far away; and when he looked up again there were guards and dogs tumbling on all sides. One man hauled his animal hand over hand to his chest, then shoved it snarling and yapping through the air at his quarry. But the leash ran out inches from Bibi's face, and the recoil sent guard, then dog, then guard, reeling end over end, until they merged with clouds of debris and were lost.

Sailing up ever faster in a whirl of dust and gravel, Bibi sensed he was being drawn into the great spiral above the crater. Remembering the fate of the Anti-gravity Hermit, he swam madly toward the rising moon, which he could just barely glimpse at the cloud's edge. But although he tried the breaststroke, the American crawl, and even the butterfly, he found himself being sucked inescapably backward.

Finally, with a thud that resounded through his entire body,

Bibi collided with a rising boulder. Instinctively, he took hold and clambered to its far side. There, with a powerful thrust of his feet, he sent himself flying out toward the edge of the vortex, passing several startled-looking guards and dogs on their way in.

Freed of the updraft, Bibi passed into a patch of clear air, and saw the glow of the station below. Now sweeping earthward, he intersected with another boulder, and again took hold, tumbling with it toward the heart of the compound, where a matrix of lights and machinery still whirred in the night. Fighting for control, Bibi managed to get his feet beneath him; at the last possible moment he shoved himself clear of the rock. Halting in midair, he watched as the projectile sailed down toward the center of the station. When it hit, there was a flash and a rumble, and the shock waves of a gigantic explosion.

Moments later Bibi found himself drifting gently back to earth. The great cloud, to his amazement, was funneling itself rapidly back into the crater; on every side was the patter of falling debris. He landed lightly on the ground and brushed himself off.

Well, he concluded, feeling about his clothes and rucksack to make sure everything was in one piece, *I guess that's that.* But as Bibi made his way out of the now-darkened compound and back into the desert, hearing distant, confused shouts and barks as the guards and dogs touched down, something occurred to him. He checked, then rechecked the button-down pouch in his jacket where he usually kept his most important items. Then he patted himself over again.

Hmm, he thought to himself, as he stepped back into the night. *I wonder what could have become of my wallet?*

8.
DESPAIR

Perhaps Bibi's encounter with gravity had some lingering impact on his spirits; for on leaving the desert he sank into the deepest gloom he'd ever known. At the moment of destroying his journals he'd felt free, powerful, an animal uncaged from the trap of his own mind; but as time came between him and the event, he began to feel directionless, oddly stifled. Maybe it was the unsettling end of the Anti-gravity Hermit, the wisest being he'd encountered in all his travels. Or that he'd been searching so long now for the Hubcap King with no results. Perhaps, too, it was the mood of the country—for as Bibi continued to wander with increasing aimlessness over the land, America was beginning its slide into the Fifth Depression, a period historians would later describe as its darkest hour.

Everywhere Bibi went he met legions of the homeless, gaunt and unshaven, wandering in search of a day's work or a handout. It was said that for five states in either direction no one had a job. The world, which had always felt fundamentally kind and boun-

tiful to him, seemed suddenly full of hard, sharp things for people to hurt themselves on.

With no clear idea where to head next Bibi drifted, along with
thousands of others fleeing the onset of winter, down toward
the Bayou, one of the few regions of the country he'd never visited, having reasoned there could be no valleys of any sort in this
vast and tangled swampland, where the slightest dip was filled
by water.

In those years all it did was rain. Bibi joined the gangs of
haggard and hopeless headed south along a power-line access
road that paralleled the great river at the continent's center.
Known to the initiated as the Hobo's Highway, this crude dirt
thoroughfare twisted along the riverbank for nearly a hundred miles, providing a mud-ridden but authority-free route for
those who used it, while the electric wires hummed and
sparked their way overhead. In the evenings the travelers gathered in shantytowns of cardboard and sheet metal, nicknamed
"Kirbyvilles" in mock homage to the new president, and passed
bottles of whatever came to hand, sharing the stories of their
lives.

Despite the darkness of his spirits, Bibi continued to ask
everyone he met if they'd ever happened upon a place called
Hope Valley, but given the circumstances, the question came
to seem more and more absurd. He began to feel increasingly
separate from everything around him. Time, as Bibi now saw
it, was not something which passed, but something one passed
through, much as you had to pass through space to get from
one place to another. The only difference was you could never
stop or turn back. Or could you? He had turned back once,
hadn't he—or, had he, in the heat and dust of the desert,
merely imagined it? That moment now seemed increasingly
remote. He'd crossed the Great Desert many times, yet the
wasteland of time still stood before him; and the weariness of
his journey across the continent was nothing compared to his
unceasing, unstoppable expedition through time.

It was on one of these evenings, as the rain sluiced down and the travelers huddled around oil-can fires telling stories, that Bibi ran into an old friend.

"Cheeerrrss to you, Stranger," drawled a bedraggled, greyish fellow who sidled up to where he stood. The newcomer held up a white disposable cup, winked at Bibi, then took a slug and fell back, reeling. "Lordie—there's nothin' like a shot of Ol'Dogbite in Styrofoam. Sorta eats away at the cup, you know, so what you end up with's half whiskey and half dissolved Styro— Man, that stuff's liquid lightning!" With that he took a graceful and some-how familiar leap into the air.

Sure enough, it was the Gravity Man. The poor fellow had fallen on hard times since Bibi saw him last, cavorting with the acrobat troupe the night of the farewell ball at Peter's estate. The Bolivians, as it turned out, had betrayed him, leaving him abandoned and penniless in the slums of La Paz, from whence he'd spent the last years working his way back, first as a banana picker, then a rural telephone worker, and finally, as lookout from the mast of a ship.

"All my dreams are shattered," he told Bibi. "I'm too old now to ever conquer gravity. All I have left is this." He peered into his decaying cup and took another slug. " 'Course," he sputtered in admiration, "I could do worse!"

The Gravity Man was fascinated to hear of Bibi's recent adventures. "Just imagine," he marveled, "the government and I have been on the same track all along!" But then his tone grew somber. "Still, you shouldn't be wandering around out here in the open without any cover."

"What do you mean?" Bibi pointed to the rain poncho he'd fabricated from a trash-can liner.

"No," answered his companion. "I mean your face." He peered at Bibi in the darkness. "But surely you realize you're a wanted man?"

· · ·

Some time after midnight, in the midst of a renewed downpour, the two made their way up the steps of the post office in a nearby town. At his friend's insistence Bibi had donned dark glasses and an oversized fisherman's cap, and stuck a bit of squirrel tail salvaged from a roadkill to his upper lip as a makeshift moustache.

"There you are." The Gravity Man pointed his flashlight through the glass. Sure enough, from a poster inside, Bibi's likeness stared back at them—or to put it more accurately, faced toward them—for the eyes were closed. The silly grin and baby-smooth cheeks identified the source as his driver's license photo, taken sometime during high school.

"My wallet!" Bibi patted his pockets automatically. "I'd wondered what happened to it."

The two stood and regarded the image. It would be hard to imagine the shutter going off at a more awkward moment; in addition to the closed eyes and unfortunate grin, Bibi's left hand was frozen in air just below his chin, as though he'd reached up to scratch an itch and had been caught in mid-motion.

The sign below the poster read:

WANTED
FOR DISRUPTION OF GOVERNMENT ACTIVITIES
AND ACTS OF INDUSTRIAL SABOTAGE

FREDERICK G. BROWN II

!!$$BIG$$!!
REWARD
SHOOT FIRST, ASK QUESTIONS LATER.

"Shoot first? . . ." Bibi repeated numbly.

"Look at the bright side," remarked his friend. "At least they don't know your *real* first name."

At that moment Bibi heard voices from the darkness behind them.

"Hey, how come that guy's wearing sunglasses at night?"

"Sure looks suspicious to me."

"Do you suppose it could be that Brown character?"

To which a chorus of voices responded: "Shoot first, ask questions LATER!!"

A volley of shots exploded from the darkness. Bibi dove for the deck, barely glimpsing the ragged tangle of men and guns who surged at them from the shadows. But the Gravity Man, recognizing the opportunity he'd been waiting for his entire life, leapt from the stairs and soared high into the air. As though carried by a gust of wind, he sailed up and up, higher than seemed possible, over the heads of the pursuers into the blackness beyond.

Like a single beast the posse turned and, in a flurry of shouts and gunfire, was gone.

Some time later, Bibi made his way back through the dripping underbrush to the outskirts of the encampment. There he found the Gravity Man, who'd eluded capture by perching atop a telephone pole as the posse thudded past in the night, and was watching for his arrival from the upper limbs of a magnolia tree.

"I guess," Bibi called up to him, "you managed to defeat gravity after all."

"Guess I did." His friend laughed, then bounced down a limb or two and reached out to straighten Bibi's squirrel-tail moustache.

"You look," he said, "like Alvin and the Chipmunks having a really bad day."

The next morning, hoping to pass for one of the new breed of ascetics that had lately begun to roam the land, Bibi shaved his head, shed his clothes, and donned his trashbag parka, the closest approximation he could find to holy attire. He took leave of the Gravity Man, who was headed out on a pilgrimage to the site of the great crater.

"Good luck in the promised land," Bibi called, waving him off. "And thanks for saving my life!" But a renewed sense of melancholy settled on him as he watched his friend bound down the road in a series of astonishing leaps, looking for the moment almost young again.

Alone once more, Bibi took to the banks of the river and headed south. He kept to himself, avoiding the groups of armed men he sometimes saw questioning other travelers; but more than once he had to endure their scrutiny as he passed, sweating in his plasticine cassock, eyes lowered in apparent contemplation.

One afternoon, as Bibi walked the riverbank in this fashion, a tattered youth flung himself from the shrubbery beside the path and blocked his passage.

"The sun rises in the east and sets in the west," the fellow challenged him. "Where, then, do I meet myself?"

"Excuse me?" Bibi replied.

The youth stared at him. "He who has committed no fault requests my pardon!" With that he dropped to the ground, then rose and began to trail along behind him. And although the fellow's presence made him more than a little nervous, all Bibi's attempts to drive him off proved futile.

A few days later another man confronted the pair.

"The sky is up and the earth is down," he asserted. "Where is the realm of Truth?"

"I don't understand," responded Bibi.

"Of course!" exclaimed the man. "In the emptiness of non-conceptual awareness. Why didn't I think of it myself?"

He, too, began to trail behind.

By the time the river dispersed in the vast delta of the Bayou, Bibi's group of tagalongs had grown to more than a dozen, all clad as he was, in converted trashbags scavenged from roadside bins. As the odd band grew, it began to attract attention. Passersby stopped to take pictures; and one morning a group of horsemen accosted them as they walked along a deserted stretch of road.

"Ever run across a fella by the name of Frederick G. Brown II?" questioned the leader, waving a shotgun around his head.

"Brown is nothing but Nworb backwards," replied one of Bibi's followers enigmatically.

"The nature of existence is inherently nonexistent," answered a second.

"You are yourself what you seek!" cried a third.

With this the posse's eyes fastened on their leader.

"He *is* kind of tall," remarked one of the men.

"His eyes *are* blue," said another.

"What better alias," added a third, "than to be on a search party for yourself?"

"Get 'im!!" they shouted.

And in a burst of hoofbeats and gunfire they vanished into the distance.

Nearing the southern edges of the continent, Bibi and his followers passed into the Bayou, where moss-laden trees nodded their heads over the waters and murmured to each other in the evening breezes like old men. Nights here reminded Bibi of his time on the river with the Professor and Peter and the rest so long ago, and as he sat in the twilight his heart often swelled with thoughts of that unrecoverable past, and his own fading youth.

One evening, as he slept beside the Hobo's Highway beneath the power lines, Bibi had what was perhaps the strangest dream of his life. There had been a storm and, still within the dream, Bibi was awakened by the spitting crackle of fallen wires as they snapped along the ground. The walls of his cardboard hut glowed fluorescent yellow. He clawed free of his bedroll and stumbled into the night. Cables writhed along the earth like glowing snakes; the air was sharp with the tang of ozone. He suddenly remembered that his Uncle Otto, who used to work for the power company and would know what to do, was sleeping nearby. He burst through the door of a neighboring hut and shook the figure inside, but a surge of light went up to reveal the sleeper's face as one he'd never seen before. He hurried to the next shelter, and the next, but nowhere found a face he recognized. The camp had become a whirl of sparks, decked about with heaps of fluorescent slag; cables heaved this way and that, spitting fire. Coming to the last hut, Bibi tore his way in and shook the sleeping figure. This time the sleeper awoke and rolled over to stare at him in the pulsing glow.

The face was his own.

The next morning Bibi rose while it was still dark and slipped away into the underbrush, abandoning his followers, who'd stayed up far into the night discussing the distinction between "each" and "every" and were sleeping too soundly to notice. They'd camped no more than a day's travel from a major port city, located on the delta where the strands of the river lost themselves in the sea. Like many such cities, it was a haven for smugglers, gamblers, and pleasure-seekers. Famed for its libertine atmosphere and general ambience of around-the-clock gaiety, the place had attracted a huge population of down-and-outers hoping to forget their troubles and make a few dollars by any means possible.

It looked to Bibi like the perfect place to acquire a new identity.

Pausing some hours after dawn in an alley at the outskirts of town, Bibi pulled out a pocketknife and sliced open one of the seams of his rucksack. In the lining he had long ago sewn three gold coins Peter's father had pressed upon him in case of emergency. They were his last physical remembrance of life on the estate.

Bibi spent the first on new clothes, a pair of shoes, and a broad-brimmed hat—appropriately stylish for his fresh beginning on the Delta. The second he traded for a new birth certificate and social security card at a storefront in the neighborhood known as Plump Village.

"Welcome to Nu-U," the receptionist said mechanically as he walked in. "Can I help you?"

"I need a new self," replied Bibi, not knowing how else to put it.

"Hey down, don't we all," replied the woman, a beige-skinned beauty of indefinable ancestry. She pulled a form from her desk and, pen poised above it, looked at him expectantly. "So dish me the poop, Boob."

"Huh?" replied Bibi.

"How you gonna bop, Pop?"

Bibi stared at her blankly.

"Your name, country boy, your name. What's it gonna be?"

"Oh." Bibi thought for a long moment. "Bobo," he answered at last. "Bobo . . . Le Blaque."

The woman looked at him with sudden admiration. "Hey down, big Boob!" she grinned. "You gonna bop all the way to the top!"

At a shop a few doors down Bibi traded in his last coin. He emerged hours later, still groggy from anesthetic, with a shorter nose, a nobler chin, and an enormous weight removed from his shoulders—although the doctors could do little about the blue of his eyes; and Bibi opted at the last moment to keep the Australoid scar on the back of his hand, for old times' sake.

With a bit of change left over from his first two transactions, Bibi checked into a skid-row hotel to recuperate.

. . .

Unbeknownst to Bibi, a large, jolly man wearing sunglasses and a bright striped suit entered the Plump Village storefront the morning after Bibi purchased his papers.

"Hey up, Boon Baby," he greeted the receptionist. "What way fine mood you be boppin' this grand A.M.?"

The receptionist looked at him. "You coulda skipped the suit, Boob," she replied. "Not to mention the lingo. So what dirt you be diggin' today?"

All traces of jolliness drained from the man's face. He dropped an eight-by-ten of Bibi's driver's license photo onto her desk.

"We want this guy. We want him bad."

The receptionist glanced over the image. "Why you boobs always got the same lousy pictures, eyes squinted up and face just a-grimacin'?" She handed it back. "Never seen 'im."

The man's hand struck across the desk like a rattlesnake. He grabbed the woman by her blouse and pulled her halfway across the desktop.

"Spare me the art critique, sister. You ought to know we're entirely prepared to put you out of business. Not to mention ruin your life."

"O.K., O.K.! Just set me loose so I can think, hey? These duds cost a fortune!"

The man released her. She sank back to her seat and brushed the wrinkles out of her clothes.

"Now that I think on it," she said, "I mighta run across a boob who looked like this someplace." She put a finger to her forehead. "Seems to me his name was . . . Bubba. Yeah, that's it. Bubba LeBeige."

By the time the man returned a few days later he found the storefront closed and the operation moved on.

No one in the neighborhood seemed to know a thing about it.

· · ·

To one accustomed to the silence of the wilderness, the sirens and gunfire, shrieks and car horns of the city took more than a little getting used to; and it was during Bibi's first few nights of restlessness that the Terry Cloth Man began to haunt his dreams once more. Face rough and porous, beaded with sweat, he loomed over Bibi's bed and leered moistly.

"Is this all I am?" he mocked.

"Why bother?" he jeered.

"Life is a Naugahyde seat cover with no stuffing!!" he taunted, until Bibi woke panting and clutching his pillow in terror.

It was during this period, too, that Bibi came to grips with an unsettling phenomenon: most of his life appeared to be missing. It was all a horrendous blur really, when he examined it, so disheveled and out of sequence he could never put it back in order. Why, there were weeks—months, even—that had been completely forgotten, sucked into the abyss of time never to reappear.

Our hours, he thought, *our days, are constantly being misplaced, like ballpoint pens in the pockets of consciousness . . .*

And if he couldn't remember them, who was to say they'd happened at all?

It became painfully clear to him that nothing in life was really his own. What he thought of as "Bibi" was an assemblage of memories and anticipations: a set of Chinese boxes, one inside the next, each utterly empty.

"It's like this hotel," Bibi mused to the maid, a half-Maori mother of nine who worked nights for an escort service. "Life is just a dingy boardinghouse, and you and I and everyone else have checked into our own private rooms. The walls are thin and the windows are dirty, and all you can see through them is a brick wall and maybe some trash in the alley below. Sometimes from the floor above or the next room over you hear a thump or a distant vibration—and you have to deduce, from these clues alone, who or what is out there."

"Hey down, big Boob," the woman responded, with a sad shake of her head. "You gone down on the jones big time!"

Bibi's father and his other ancestors began to join the Terry Cloth Man in his dreams: dreams from which he woke sweating and shouting, with no idea who he was, or where, or why.

He spent hours staring at his new, foreshortened features in the mirror. His face was gone. His past had vanished. Who was he?

Bibi stayed on at the hotel. He tried jobs: desk clerk, janitor, night watchman.

He took to drinking.

At a loss for how to spend his time, Bibi began to frequent the cafes and speakeasies of the waterfront—places with names like "The Salivary Paradise" and "Nude Buffet."

"To the pointlessness of life!" a man toasted him the first time he came through the door of one of these places. "Ain't despair grand?"

And to those waiting out the bad times in the dives and coffeehouses of the Delta, indeed it was. The company of others who shared and even exalted his misery bred in Bibi a manic, desperate energy—helped along by the liberal servings of absinthe-and-espresso cocktails, popularly known as "Levelers," which he'd taken to consuming. Bibi danced as the balalaika and trombone quartets which were all the rage that season bumped and ground their rhythms into the night—a band known as The Curculios, in particular, inspired a popularity bordering on hysteria—and listened while bearded bards barked poetry into crowded, smoky clubs. One recent poem, titled "Groan," had sparked a near-revolution in the nation's literary circles, while another, poet Anna Graham's bleak yet quirky "Hyena Rumps," seemed poised for similar success.

Bibi consorted with geniuses known and unknown, including the authors of *Angry Plums* and *Why Should the Sun Bother to Come Up?* He became intimate with Trudy Mug, the pioneering woman writer credited with coining the phrase

"The Lost Generator" to refer to the runaway industrialism of the modern era. He grew close to underground writer Chuck Kowskiboot, who'd been laboring for seven years on a minimalist novel titled—and consisting of the single word—*The*. Bibi lost himself in the scene, becoming immersed enough to convince himself for a time that depression was the most honest form of satisfaction available. He grew a goatee and learned to smoke cheroots. But he always had to make his way at last to his grim, lonely room and face his emptiness alone.

Bibi began to find life increasingly irritating. He felt stifled by his own body hair. *Of what possible use,* he asked himself, *is this hair on the backs of my fingers?* Knobs broke off of things. Meals burned. When he needed something he couldn't find it. He became impatient with store clerks, waitresses, the hotel staff. Sometimes, for the first time in his life, he was just plain mean.

Around him, all he saw was suffering. The janitor had eczema; the concierge, lumbago. The streets were jammed with drunks and beggars. Above all, life was so messy—a fabric continuously unraveling, with only the vaguest pattern to any of it. He wished he could return to the time before the gravity pit, any time back then, and live there forever.

Bibi came to distrust happiness, for he saw it could not be counted on, but came and went as it pleased. And being distrusted, it came less and less.

He tried to regain his youthful sense of the world's dreamlike nature, but failed entirely.

Omigod, he told himself. *This is real.*

One morning, after a long night on the town, Bibi entered the lobby of his hotel to find it filled with jolly men wearing sunglasses and striped suits.

"LeBeige?" the desk clerk was saying as one of them looked on. "Let me check my listings . . ."

"Also known as Frederick G. Brown II," added the questioner.

"What's the 'G' stand for?" asked one of the staff.

"Gulliv—" began Bibi, automatically.

"What's that?" responded the head of the suits.

"Nothing," answered Bibi, carefully checking his mail.

The maid was swiveling a wanted poster with Bibi's former likeness on it around in her hands. "You boobs got the dough to buy them suits," she said, "how come you can't come up with a better picture?"

"—armed and presumed dangerous—" the man near the desk continued.

"Only to himself," muttered Bibi.

"Did you say something?" smiled the fellow, but Bibi was too absorbed in a mail-order bird-feeder catalog to reply.

"Hey down, Bobo," the janitor called to him from across the lobby. "These boobs wanna know if we've ever run across some bad ol' boy named Bubba—strange-looking fella, to judge from his picture."

Bibi shook his head, which was still pounding from last night's libations, and closely examined a two-for-one special order form.

"—credited with starting a nationwide cult—"

"—blew up a government installation—"

"Got a Le Blaque," the clerk spoke out. "Afraid that's the best I can do."

"In . . . dust . . . real sab-o-tage?" the maid was reading from the poster. "Why can't you boobs use plain English?"

After a prolonged series of questions, during which Bibi had to struggle manfully to prevent his breakfast from squirming back out the way it came, the men in the suits left.

As a precaution Bibi moved that afternoon to a rooming house on the other side of the city, in an area known as the Norwegian Sector.

. . .

Over the next five months Bibi moved five times—twice when the men in suits got too close for comfort, once when a sewage pipe emptied itself into his heating duct, and the rest because he couldn't pay the rent. During this period he was mugged seven times, witnessed five assaults with deadly weapons, and participated in three outbreaks of mass hysteria.

As the bad times grew worse, the wail of police sirens and ambulances in the city became almost continuous. Even more unsettling to Bibi were reports of dozens of mistaken shootings by those pursuing the reward for Frederick G. Brown II; and although there seemed little it he could do about it, Bibi felt somehow responsible.

His doubts deepened. What *was* life? Did it really mean anything, or was it simply some absurd, tragic accident? What did *meaning* mean? Such thoughts crowded Bibi's head day and night like a horde of men in striped suits, till he wanted to reach out and adjust the horizontal hold on reality.

Reflecting that nothing he'd ever thought had seemed to do him much good, Bibi resolved to empty his mind and start anew. With this intent he doubled, then tripled his alcohol intake. But the drink didn't wash his thoughts away; it merely dissolved them into smaller pieces and sloshed them around until he ended up more confused than ever.

He wandered the streets of the city, watched people stepping along the sidewalks, moving their mouths—speaking through the same apertures they used to eat. *Here I am,* Bibi thought, *the end product of four billion years of evolution—and I haven't got the slightest idea what's going on.*

The moon hung in the night sky like a pale, withered fruit, always out of reach.

He stopped writing his mother.

• • •

Time passed. Down on his luck, out of work for the eleventh time, Bibi applied for a position at a club called "Humps Galore." The marquee featured a neon-rimmed camel which romped up and down while a bikini-clad maiden clung to its back. The current attraction was Rana, Queen of Toads, whose stage act featured amphibians emerging from every conceivable orifice.

"Whaddaya got to offer?" asked the proprietor, a deeply stooped, cheroot-chomping fellow known as Humps, when Bibi showed up at the door. "Entrail act? Bestiality? How about vegetables? Haven't had a good veggie act in years!"

"I'm here to apply for your job as janitor," Bibi replied humbly.

The boss looked him up and down, snorted a few times, then shrugged.

"You're on!"

Bibi worked diligently at his new job for the better part of the next year. Having been ejected from his last formal dwelling place, he moved into a cubicle behind the men's room, where he slept on a bare mattress, eventually earning the nickname "Slops" for his efforts. Although at first Bibi made the best of the situation by asking every customer he encountered whether they'd ever heard of Hope Valley or any sort of hubcap ranch, with the passage of time his efforts grew weaker. His past insights, his trust in the worthiness of life became increasingly unreal—and try as he might there seemed to be nothing he could do to turn the situation around.

In search of new diversions, Bibi began to dabble in the many means of mind alteration available on the Delta. One popular substance, administered as a liquid into the ear canal, caused users to recall childhood events in such vivid detail that they seemed to be reliving the past; but after revisiting the scene of his father's bug-eyed suicide three times, Bibi had to conclude that this particular form of escape was not for him.

Another drug created such a precise illusion of becoming an animal that those under its influence had been known to kick or bite unexpectedly, to urinate on furnishings, and even to engage in sudden and unpredictable stampedes. But after spending far too many hours in the form of his childhood dog Buster, and sniffing out his father's body from beneath his backyard rosebush again and again, Bibi was forced to abandon this diversion as well.

But perhaps the most widely used of the currently fashionable chemicals was Gendamine, a substance which produced the undeniable sensation of being a member of the opposite sex—with the predictable side effect of sometimes provoking complete insanity in its users. On the one occasion Bibi submitted to its influence, however, he had to be forcibly restrained by the club staff from slicing off the ring finger of his left hand with a broken bottle—an effect none present had ever encountered before.

On the whole, Bibi had to conclude that his experiments with such avenues of escape had not been successful. He thought with longing of his experience in the Canyons of Time and the ecstatic weeks of freedom which followed—but what good was ecstasy, he asked himself, if you couldn't hold on to it? His old life was a dream, he told himself, and this one was too—and there seemed little hope of awakening from it.

In the wake of the crash, however, everyone seemed to be drifting down to the Delta; and one evening a pair of old friends showed up on the dance floor and roused him from his inertia. To Bibi's amazement the General recognized him immediately despite his changed features.

"Got no mind to get in the way, so all he sees is your essence," explained his new wife, the woman with no chin, who after a long courtship had fallen for the old soldier's charms and was now accompanying him on a honeymoon tour of the country. The aging warrior proved to be as frisky as ever, and in the exuberance of their reunion the three danced till the wee hours of the morning, rediscovering their proficiency at the mambo, the tango, and other classics they'd mastered so long ago.

Although the General had little recollection of anything that happened before he'd entered the club, the woman with no chin—whose name actually turned out to be Doreen—was able to fill Bibi in on recent events at the estate. With the collapse of the money market, chaos had overtaken the city. Peter, Cilantro, and the family had been forced to barricade themselves inside the mansion, together with the bridge-dwellers and various hangers-on, while the Professor feverishly attempted to finish the research necessary to gain mastery over fate. But they were soon overcome by gangs of marauding businessmen, who swarmed into the countryside in search of plunder, clad in the tattered remnants of business suits and carrying briefcases crammed with weapons. Forced to flee under cover of night, the group had dispersed; their current whereabouts were unknown.

Though Bibi's spirits sank to hear of the troubles of his friends, he did his best to distract himself through redoubled alcohol consumption and increasingly vigorous footwork. The three pranced ever more madly until Bibi, whose stamina had been somewhat compromised by his new lifestyle, was forced to take a breather in one of the booths while the General and his bride danced on.

The next thing Bibi knew, he awoke to find the club empty, sun streaming in through the windows, and Humps standing over him.

"Slops!" the proprietor was saying, shaking him by the shoulder. "Slops, wake up!"

"Oops! Sorry, boss," Bibi scrambled to his feet. "Guess I sort of laid down on the job, didn't I?"

"Forget that," crowed his employer, chomping away at his cheroot. "You were magnificent!"

"I was what?" Bibi rubbed his eyes as he strove to comprehend this new turn of events.

"Last night—on the dance floor. Slops, you've been wasting your talents!"

"Wasting my what—?"

"You're promoted!"

Within a matter of weeks Bibi's act, titled simply "Bobo Le Blaque, Exotic Dancer," had taken the city by storm. Although his early performances stuck close by the classic styles which had brought his success, Bibi soon set off for more adventurous turf, drawing on his travels and his life in the wilderness for inspiration. People flocked from all over the Delta to see his unsettling "Asylum Mambo" and the oozing "Quicksand Waltz," not to mention his elegant, fiendishly difficult to choreograph "Creosote Spider Ballet."

"I don't care what he does, so long as he strips down to a G-string before doing it," a grinning Humps told a news team, adding that his only regret was that he'd been unable to locate the General and his bride to make the act a threesome. Indeed, it was reported that the club had never done so well in all its years; and patrons were often heard to say that Bibi had transformed the caliber of the place entirely.

Within a short while Bibi had moved to an elegant up-river apartment building, protected from the increasingly dangerous local gangs by around-the-clock patrols. He grew friendly with politicians and celebrities, and became a fixture of the local society columns. He even made occasional television appearances. For a time Bibi was so diverted by his success that he nearly forgot his despair; and he abandoned his faltering search for the Hubcap King altogether.

But then there were the nightmares, populated by his ancestors and the grinning spectre of the Terry Cloth Man, which increased in direct proportion to his popularity. And the men in the striped suits, who seemed to be everywhere these days, standing about, smiling at him; they'd even taken to coming to his shows.

The crowning blow came when a letter, forwarded through a series of addresses, finally caught up with him at his apartment:

Dear Bibi, it began (actually the name had been scratched out, not as heavily as he might have hoped, and replaced by a crudely lettered "Bobo" inserted over the top—for in his last letters, more than a year ago, Bibi had filled his lone correspondent in on his new identity):

I hope this letter reaches you wherever you are, and that as you're reading this you're still alive and not in jail or anything. I'm afraid I have some bad news for you. I saw a news report on television the other night—you know how I like to watch "America Right Now" in the evenings while I do my needlepoint and eat my dinner and wonder where you are. Sometimes they have the most remarkable stories. Last week there was this show about a woman who had no hands but lived a perfectly ordinary life using only her feet for everything. She'd got to where she could use her toes just like fingers. There was this close-up and they looked just like any usual set of toes, but she could make the bed and dial the phone and even wash dishes with them.

Anyway, this program I'm writing to tell you about wasn't about her. It was about a guy who ran some sort of junk farm in one of those leftover bits of the Frontier. I couldn't tell exactly because I couldn't get my hearing aid adjusted just right—I think they called him the "Wheel Cover Pontif," or something of the sort. The story was about how he had died and they were putting him in the ground, but it wasn't in any kind of ordinary coffin. It was in some

*old car from the '50s. I think they said it was a Plymouth. I
mean, they were burying the whole car, with him in it. Or
was it a Pontiac?*

*I couldn't really tell for sure—they only had these old
photos, since because he was dead and all they couldn't
show much of him on the TV camera—except when they
had a shot of his body in the front seat as the car was being
lowered in, and then he just looked like a big doll or
something. Anyway, all old men look pretty much the same,
don't they, with their big ears and noses, especially in those
black-and-white photos that turn brown after they've been
sitting around for a long time.*

But I couldn't help but think it was your Uncle Otto.

*I'm sorry. You know I was very fond of him, too. Maybe
this is a good time to start thinking about a career?*

*Are you eating your vegetables? Please write back and let
me know what you're doing.*

Love, your Mom,
Millicent Brown

P.S. I hope you're not dead.

My whole life has been a waste. This was all Bibi could think in
the wake of the letter. He continued to go through the motions
of living, but something inside him had collapsed. The world
seemed a sham, a painted backdrop for a show that would never
go on. Perhaps the Man with the Terry Cloth Face had been
right, he thought. Perhaps it was all for nothing. He turned almost savagely upon his old beliefs. Time, the Universe, and
America, indeed—how could he have been so naive?

In desperation, Bibi took to prowling the brothels and drive-
through sex parlors of the waterfront—known as "Quickie
Lubes" or "Lovin' Ovens" in local parlance. Here he sampled

every pleasure known to humanity. He tangoed with transvestites, tangled with transsexuals, sampled sadism, and muddled his way through masochism.

For a time he frequented an establishment that specialized in unusually sized humans. Here he bedded a taciturn Peruvian giantess nearly eight feet tall, whose breasts were each larger than his head, and a giddy Lithuanian midget named Anastasia—as well as a woman known as Twigs, whose limbs were so thin it was like making love to a bird. He visited sex-with-animal parlors, sex-with-vegetable parlors; he was even, it was rumored, seen leaving a place known as The Cathouse, which featured liaisons with endangered species.

Nothing satisfied him.

At last, after marshaling his courage one evening by downing eight or nine "Green Lizards" at a local drinking establishment, Bibi got up the nerve to knock at the door of an outfit known as The One-armed Bandit, which specialized in deformities. After making his way through several rooms full of hunchbacks, harelips, and hermaphrodites, and dodging a pair of Siamese twins who persisted in blowing in both of his ears at once, Bibi managed to locate the proprietress.

"Nine fingers?" responded the Madam. She lifted one eyebrow as Bibi confessed his inmost desires. "I'm afraid we don't carry them." As she showed him to the door, Bibi could have sworn he heard her whisper to the night clerk: "Jesus, some people are weird!"

At last, after working his way through the entire district, avoiding only one particularly seedy establishment whose specialty was necrophilia, Bibi managed, at great expense, to arrange a liaison with a woman who had only four toes on her left foot.

It gave him no pleasure.

In his more introspective moments, Bibi often felt he didn't have the heart for this life. But he no longer knew what he did have the heart for.

. . .

Months passed. Drunkenness became Bibi's most familiar companion; he slipped into it as easily as one might slide into a favorite chair. After his show one evening, he stopped by a club called The Omnidiabolic Telegraph Agency to speak with a new acquaintance, a half-Samoan alligator wrestler named Charles. The idea had been to discuss the possibilities of putting a joint stage act together, but after downing five or six "Boilermakers," Bibi found their conversation headed for deeper waters.

"I saw into the nature of time once," Bibi confided woozily. "It was sort of like an . . . express train, I think. Running backwards—or was it forwards?"

"I'm with you, Boob," commiserated his companion. "I once saw into the nature of chopped liver. I was on a twelve-day Retsina binge, and—"

"Actually," Bibi went on, "it was more sort of . . . reversible . . ." he groped for words, "like one of those jackets you can wear inside out or the other way around. In a way it was—" He stared off into nothingness. "I mean, it was hardly even . . ." He trailed off altogether. "I don't remember what it was like, goddamn it!" Bibi burst out. He slammed his fist on the table so hard the glasses leapt in astonishment and half the place turned to stare. "I saw it," he cried. "I saw into the nature of time—and I couldn't hold on to it!" With that he broke down sobbing and laid his head on the table.

"Hey down now, Boob . . ." Charles awkwardly placed a hand on Bibi's shoulder. "Barman," he called, "bring Bobo another Boilermaker!"

The speakers below the ceiling were blaring out a popular tune called "My Sweetheart the Moon."

Bibi felt like he'd come to the end of everything.

Later that evening they were joined by Kowskiboot, who was

even more depressed than usual. He'd just received word that Patagonian writer Mariel Borquez had published a novel more minimalist than his, titled simply "T."

"Brilliant idea, huh?" spoke up author Brusque De Entraila, who was drinking at the bar. "It's a quick read, doesn't require translation, and provides enormous freedom of interpretation for the reader!"

"Not to mention the obvious Christ imagery," added another writer, Dick Bratwurst, spreading his arms in mock-crucifixion.

"Well, it's sure succeeded in martyring me," moaned Kowski-boot.

"Hold on just a minute," broke in a visiting author from overseas, who'd taken on the name Kentucky Coyote, and was known for jotting down everything that happened so it would not be lost forever. "What was that you just said?" she scribbled away, "I need to get it down exactly—"

"I said 'Seven Years Down the Tubes,'" growled Kowskiboot, glowering into his drink. But then he brightened. "Hey, that wouldn't be a bad title for a novel!" With that he pulled a pen from his pocket and a cocktail napkin from beneath a glass and began scribbling away, too.

Bibi peered darkly into the smoke-filled shadows of the place. He wished they would all go away and leave him alone. He wished the entire world would vanish.

But the usual evening festivities were about to begin. A poet who'd taken the name Lance Quiver mounted the stage and announced: "This piece is called 'Daughterette' ":

> the moon is rising up above
> the unknown chairs of my chest
> —and might my friendly countenance dissuade
> each passerby
> from asking:
> Wherefore didst thou run in pursuit of thy pestilence?

The scattered applause was broken by a disheveled bard, Thumb Stays, who lurched onstage and grabbed the mike, shouting:

> *Hey down now moon, oh luminous Boob of the sky!*
> *Dig it on down, boon Doggie—*
> *May you bone in tune at noon!*

The audience broke into howls of encouragement. At this Raze Kilo, a longtime veteran of the scene, stood up and proclaimed:

> *Two roads diverged in a wood—*
> *and I, all too aware of the possibilities,*
> *stood paralyzed for a lifetime!*

The crowd went mad.

Bibi didn't understand any of it. But then, he no longer felt he understood anything else, either. He was just about to order another Boilermaker when the door of the place burst open and a horde of men in striped suits swarmed into the club. This time they weren't smiling.

Without stopping to think, Bibi kicked over the table and rolled between the legs of a three-hundred-pound transvestite in a baton twirler's uniform, who was prancing just behind Kilo as he came offstage. The leader of the suits struggled through the crowd.

"Brown," he shouted across the room. "Frederick G. Brown II. We know who you are!"

"Isn't his name Bobo?" interjected Charles, rising to his feet and tripping over a table leg.

"But wait!" called the head suit. "We aren't—I mean, we don't—"

Bibi mamboed through the throng on the dance floor, limboed beneath a beer sign, and sprang for the top of the bar. The momentum carried him halfway down the counter, beer mugs going everywhere.

"Hold on a minute—" shouted someone above the uproar. "Did he say Frederick G. Brown II? Doesn't that mean—?"

A chorus of voices finished the thought for him:

$$"MONEY!!!"$$

The place exploded. Lance Quiver dove for Bibi's ankles and collided with a fortune-teller who'd just set her act up on a barstool. The man in the twirler's outfit, mistaking him for Bibi, brought his baton down on Quiver's head. A fellow in a giant rabbit costume socked the baton man in the jaw, sending him to the ground. Crystal balls and tarot cards spilled across the floor. The drunken Quiver grabbed Kilo by mistake. "I've got 'im!" he hollered. "I'm rich, rich, rich!"

Bibi rolled off the bar and landed in a sinkful of ice.

"Wait a minute!" shouted the leader of the suits. "Actually, the reason we're here is—"

His words were lost in the chaos. Kowskiboot went sailing over the bar for no apparent reason, smashing the mirror and tipping over a row of whiskey bottles. Quiver came behind him, flung like a rag doll by the enormous bunny. He intersected with the bartender, who crashed into the cash register. The drawer sprang open, and money went everywhere. Erupting in hysteria, the crowd surged toward the cash. Bibi crawled out along the back side of the bar and into the hallway that led to the bathrooms.

Amidst the confusion a band was trying to take the stage, but Charles, mistaking an alligator-skin trombone case for the genuine article, seized it and went rolling end over end across the dance floor.

The hall proved to have no exit. Bibi turned back toward the entrance, only to bump into Kowskiboot, who was crawling awkwardly along on his knees with a fifth of whiskey in each hand.

"Here," the old fellow winked, handing him a bottle. "You'll be needing one of these."

Bibi grabbed it and took a slug. "But how am I supposed to get out of here?"

Kowskiboot shrugged. "Bathroom window?" he suggested, then tilted to one side and passed out on his back.

Bibi heard the bar tip over in the main room. He started for the men's toilet, then on second thought doubled back to the women's room and locked the door. He heard shouts and crashes as the first members of the crowd streamed into the hall, only to trip over the prostrate author.

"He must be in here!" someone shouted outside the men's room.

Bibi heard the adjacent door go down with a thud. Confused voices and shouts.

"Try the other one!" he heard someone cry as he clambered atop the toilet tank and smashed the window with the whiskey bottle. Bibi heard the latch rattling behind him as he wriggled through the opening, then the slam of the crowd breaking in. Then he was on his feet in the alley out back, running faster than he'd ever run in his life.

Practically the only ones left standing in the ruined club were Kentucky Coyote and the leader of the suits, neither of whom had participated in the mayhem.

"Hmm," Coyote mused, glancing about the new emptiness and scratching her head. She jotted on her notepad a title that had just come to her. "A Place to Oneself," she read aloud. "No, that's not quite right. A Room for Oneself? No . . ."

"The funny thing is," the man in the suit said to her, "the only reason we stopped by was to let Brown know that, just as we'd finally figured out who he was—the key, you know, was the scar on his wrist, you can just barely see it in that photo—"

"Hold on just a minute," Coyote responded, pen flying, "this is all very, very interesting . . ."

"—just as we're sure we've got him, what happens but the government goes bankrupt. We're out of a job. Off the case. I was just gonna offer to buy him a drink!"

Bibi kept running till his legs would no longer carry him. At last, when he was sure he was safe, he collapsed on a park bench and breathed for a while. Then he rose to his feet and walked on through the city.

Having no idea which direction to go, he turned down a broad avenue, past the usual late-night array of seekers and lunatics. A mist was beginning to gather along the street; snake charmers and organ grinders peddled their acts while sirens howled in the distance. A performance artist stood in the middle of a sidewalk that had just been poured by a night crew, feet immersed in the rapidly hardening concrete, playing a violin. A street vendor tried to sell him a stuffed armadillo.

An evangelist shouted from a corner: "Absolute knowledge? Our compasses indicate only relative North!" Spotting Bibi, he shouted across the street: "What's it all about, Boob? What are we?"

Bibi didn't know. He wasn't sure he cared anymore—but then, he couldn't not care, either. He walked onward through a gathering fog, whose thickness his eyes could no longer penetrate.

Bibi walked for miles, fog wrapping about him like a shroud, until the lights of the city fell away and he emerged at the edge of the gulf where the strands of the river ended their seaward journey. Here the fog faded to haze and the haze to wisps of cloud. Waves lapped against the shore; moonlight fell and broke in shards upon the water. Strangely, Bibi thought it the most beautiful night he'd ever seen.

Having no notion of what he should do next, Bibi stood for a long time, watching the waves move back and forth. *Why,* he wondered blankly, *does the tide bother going out when it's only going to come back in again?* It was mesmerizing, the way his mind merged with the brightness of moon on water. Scarcely knowing what he was doing, Bibi found himself stepping forward and heading out into the light.

The ocean was warm against his skin, her touch a caress. In the moonlight Bibi could see, as he stood to his waist in the salty embrace, the reflection of a face on the surface—a face he could no longer recognize. He stretched out a finger and traced a name below it: Bibi Brown. But the words vanished instantly, and the act brought no recognition. Transfixed, he dipped his hands below the image and brought up a handful of water. He stared for a long moment at the rippled reflection in his cupped palms. Then he lifted the briny liquid to his lips and drank.

The salt seared Bibi's throat and brought him back to himself for an instant. He could see the distant lights of the city playing upon the gulf, wondered vaguely if there were sharks in these waters, decided it didn't really matter. It was Bobo, after all, who would be their victim. And who, in the end, was *he*? With that, Bibi lowered his head into the dark waters and struck out swimming.

Bibi swam with a fury—swam away the years in the clubs and brothels, the anti-gravity pit and the Canyons of Time, the Frontier and the asylum. He swam away his search for the Hubcap King, the whole continent of America, his entire lost youth. He swam with a strength that seemed inexhaustible, until at last he was empty of everything, with nothing but the stars and moon rocking above. He rolled onto his back and floated for a long time, watching the sky wheel above him. It would be so easy, he thought, to let himself go, to sink into that saltwater womb and end the struggle forever. The Hubcap King was dead. He'd squandered his life on a fool's mission. What, after all, was left for him? With that, Bibi tucked at the waist and dove into darkness.

He dove till the pressure hammered at his ears; and he dove deeper. He dove until he could dive no more; then he opened his eyes and, still kicking against the water's upward pull, stared into the stinging blankness. Not a glimmer of light penetrated. What was there to lose? Bibi parted his lips, and was just about to suck in a lungful of salty wetness, when all at once there appeared before him a familiar vision—a vision he'd seen far too many times before. It was the figure of a man, prone and motionless, with a slack, open mouth and two protruding, fishlike eyes. There were other figures around him, bent and sorrowful; as though from a distance he could hear sobbing and other sounds of pain. And as Bibi looked at the figure who had been his father, the words took shape in his mind:

Is this all I am?

To which a second, fainter voice added, like a distant echo: *Bibi—you promised!*

Darn it, thought Bibi to himself, *I knew this wasn't going to work out.* Emitting what would, on the surface, have passed for a sigh, he revolved in place and kicked for the surface. Bibi broke through several moments later, retching and gasping for air. He rolled onto his back, inhaled, swallowed water, snorted, choked till he'd caught his breath. Afterward he lay there, floating and breathing, for a long while, until he became very quiet inside. Bibi watched as the moon neared the horizon; soon he would be wrapped in wet, velvety blackness, out of sight of the shore, with only the stars for guides. But despite his exhaustion, Bibi felt oddly clear-headed—more so than he'd felt in a long time. There wasn't much he knew for sure anymore. But at least he was certain of one thing: he wasn't through living.

From the movement of the waves Bibi had a pretty good

idea of which direction the shore lay. He took a deep breath and, as weary as he could imagine, struck out in the direction he thought would bring him to safety.

．　．　．

"Whew!" the waitress exclaimed, her dishwater-brown beehive listing to one side as she looked over the new customer from top to bottom. The wind blew the door shut behind him. "Rough night?"

Bibi nodded, taking a seat at the counter. His clothes still clung damply to his flesh, and his skin was raspy where the salt had stuck.

"You look like you could use some coffee."

Bibi fished around his pockets, found a salt-smeared quarter and laid it on the counter. "This is all I have left."

"Midnight swimmer's discount," smiled the waitress, firing up a fresh pot of brew. Bibi noticed the tag on her blouse:

"Excited to Serve You:
Polly."

"Hungry?" she asked as she poured him out a glass of water.

"This quarter's all I have."

"Wednesday A.M. special," she smiled. "Breakfast free with purchase of coffee." She leaned over the coffeepot, nearly upsetting a stack of glasses, and called to the kitchen: "First Base Breakfast, Hap!" Then she glanced back at Bibi and added, "Make it a double!"

On second thought, Bibi mused, he'd have to call her hair dishwater-blonde. In fact, the way it glimmered, piled all out of kilter above her pleasant, neither-old-nor-young face, he found quite appealing. And behind her teardrop-shaped glasses were a pair of truly beautiful green eyes. Sea-green, he'd have to call them.

Polly slid the coffee urn out of the way and put a mug under the drip spout. "If you wait for the pot to fill," she explained, "it'll be daylight before you get a cup." The dark liquid trickled into the mug. "Hey," she asked him, "anyone ever tell you the difference between Hell and planet Earth?"

Bibi shook his head.

"In Hell it's exactly the same as it is here—but there's no caffeine." Smiling at her joke, she slid the cup out from under the drip and put the pot back in place. "Hey," she asked, turning back with the mug. "What's your name, anyway?"

"Bo—" Bibi started to answer automatically. "Um . . ." He thought for a moment. "Bibi," he said finally. "Bibi Brown."

"I'm Polly," said Polly.

"I know," said Bibi.

But as Polly put the coffee down before him, something caught Bibi's eye. It was something about her hands: or perhaps not so much something as the absence of something. For Bibi noticed—couldn't help but notice, as she released the handle of the mug—that if he looked closely at the second finger from the bottom, the ring finger of her left hand, he could just see that part of it was missing. All the others were complete, but through some mishap or accident of birth, this particular digit ended between the second and third knuckle, leaving a small but discernible stub.

9.
LOVE

Nine! Sweet 9! Oh lollipop among numbers, queen among numerals, poised at the summit of the single digits like a great lone finger, quivering skyward! Compared to your grandeur, what are the charms of a mere "10"—composed as it is of the two lowliest numbers, set side by side to prop each other up? Complete unto yourself, needing no other number to lend you strength—in your shadow all other digits tremble in inadequacy! Nine, 9, nine—oh glorious, glorious nine!

Like a cat with its many chances at living, Bibi had, to his amazement, surfaced once more into life. He felt resurrected; reborn. His dream had come true. The Nine-fingered Woman was Polly, Polly was the Nine-fingered Woman, and she was his, his at last! He wrote poetry, he sang, he danced—the suffering of his recent past was swept away entirely.

Her simple trailer rocked with their passion, threatened to leap from its cinder blocks with their frenzy. Water sloshed from the bathtub, the sink cracked free of the wall, legs collapsed beneath the table, sofa cover split, fabric of reality burst asunder . . .

If she were a flower, Bibi thought, she'd be a daisy, with her bright, simple good looks and her plain, wide-open features. Her smile was like the crescent moon. When he gazed into her green eyes Bibi saw, as though reflected in twin pools, the mystery of life itself.

Porcelain figures of rabbits and quail sat everywhere about Polly's trailer, propping open doors, occupying shelves and alcoves. A collection of plates with animal pictures on them hung from the walls. She had a taste for paintings of birds on velvet.

"It's not much," she'd told him, gesturing about that first morning she brought him back after her shift, ostensibly so he could have a shower, "but it's home."

"It's beautiful," replied Bibi as he looked around, wide-eyed and slack-jawed. "Absolutely beautiful."

"Um, the bath's over here." Polly started nervously down the hall in the indicated direction, only to trip over a startled-looking ceramic hare.

Bibi leapt to the rescue, but thunked his head on the low hall entry and reeled back.

Stumbling forward, Polly grabbed for the bathroom doorknob, but it broke from its mount and she went sprawling to the carpet. Lurching gallantly toward her, Bibi tripped over the same startled hare.

Polly had just enough time to rise to her knees, beehive spilling about her face, before intersecting with Bibi's downward-arcing tumble. His right arm landed across her shoulder, while his left instinctively grabbed for her hip. Her left arm went around his neck, and her right swung automatically about his waist. The forward momentum sent both to the carpet—but the momentum of love was just beginning. Their lips met, bodies linked, souls recognized their long-absent other halves and merged into one. Could it be said that the ground shuddered? That universes opened? Might one assert that the problematic, much-sought-after union of man and woman, never successfully achieved since Eve and Adam quarreled over the apple, was consummated at last in that tiny trailer-park hall-way beside the Bayou?

Actually, as the Anti-gravity Hermit would have foreseen, words could not hope to contain what passed in the ensuing eternity between these two lovers.

"Ah, Baby," Polly sighed after it was over, resting with Bibi's head against her heart as they lay together in the hallway (though in truth she must have found it rather unusual that her partner, in his post-coital bliss, was sucking at the fingers of her left hand like a contented child). "We're perfect together."

Bibi couldn't have agreed more.

Pinned to Polly's refrigerator by a magnet in the shape of an al-ligator was a list of her guidelines for living.

"I don't get it," Bibi said, reading out loud: " 'Never trust any-one who doesn't like lemons.' What's that supposed to mean?"

He was wearing nothing but a towel wrapped around his waist. He hadn't felt so good in years.

"You're got to read them all," said Polly, "every day for months. Then they start to make sense."

" 'Watch out for the full moon,'" Bibi ran his finger down to the next item. " 'It puts people in strange moods.' That must be what happened to me—lasted seven years, I think."

"Want some lemon pie?" Polly asked.

"Are you testing me?" Bibi took the plate and fork from her hands. " 'If we knew all the answers at the beginning,' he read, 'there wouldn't be any reason for the journey.' Hmm. I think your thinking is starting to sink in."

"I think *your* thinking is half the problem, that's my thinking. Now eat your pie!"

Bibi told his new love all about his travels and his search for the Hubcap King.

"Why are you laughing?" he asked her when he'd finished.

"All your wanderings over the past years—and I've never left Magnolia County."

"Never? But how come?"

"Oh, I don't know." She rubbed absently at the fingers of her left hand. "Somehow it never felt right." Polly suddenly became very concerned with the exact position of a ceramic duck on the bookshelf. She moved it a few inches to the right, then to the left, and stood back to examine the results. "Besides," she glanced at him over her shoulder, "you've proved it yourself— what am I looking for if it's not here?"

Bibi asked why she'd never married.

"I'm married to mystery," she responded, and turned to busy herself with a terra-cotta partridge. But Bibi couldn't help notice—was that a tear in her eye?

Oh, he was mad for her. When she was away his body pulsed with longing. He found himself staring at doughnuts, keyholes, the open necks of wine bottles. Walls and floors drew in and out as though breathing, and everything took on a new sense of luminosity, as though expressing a subtle internal pressure. The things of the world were again bulging with meaning, and Bibi felt so filled with the same presence it seemed his skin would crack open and fall away, and everything he thought of as himself—plans, memories, preferences, aversions—would be swept away in a fresh torrent of realization.

When she came home they'd leap at one another like crazed animals, making love again and again in her tiny candlelit bedroom, their shadows projected larger than life on the wall, images reflected in each other's eyes to the point of distortion.

He explored her every orifice: nostrils, navel, ears. In the long, steamy Bayou nights, alive with the song of whippoorwills, he moaned out loud: "I want to enter you so completely . . ."

"Yeah, Bibi?"

". . . that I touch every part—your liver, your kidneys . . ."

"Oh, Bibi—"

"Your gallbladder. I want to make love to your gallbladder!"

"Oh, Baby!"

He counted to nine while they made love, then back down to zero, occasionally even shouting "Blast off!" when the ecstasy overwhelmed him. He took her hand in his, stroked it across his body, put the stub of her missing finger between his lips. Polly didn't mind. Love was love, as far as she was concerned. One evening, as she took his straining, turgid member in hand, she whispered to him: "Bibi, look—it's my tenth finger!"

And it was. For the first time in their lives, both of them felt complete.

Polly had her own way of thinking about things.

"I don't understand," Bibi ruminated one morning as they loitered in bed, "how my life turned in on me like it did. I mean, everything was always so good, then all of a sudden—"

"All the good things in life can hurt you." Polly sat up, examined her toenails, reached for a bottle of nail polish. "It's set up that way so you don't take them for granted."

"But things change so quickly. I mean, one minute you're on top of the world, and the next—"

"Happiness comes and goes. That's why it makes us happy. Why, if it was here all the time, we'd hardly notice it."

Bibi thought about that. "You know," he said finally, "the funny thing is, if there was a key, some solution to the whole big riddle, and one day I saw it, the celestial light of realization beamed down on me, I don't know if I could take it. It might kill me."

"Maybe it wouldn't be such a bad thing," Polly said, "that kind of death."

"I'm not sure I know what you mean."

"I'm not sure I do, either." Polly spread pink on her little toe. "Bibi, Baby," she went on, "do you believe God exists?"

"I'm not even sure *I* exist. What about you?"

"I think God and the devil must have fallen into a blender or something at some point and gotten all mixed up. And we humans—we're the result."

Although she was everyone's favorite employee at the cafe, despite her penchant for dropping pickles down the shirts of customers and other acts of occasional awkwardness, it was perhaps fortunate that Polly never tried her hand at the grill; for the culinary experiments she performed on Bibi at home were of a sort never before known on the planet. A favorite concoction, which she'd dubbed "I Ching Soup" after the complex divination process she used to determine its ever-varying ingredients, ranged from the inedible to the sublime. One day it might be a porridge of celery, lime peels, and gingerroot; the next a catfish stew delicately flavored with chicory. Polly's greatest extremes, whether successes or failures, were always products of the moment, never to be duplicated, for she followed no recipes, kept no records, used no measuring devices of any kind. Sometimes she dreamed of ingredients; at times these nocturnal visions were so compelling she'd rise in the night to prepare them. Bibi would wake far past midnight and trudge down the hall to find her standing above the trailer's tiny stove top, combining corn starch with vinegar, and blackening the resultant paste in a mixture of olive oil and coconut milk.

But Polly's occult leanings were in no way confined to the kitchen. She hosted biweekly meetings of a group known as the

Amazing Light Fellowship, which, in the best tradition of their Bayou home, performed séances, divinations, and rituals for every occasion. Convinced by Bibi's still-recurring nightmares that he was not yet completely healed from his bout with despair, Polly insisted that he not only attend these gatherings, but accompany her on visits to various local healers in hopes that he might come around.

"But I feel fine—great in fact!" Bibi would say as she trundled him off in her ancient Rambler for yet another consultation.

"Denial!" Polly would respond, in a tone that brooked no resistance; and her argument was always ironclad, as any attempt at further protest could always be explained away by the same single word.

One such healer, convinced that the key to Bibi's recovery lay in the transformative powers of static electricity, responded to their visit by running down a carpeted hallway in his socks, then leaping into the air to shoot a powerful static force at Bibi through his feet. The wall at the end of the hall bore evidence of the numerous times he'd overshot his mark.

Another, who claimed to channel the spirit of Madame Curie, studied the patterns of light and dark under Bibi's fingernails before concluding that in a past life he'd gone down with the *Titanic,* and required a program of daily ice baths to restimulate and clear the memories.

"My God, what have they been telling you?" exclaimed a third consultant. "What you really need to do is follow my thirty-day raw pomegranate cleansing diet. But you must eat the seeds!"

Then there were the séances, led every Thursday night in Polly's trailer by Madame Zevar, a sprightly, elderly woman who always wore a sparkly, multicolored turban wrapped about her head and was known as "The English Channel" for her impeccable old-world accent—though there were those who claimed she'd never traveled farther than Biloxi, at least not in the flesh. These gatherings always filled Bibi with dread, for at least one of his ancestors inevitably showed up during the proceedings, to hover half visible above the kitchen sink or rock the dining table while whispering in Bibi's ear: "Life was the death of me!" And although Madame Zevar's trademark good manners never faltered, even when her eyes bulged from their sockets as she channeled the ghost of his father, Bibi's certainly did; he could scarcely wait for the evenings to end.

"See," Polly said, eyes flashing like rhinestones behind her lenses, "that proves it. If you were truly at peace with your ancestors, meeting them in spirit form wouldn't bother you in the least. In fact, you'd welcome the chance to catch up on news from the other side!"

Reluctantly agreeing that maybe she did have a point—though he couldn't entirely go along with her notion that his nightmares might be signs of actual spirit possession—he promised to approach the next gathering with a more positive attitude.

True to his word, Bibi, who'd spent the day purifying himself through a program of pomegranate fasting, saltwater enemas, and the requisite ice baths, found himself sitting in the candlelit living room of the trailer that next Thursday in an exceptional state of tranquillity and openness. Present were Hip and Hap, the owners of Polly's diner—balding, paunchy men in their fifties who wore identical sleeveless tee shirts and were distinguishable only by the slightly differing lengths of the half-smoked cigars which protruded from their mouths. So similar were the two, in fact, that the diner's resident derelict, an elderly poet named Corsica, who was also in attendance, had always interpreted their twinlike appearance as a double-vision phenomenon brought on by drinking, and never for a moment dreamed the place had more than one owner.

Also present were Muriel and Delilah, representatives of the Magnolia County Dearly Departed Appreciation Society; Isis, a self-described apprentice sorceress with flowing hair, rippling scarves, and feathers, crystals, and medicine pouches affixed to every conceivable region of her body; and Polly's next-door neighbor, Jeremiah the Survivalist, in his trademark army fatigues and French Foreign Legion cap.

Madame Zevar began the session with the participants holding hands around the table while she delivered a traditional spirit-summoning chant which she herself, or so she said, had translated from the ancient Mesopotamian:

> *All you shades on the other side*
> *Listen now as those who've cried*
> *At your loss so sad and tragic*
> *Call you back here with our magic!*

Bibi had begun the evening in an unusually receptive state, but the chant must have sent him over the edge, for no sooner had the usual dank chill fallen upon the room and the eerie scent of persimmon blossoms pervaded the atmosphere as always, than he found his mouth opening as though of its own accord, and emitting the words: "Why bother?"

All present, including Madame Zevar, who had just commenced to shuddering and delivering her usual string of incoherent syllables, turned to glare at the interruption.

"Why bother?" repeated the medium, eyes opening wide and her cordial smile dropping to half-mast.

"Bibi," hissed Polly, leaning across the table. "You promised!"

"I'm sorry—" replied Bibi, who was as unsettled as anyone by his inexplicable behavior. "What I mean is . . . I'm just plain bored!"

At this Madame Zevar rose to her feet. "Young man, have you no respect for the dead?"

In place of his intended apology, Bibi found himself responding: "Life was better before I knew so much!"

"Then perhaps," snapped Madame Zevar, "you'd better leave before you learn anything else. Or shall I?"

"No, no, Madame Zevar," pleaded Polly. "Please stay. I don't know what's come over him."

Bibi, whose tongue was no longer his own, carried on, crying: "I haven't got a clue!"

"Nor have any of us," ventured Muriel. "And that's why we members of the MCDDAS strive to remain open to every possibility, and continue to honor the spirits of those we have loved who are no longer—"

But the no longer remotely polite channel cut her off, shouting: "This is an outrage!"

No one was listening to her anymore. Bibi, who had climbed during this exchange to the top of the table, now stood rocking at its edge. He leapt from its surface, crying: "The future is bright, but I never seem to get there!"

Isis, meanwhile, had backed up against the refrigerator, where she was waving a crystal cross and chanting an incantation in ancient Cyrillic, while Corsica took advantage of the diversion to creep over to the liquor cabinet, where he cracked open a bottle of Creme de Menthe and took several deep pulls.

Bibi, on his feet again, now seized a banana from the fruit bowl, brandished it about, and plunged it like a saber against his belly, moaning as he sank to the floor: "When all is said and done I'm just like everybody else."

At this Jeremiah grabbed an apple from the bowl, plucked its stem, then lobbed it into the center of the living room and rolled to a defensive position under the table with his fingers in his ears.

"Do you suppose we should call a doctor—?" suggested Delilah, backing away from the commotion.

"C'mon, Hap," said Hip, picking up his hat. "Sadie's never gonna show up with all this racket going on."

"Or Susie," replied his partner, and together they walked out the door.

To which Bibi, writhing on the floor in an apparent agony, responded: "God . . . arrrrgghhh! . . . stood me . . . up!"

"Omigosh," exclaimed Polly, dropping to her knees beside him. "I think I know what this is about! Bibi, oh baby—"

"Dad gum-it!" replied her lover, emitting a stream of gargling and hissing sounds. "At last I've found the cure for all life's ills!" He kicked his legs and clutched his hands wildly about his throat.

"Madame Zevar," Polly called to the medium, who'd backed into a corner with her turban unraveling and a stricken look on her face, "it's his ancestors, Madame Zevar. They're coming through him!"

Bibi twisted and trembled as he lay on the carpet. "Aaargghh . . ." he cried. His back arched in torment and his lips worked as though trying to form words. ". . . Ooohhh!" At last Bibi managed to spit out a final sentence:

"LIFE IS A NAUGAHYDE SEAT COVER
WITH NO STUFFING!!!"

With this he convulsed upward, then suddenly relaxed.

A hush fell upon the room as everyone waited to see whether there would be another outburst. But Bibi remained silent; and after a moment Isis stepped forward and pointed a shaking finger at his outstretched body. "Look," she whispered. "Look!"

And while there are those who would later dispute it, all present, with the exception of Madame Zevar, later swore that they saw Bibi's unconscious form lift into the air and hover several inches above the carpet for a long moment, before slowly settling back to rest.

At which Bibi sat up, looked about, and asked blankly: "Is this all I am?"

"I don't think so, Baby," replied Polly, taking him into her arms. "I don't think so."

. . .

That night Bibi awoke from a terrible dream in which he watched his father stuffing marbles up his nostrils, one after another, until he was asphyxiated.

"Daddy," he woke shouting. "Come back—I love you!"

Polly held Bibi in her arms for many hours after that, during which time he cried many years' worth of tears—for he had never, even as a child, really mourned his father's passing.

The next morning Bibi had to admit he felt a lot better than he had in ages—in fact, maybe ever. And as for his ancestors' nocturnal visitations, they ceased from that day on, never to return.

The banishment of his nightmares, however, was far from the only impact Bibi's debut as a channeler had on his and Polly's life together. Two other results followed in short order—the first being that Madame Zevar, who'd never channeled more than two or three spirits at a time, let alone a dozen, didn't come to the gatherings anymore; and the second being that nearly everyone else in the neighborhood did. Jeremiah needed to contact his buddies who'd been lost in the government's tragic debacle in Madagascar; Muriel wanted to discover where her husband Vernon had hidden $500 in lottery winnings the night he drove off the Robert E. Lee Bridge; Isis was seeking to connect with the spirit of Joan of Arc, who she was pretty sure she'd been in a past life, though she thought she ought to check with the source just to make sure. Then there was Claude, a shrimp fisherman from down the road, who needed to know where his drowned first mate, Jacques, had left the key to the engine room; Marilyn, the southern belle, who wanted to ask her departed high-school beau, Foyell, if it was all right to marry someone else now that thirty-eight years had passed; and an endless procession of other mourning, woeful souls looking for a moment's relief from their sorrows.

Bibi, unable as always to resist a plea for help, channeled them all. He staggered again and again out of the Madagascan forest, riddled with bullet holes and shrapnel, to let Jeremiah know it was really all right that he'd survived. He suffered the drowning agonies of Jacques, to return soaking wet from the other side, key in hand. He brought release to Marilyn with the transmission of Foyell's blessings, and ecstasy to Muriel with the revelation that the money was rolled up in a tin of Vernon's pipe tobacco in the top dresser drawer. And he marched stiffly around the trailer before the eyes of the amazed Isis, chanting: "A free Christendom for all Europe!" before gently letting the sorceress-in-training know that she was actually the incarnation of Joan's sister Jane of Arc, who'd lived well into old age as a washerwoman.

As word spread, they had to expand séances to Tuesdays, then Mondays, and finally to every night of the week to accommodate the crowds that came from all over the Bayou, spilling from the tiny living room out into the yard; some even stood on one another's shoulders before the windows, in hopes of catching a glimpse of the legendary channeler hovering in midair, as he was rumored to do while at work.

But through all the confusion, Bibi and Polly's love remained strong. Regardless of how many people were waiting outside for night to fall, they'd station Isis, who'd become Bibi's informal assistant, at the gate, then pull the shades and light a candle, and spend hours lying in bed, gazing into one another's eyes.

"Have you ever thought," Polly mused, "how perfect the names for the colors are? I mean, take blue for instance—it's just so . . . *blue*. To think that when they were making the names up they might've called it yellow instead . . ." She smiled her moonlike smile.

"Polly," Bibi mused back, "if we took away everything we ordinarily think of as ourselves—our favorite music, the food we like, the color of our hair—what do you suppose would be left?"

"Why, nothing, of course," replied his love. "Bibi, you ask the weirdest questions."

But Bibi was no longer listening. He was staring, eyes inches from her face, at Polly's two noses—one ordinary, the other enormous and transparent. When he closed his right eye, one nose vanished; when he closed the other, the remaining nose jumped to the other side. He lay there for a long time, winking and making her nose jump back and forth.

"Do you love everything about me?" Polly asked one afternoon.

"Of course I do," Bibi replied.

"Even my spit?" she persisted.

"Your what?"

"I want you to love my spit!"

She told him everything—almost.

"So . . . what happened to it?" Bibi finally got up the courage to ask one morning, taking her wounded finger in hand as they lolled in bed with the windows open and the sun streaming in.

Polly merely smiled, a bit wistfully. "A girl's got to have at least one secret."

Which made her, as far as Bibi was concerned, more mysterious and desirable than ever.

They made love every way possible. They made love quickly, and they made love very, very slowly. They felt every nuance, every tender tendril of each other's movement. They came to feel as if they knew every cell in one another's bodies.

Polly was a mysterious creature to him—sometimes soft and open, other times closed up like a book, her pages written in a language he could never understand.

They practiced complete surrender, kissing one another's open eyes.

. . .

Meanwhile the spiritual situation was continuing to get out of hand. Especially after Bibi, while attempting to channel the grandfather of an eczema-ridden crawfish trapper, was accidentally taken over by the ghost of Louis Pasteur, who cured the fellow's skin problem instead.

Word spread through the throng outside, who began shoving their way toward the trailer in a frenzy.

"Seborrhea!" shouted one man incoherently, as he burst through the screen door, heedless of the locked frame.

"Gout!" cried a woman, clawing at the kitchen screen.

"Shingles!" yelled a man who was halfway through the bathroom window.

"Diverticulosis!" came the cries from the darkness.

"Gingivitis—"

"Piles!"

"Halitosis . . ."

"Warts!"

Bibi cured one man of dandruff, and his wife of a toothache. He cured a child of colic, and her mother of gallstones. He cured an elderly ex-curate of impotence and a teenaged boy of acne. He cured through the night and into the dawn, then collapsed on the couch with the wreckage of the evening strewn about him.

The next night the crowd had doubled. There were so many people, in fact, spilling out the driveway and winding down the road to the trailer park, that Polly could scarcely guide the Rambler through them when she came home from the diner. Again Bibi stayed up till dawn, healing epileptics and syphilitics, rheumatics and insomniacs, hysterics and hypochondriacs. He cured victims of Crohn's Disease, Legionnaire's, Alzheimer's, chronic fatigue syndrome, and herpes; and still they came.

The yard grew piles of abandoned crutches, leg braces, crosses dragged for miles by the faithful, even wheelchairs. A news team came from "America Right Now" to film a feature titled: "Bibi Brown: Man or Myth?"—and after the commentator's migraine headaches mysteriously cleared up, they sent back a second team to shoot a sequel called: "Bibi Brown: The Genuine Article!" Crowds backed up all the way to the highway. Testimonials tacked to the Cyclone fence told the story of cure upon cure:

"Bibi saved my son."
"For the first time in seventeen years I am free of
    pain."
"Thanks to Bibi I can walk."
"I can hear."
"I can see!"
"My back doesn't hurt."
"My nose isn't running!"
"Praise be to Bibi."
"Blessed be Bibi."
"All hail Saint Bibi!"

Then things really began to turn strange. "Look what I found," announced Isis one day, holding at arm's length a dead chicken she'd discovered hanging from the doorknob.

Polly, rather sensibly, cooked it for lunch; but this was only the beginning. The next morning they found a toad lying belly up on the doorstep, and the following day a pile of what appeared to be sheep entrails. Later that week they noticed a row of horseshoes tacked upside down along the base of the trailer, and an ungodly mass of hair mixed with mucoidal secretions below their bathroom window.

Shortly thereafter Bibi's hair began to fall out, while Polly developed a rash on the soles of her feet. Isis began to have unsettling dreams of satyrs and apes. And it didn't stop there. Soon Bibi lost all interest in food. He became haggard and gaunt. Red marks appeared on his palms. He saw things in the backs of closets and under tables; strange things that slunk back into the darkness and weren't there when he turned on the lights.

Polly started hearing voices. "One BLT, hold the mayo," they'd cry, or "Home Run Dinner, no gravy!" until she thought she'd go mad. Isis developed an itch in the center of her head that she couldn't reach, no matter what she stuck down her ears.

And still the afflicted came.

Bibi healed every night till dawn, then collapsed on the sofa, too tired to walk down the hall to the bedroom. He and Polly scarcely had time to speak anymore; soon their intimacies ceased entirely. He stopped eating altogether. First he had to sit down between healings; then during them; and before long he was conducting sessions from a horizontal position on the couch, which he scarcely left day or night except to go to the bathroom.

It was at the peak of this desperate state of affairs that an unexpected visitor dismounted from a bus at the highway. Brandishing an umbrella, she cleared a path through the crowds and wound her way in and around the tent city which had grown up beside the trailer. She stepped past mounds of crutches and assorted debris to mount the steps, wisps of white hair poking from beneath her hat, satchel clasped firmly in one hand. She knocked authoritatively at the screen door, where she was greeted by a peaked, jaundiced-looking Isis.

"I'm sorry, healings don't start till sunset," the ailing apprentice greeted her.

"*I* happen to be in perfect health!" responded the visitor. With that, she pushed past the startled doorkeeper and crossed the living room to the sofa.

"When I said it might be time to get started on a career," she said, on glimpsing the pale, prostrate healer, "this wasn't exactly what I had in mind!"

"Mom!" Bibi greeted her, scarcely able to raise his head. "I know . . . I must look terrible, but at least—"

"—at least you're not dead!" the good woman finished the sentence for him. "Still, it looks like I arrived just in time." She leaned down and embraced her son, then drew back and examined his new features for a long moment. "I don't know about that chin, but I like the new nose. Rather an improvement on the Brown version, I must say!"

"I've been meaning to write—" Bibi began.

"Of course you have."

"But how did you find me?"

"The television program, naturally. I could tell immediately that things were going to get out of hand."

"And," responded Bibi, "that's exactly what they've done." He was silent for a long moment; then he groaned, mustered all the energy he had, and swung his feet unsteadily to the floor. "So now that you're here"—he drew a deep breath—"let's see what we can do to turn the situation around."

The first item of business was to get Bibi some rest. That night Millicent stepped onto the front stoop and, waving away with her umbrella the half-dozen paraplegics, seven or eight cancer victims, and eleven or so heart patients at the front of the crowd, announced: "Tonight is my son's night off. He needs some sleep!" In response to the collective moan which answered her she added, "You've all suffered this long. You can survive another day!"

This provoked some jostling about in the group, but none proved willing to oppose the mother's fierce gaze. Having given the crowd a final glance of warning, Millicent went back inside and sat down with Bibi, Polly, and Isis at the kitchen table.

"Now explain to me," she began, "exactly what has been going on."

"Well," Bibi said, "it looks to me like some kind of a curse or something must have—"

"What?!" interjected Polly. She leapt to her feet, looking wildly about the room. "I'm telling you, the Center Field Special is— Oh." She relaxed. "Yes, there's no doubt about it. We've been hexed."

"I can't imagine why," said Bibi, "when we're doing so much good for everyone."

"Except yourselves," put in his mother.

"But who," asked Isis, jiggling a finger desperately in her right ear, "would do such a thing to us?"

"Shouldn't be hard to figure out," said Millicent. "Now tell me the whole story from start to finish."

They told her everything, from the first séances through the channeling sessions and into the healings. Scarcely had they finished when Millicent announced: "It's Madame Zenkar."

"Zevar," corrected Polly. "But why? We were always so good to her."

"Professional jealousy?" suggested Isis.

Bibi nodded. "She wants what I've got."

"And you don't need it anymore," said Millicent. "Or at least, it doesn't look like you'd survive having it much longer. So what should we do?"

Bibi shrugged. "Why not give her what she's after?"

"But how?" asked Polly.

"I imagine the spirit world operates on the same sensible principles as this one," said Millicent. "I propose we arrange a trade."

As soon as they'd finished dinner Bibi, Polly, and Iris arranged the room, as in the early days, for a séance. Scarcely had they dimmed the lights and lit the candles when Bibi slipped deeply into a trance and the scent of boiling milk filled the air.

"It's Pasteur," said Isis. "I can smell it!"

Sure enough, Bibi opened his eyes and in an unusually resonant voice addressed the group: "Can I do something for you, ladies?"

"Doctor Pasteur," began Millicent, "you know I've always admired your work—"

"But of course," replied Pasteur. "Still, I must inform you that spirits, having nothing to gain or lose by it, are not overly susceptible to flattery. I suggest we cut to the chase."

"Yes," replied Millicent. "Certainly. It's my son Bibi—"

"An excellent channel. Perhaps the finest I've inhabited. But not looking so well these days."

"But can't you do anything, Doctor Pasteur? I mean, all your experiments with the um . . . vaccines, and everything—"

"My many innovations are well known to me. Unfortunately, we spirits can't do a thing in cases where black magic has been practiced. It's against the rules—domain of the devil and all. Don't want to tangle with him!"

"No, no, I guess you don't. But isn't there anything you could do? I mean, if you left Bibi and found someone else . . ."

"Madame, I don't know if I can adequately express the joy it has brought me to resume my work, and the good I have been able to do by it. One might almost say it's restored the meaning to my life—that is, er—death."

"But it might kill him!"

"Being dead," replied the doctor, "is not so bad as people think."

"But supposing," persisted Millicent, "you found a . . . better place to work?"

"It would have to be someone exceptionally talented," replied Pasteur after a moment. "And in order for me to come through at all, he or she would have to be as innocent, as open, and as—forgive me—a trifle clueless, as our friend Bibi. Or they'd have to want the power of healing very badly."

"I think I know just the person," said Millicent.

A simple phone call—the only such communication ever known to have occurred during a séance—proved sufficient to strike the deal.

"Is this Madame Zenon?" asked Millicent when the unhappy medium picked up the receiver.

"Zevar," corrected the voice on the other end. "What can I do for you?"

Millicent paused to turn up her hearing aid. "Are you a mother?" she asked.

"I have two grown sons," replied the channel. "One lives in Cincinnati, and the other—who is this?"

"Bibi's mother. Madame Zonar, he looks terrible. We've got to do something. I have the ghost of Louis Pasteur on the line for you."

"Zenkar," replied the medium. "Er . . . Zevar! Well, by all means, put him on!"

It took no more than a few minutes for the good doctor to strike the deal.

"So," Pasteur spoke into the receiver as the conversation concluded, "you say you're willing to provide me with a fully-equipped laboratory and remove the hex from this fine woman's son in exchange for my changing, as it were, my place of residence?"

Whatever the reply was, it must have pleased him, for he hung up the phone with a broad smile on his—that is, Bibi's—face.

"Au revoir, ladies," he said in parting. "It has been a pleasure." With that he bowed deeply in their direction—and he must have been so eager to depart that he vanished before the movement was complete, for Bibi's body pitched forward in mid-bow and nose-dived to the carpet.

"What—" he began, rising to his knees and looking confusedly about. "That is . . . does anybody know where I can get a sandwich? I'm starved."

Millicent, meanwhile, had stepped out onto the front stoop. "Attention!" she called into the sea of suffering. "As of this evening the new site for healings will be 666 Live Oak Lane!"

A short while later Bibi, Polly, and Isis, who after weeks of near-starvation were eager to make up for lost time, had all assembled in the kitchen. Bibi was just about to bite into the biggest sandwich ever created, however, when something captured his attention. His eyes, as he lifted the sandwich to his mouth, caught sight of his left wrist, where his old Australoid scar still dwelt. While the others looked on, Bibi, as though in a trance, put down his meal and lifted his right hand slowly. Then, in the last act of healing he was ever known to perform, he placed his palm over his boyhood wound. When he lifted it the scar was gone, leaving the skin as supple and unmarked as a child's.

Within a few hours there was only one person left standing outside the trailer. A pale, stooped figure, who had not come for healing, he dripped with sweat in the Bayou night, and stared fixedly over the chain-link fence at the silhouetted forms behind the curtains, drawing whistling breath through pursed lips, watching.

But by the next day when Bibi and Polly awoke, well after noon and entwined once again in one another's arms, they looked out the window to find not a soul remaining.

It was only a couple of mornings later that the two rose to find Millicent standing in the living room with her satchel packed, hat on her head, umbrella firmly in hand.

"Mom—" Bibi began.

"Mrs. Brown," protested Polly, "you've only just gotten here! Can't you stay a few more days?"

"No," Millicent responded firmly. "I've intruded on your lives quite enough. You've got—intimacies to resume. There's a half-finished needlepoint back home calling my name. And besides, my African violets need watering."

"Can't we at least drive you to the bus station?"

"I left the driver with explicit instructions to pick me up at 9:30 this morning, at the same place he dropped me off."

"But Mom," said Bibi, "what's come over you? I've never seen you so . . . determined as you've been on this visit."

"I'm channeling the spirit of Catherine the Great," Millicent responded with a wink. "Mothers can do these things."

"It's no use," Bibi said to Polly. "Once she's got her mind set on something—"

They followed her out onto the front stoop.

"It was wonderful to meet you, Mrs. Brown," said Polly, stepping forward to embrace her and tipping over a pot of marigolds. "Thanks so much for everything."

"It was wonderful to meet you, darling. I want you to know I fully approve . . . and I'd be happy to return anytime I receive a formal—that is, *printed,* invitation." With that she delivered another wink and embraced them both.

"Do get started on a sensible career," she told Bibi. "Why, before you know it you'll be thirty! Try to write a bit more often. And—"

"I know," said Bibi. "I know. Don't kill myself."

His mother smiled. "Somehow," she said, "I'm quite sure you won't. You've got Otto's blood in you, that's for sure—God rest his soul!" With that she dismounted the stairs. "Oh," she turned at the bottom. "You'll find I've stacked all those messy crutches and trash and whatnot on the side of the trailer. All you have to do is call the junkman to haul it away."

And as her small, determined figure receded into the distance, satchel clutched in one hand and umbrella in the other, a salty rain, from two very localized centers of precipitation, began to fall over the edges of the stoop and into the tiny, dusty yard.

. . .

Following the transfer of his powers to Madame Zevar, Bibi and Polly's life together became again very simple and quiet. Bibi took work at the cafe, where he enjoyed talking to people and waiting on customers. He and Polly resumed and deepened their love life. He began to experience a certain magic in everyday existence, a pleasure in the circularity of time, in repeating the same actions every day, taking a shower, doing the dishes—

"Of course," Polly said when he tried to explain it to her. "The miracle isn't healing the sick. It's you and me lying in bed together, or just sharing a meal. I mean, how preposterous it is that we're here on Earth in the first place. It would have been much more likely never to have happened at all!"

As the days passed, Bibi came once more to recognize that none of his theories about life had ever matched up to the simple fact of living—or to examine it from another angle, it was his thoughts that had led him astray. His ideas had been life preservers, floating him along the surface of existence—and one day they'd just deflated.

Bibi reflected back upon the one undeniably clear moment in his past: his insight in the Canyons of Time. The answer, clearly, was to be found at a level deeper than thought—or, as Polly put it, maybe the only way to find out what you *really* think is to get rid of everything you *think* you think. This notion struck a loud chime in the belfry of Bibi's soul.

He began working to clear his mind.

Bibi spent hours sitting on the back porch, observing the thoughts that came into his mind, allowing them to drift in one end and out the other, like trains into a station—trains he'd had no choice in the past but to board; trains which had led only to other stations and other trains, till everything was in such a frenzy he forgot where he was headed to begin with. Now, after he sat quietly for a while, his thoughts came and left without him. Soon they passed through without stopping; and after some months of practicing in this fashion they scarcely came at all.

He began to find it possible, at least in moments, to suck back all the meaning he'd projected onto the world, to withdraw the tendrils of thought from the objects they'd wound themselves about. Freed of meaning, the world began to feel so light, so airy, it seemed he could carry it around with him.

Bibi could feel it, and he knew—someday he'd be free.

As her lover's spiritual investigations resurfaced, Polly might come home to find him standing naked in front of a mirror, prodding and tapping about his body.

"Bibi, what are you doing?" she'd ask, beehive all a-kilter, as she opened the fridge to see what chance might provide for the evening's soup.

"I'm trying to figure out where the world leaves off and I begin."

Or she'd find him frozen in position, neck craned back, staring in wonder at the walnut veneer of the ceiling trim. In an attempt to deepen his awareness, Bibi placed pieces of glass on the floor and went barefoot among them, left knives jutting from drawers at odd angles. He tacked notes all over the trailer, some of which shouted "Remember!" or "Pay Attention," and others: "Wake up!"

He began to notice the spaces between sounds. There were more spaces, in fact, than sounds themselves.

At times it seemed as though he could *see* silence.

Bibi sensed there was something beneath the shifting surface of appearance; the bottom of the river, something beneath the unending flow. At times, he could almost feel it under his feet. He may, he thought, have missed his chance to find the Hubcap King—but he'd managed, through his own efforts, to find a measure of peace and confidence; and, for a time, he thought his search was over.

Polly threw a great surprise bash for Bibi's thirtieth birthday. Everyone was there: Hip and Hap from the cafe, Jeremiah the Survivalist, and all the healers Bibi had visited since moving into the trailer. Madame Zevar, who'd finally decided to forgive him, was escorted by Dr. Pasteur, whose consciousness swapped places with hers so freely that half the time Bibi couldn't tell whom he was talking to.

As the night wore on, however, things became increasingly heated. Isis, who'd graduated at last to full sorceress, discovered during a conversation with another white witch that both had been Cleopatra in a past life, and they got into a shouting match over which breast the asp had bitten, the left or the right. In a corner Jeremiah and two acquaintances were comparing scars where they'd been incised by aliens. A medium and two channels got their signals crossed while trying to bring through the Holy Trinity, and ended up being taken over by the souls of the Marx Brothers instead. Meanwhile several other guests huddled around an astrological chart, comparing the signs of their pets.

"I thought Rex was a Pisces rising," said one.

"Aries," countered another.

"That Virgo moon," interjected a third, "is what makes Felix such a good mouser!"

Finally it was time for the cake, a triple-layered white chocolate masterpiece prepared by a psychic named Io, who'd plundered the brain of Julia Child for the recipe.

As soon the room was darkened and the candles lit, however, the guest of honor commenced to shudder and quake, emitting horrific moaning sounds. "I—" Bibi began, in a tremulous voice that was surely not his own, "am the soul of Lazarus, come back from the dead!" His eyes gaped open and arms groped skyward, while the rest of the company exchanged startled, worried glances.

Then he relaxed. "Just kidding," Bibi said, grinning, and blew out the candles.

Perhaps it was growing older, or some by-product of his mind-clearing exercises, but as time passed and he delved ever more deeply into himself, Bibi began to notice an unsettling phenomenon. Although on the one hand he felt satisfied, full to the brim with life, when he looked more closely he still found a vague sense of unease, like a hunger that groped about his insides. It was small at first: an empty spot, about the size and shape of an egg, at the center of his contentment. But to Bibi's dismay, the more attention he paid to it the more the spot grew, till it became the size of a softball, and finally an ostrich egg.

When he shared his feelings with Polly she replied: "Well, of course, Baby. I'm not your food. Your food is your food, and you have to find it, just like I have to find mine. We might help each other out—but if we try to feed off one another we'll never be satisfied." She turned to busy herself with straightening up the trailer, but Bibi felt a wetness beginning to well up in his eyes; and in the kitchen, where Polly was dusting a row of ceramic chickens, a stream of briny droplets was beginning to splash on the counter below her.

Bibi's old questions began to haunt him again. He spent hours staring into the mirror, nose to nose with his altered reflection, which he still didn't quite recognize after all these years. Or he'd sit around pinching his skin, staring at the spot where his Australia-shaped scar used to be.

"Bibi, what are you doing?" Polly would ask.

"It just doesn't seem real. *Is* this all I am?"

It occurred to him for the first time that his face, the face Polly loved, was not his own. Why, she'd never even seen the original Bibi!

For that matter, who was Polly? Was that face, that flesh, the heart and mind he loved so much, the real her, or only a container? Who *was* the real Polly? Her mind? Feelings? Soul? Whoever she was, in essence, began to seem infinitely unreachable.

What, then, was love?

For the first time it occurred to Bibi that their time together might not last forever.

One evening just before closing, Bibi was half listening to the conversations in the booths as he mopped off the counter at the diner.

"Gross national product—"

"The national debt!"

"Freedom."

"Today's youth!"

"Pull yourself up by your bootstraps—"

"Sports!"

Bibi had heard it all before. But then one of the conversations began to separate out from the others and he found himself taking a sudden, compelling interest.

"—strangest thing I'd ever seen, yard all full of contraptions—tractors, printing presses, cranes . . ."

"Just sittin' there doing nothing?"

"All carefully arranged, lined up in the most perfect order—and the whole of it covered with hubcaps, from one end to the other—"

"Hubcaps?"

"Never seen anything like it. Folks out there seem to think he's some sort of wise man or something. But if you ask me—"

Before he knew what his feet were doing, Bibi found himself beside the table.

"Did you say hubcaps?" he asked, scarcely able to speak above a whisper.

"Thousands of 'em," the speaker nodded. "Everywhere."

"Do you by any chance know the name of this guy?"

The man screwed up his face. "Seems to me it was . . . I don't know . . . Black?"

"Brown," murmured Bibi.

"That's it."

"But . . ." Bibi heard his voice speak. "You mean he's alive?"

"If you call spending all your days in a junkyard 'living.'"

"Where'd you say this place was?"

"On the great northern plains, just outside the badlands on the edge of the old Indian territories. Can't miss it. Last patch of real Frontier left in the nation."

Bibi had to make change for the pair three times before he got it right. After everyone had gone he sat for a long time on a stool by the counter in the empty, lighted restaurant. Alone, revolving this way and that, staring out the broad front window into the night.

All in all, as couples do, Bibi and Polly repeated the same conversation about the hubcap ranch forty-three times:

"You *have* to go, Bibi. It's been the focus of your entire life."

"I know. How soon can you be ready?"

"Bibi, I can't go with you." Polly suddenly decides this is the right moment to reposition her porcelain duck collection.

"But why not?"

"Oh, Bibi." She moves one of the drakes slightly to the right. "You know I've never left Magnolia County."

"Just come for a week or two to check it out."

"And then what? I'd ruin it for you, Baby."

"What do you mean?"

"Besides, Hap and Hip need me at the cafe."

"Please, Polly."

"And my customers. I can't see somebody else dishing up their breakfasts."

"At least consider the possibility—"

"No one else knows how to make the coffee machine work

right. Besides, the salt and pepper shakers—if I left it to Hap and Hip, they'd never fill them. And who's going to see that Corsica gets home all right?"

"Maybe I'll just go for a week or two."

"A week won't do it. A month won't. Besides, your going will change everything between us." By now she's got the whole family of ceramic waterfowl repositioned in descending order of size. "For that matter, so would not going."

"That's what I'm afraid of."

The days passed and Bibi didn't go.

He became restless, distracted. Having found love at last, how could he leave it?

They began to argue, over little things at first—a dirty spoon on the counter, the Rambler's gas tank left unfilled, which TV program to watch.

They stopped having conversations, no longer knew what to talk about. They made love less and less.

Finally the day came when Bibi returned from work to find Polly's car missing. Everything else was gone, too. Clothes, dishes, television, ceramic figurines . . . she'd cleared out everything, 100 percent.

A note on the counter read:

Bibi, Baby:

I'm out of here. And you are, too.

P.S. You gotta go, Baby.
P.P.S. Don't try to find me, it won't work.
Love, Polly

P.P.P.S. You are the one true love of my life.

Now, thought Bibi, he finally understood what love was.

He cried for a week and two days, alone in the tiny trailer.

Then he dug his old rucksack out of the closet, patched up a few seams, and set out on the road again.

10.
THE QUESTION

America had changed since the last time Bibi paid any attention to it. The trashbag saints had gone nationwide, rustling up to passersby in hopes of a handout, cornering citizens with conundrums, and bemoaning the fate of their leader—who, they explained to anyone who'd listen, had been kidnapped, or worse, by the still-bankrupt government. In addition to their plasticine cassocks, each now wore a miniature picture of their founder dangling from a neck chain. Under the guise of listening to one of their riddles, Bibi peered at the image, and again recognized his driver's license photo with the closed eyes and silly grin—although to his relief, the redesign of his current features kept any of his followers from realizing how close their leader really was.

"Government thought he was an alien, so they liquidated him," explained one man.

"Nah, forget that UFO story," said another. "They just can't afford to have ascended masters walking around in public—it's bad for business."

"Anyway, it was only his physical form they imprisoned," asserted a wide-eyed young woman. "His essence is always with us."

"I'll bet," said Bibi.

A fourth acolyte leapt in front of Bibi with outstretched hand. "If I hit you up for one quarter," he asked, "and the next guy for another, which is the real coin?"

Bibi held up his thumb and forefinger in the shape of a zero and walked off.

The time rush was on in earnest, and the government had installed billboards everywhere, urging those in need of work to head west to the time fields, where the riches, it was said, were infinite.

YOU'LL HAVE ALL THE TIME
IN THE WORLD

read one such advertisement; and a chain of savings institutions had sprung up that specialized in temporal investments, their marquees bearing the motto:

BEST NATIONAL:
YOUR VERY BANK AND SHOAL OF TIME

The country's political scene was changing, too, as Bibi discovered when he glimpsed a familiar face speaking from a television in the window of an appliance store and went in to listen.

"Can we not have decency among the streets and building blocks of our communities, thereby summoning in a new sanity of rapprochement and charm?" the lumpy-faced speaker was urging his listeners. "For our children are the future of tomorrow, and must be cast in the indelible mold of our forefathers if we are to withstand the tornado winds of our collective destiny! Remember: today is but the tomorrow of yesterday. Yesterday is but the past of today. And tomorrow—yes, tomorrow is our finest hour!"

As he reached the climax of his speech, the speaker, in a boldly unorthodox gesture, leapt atop his desk with arms upraised, summoning a round of applause from the onlookers in the shop. It was, of course, Bibi's old friend, the Potato Man.

"That new president is an odd-looking fella," remarked the proprietor. "But I sure do like what he has to say!"

Bibi found the cities more crowded than ever. In the wake of the Nova Scotian accord and the free trade agreement with Trinidad's President Xenar, immigrants of all types had thronged across the borders, turning the streets to a kaleidoscope of skin tones and a cacophony of dialects. Many of the continent's native people, squeezed out of their ancestral lands to make room for highways under the government's Manifest Destination program, had relocated to the cities as well; and animosities ancient and new kept the melting pot in a constant simmer of tension.

After a week of travel by thumb, foot, and freight train, Bibi noticed his surroundings beginning to change. Fields and farms, train tracks and grain silos gave way to rolling stretches of prairie, and he knew he was nearing his destination: the great northern plains. Despite all the changes in the country, the land here was still vast and uncontained; towns were few, and Bibi found himself wondering why the government had seen fit to wage so many years of war against the region's native inhabitants when nobody seemed to be using the space anyway.

The mid-summer nights were warm, and though his heart often ached for Polly, Bibi rejoiced to be making his home once more beneath the open sky. The moon hung above him like a great silver fruit—so near he could reach out and pluck it. As in his early days, he often took from his rucksack the tattered photo of his uncle he'd treasured these many years, and examined the faded image by candlelight. It hardly seemed possible that after so many adventures he was at last on his way to see the Hubcap King.

. . .

Bibi had a complicated series of directions to follow amidst a maze of interlocking dirt roads, and was relieved when he came upon a tiny gas station and grocery at one of the junctions.

"Hubcap King?" the owner said, as he scrawled out a crude map on a napkin. "Why, that old fella's crazy as a coot!"

Late that afternoon, as the sun slid toward the horizon, casting long shadows across the sea-like expanse of grassland, Bibi topped a hill to find a sprawl of rattletrap buildings and machinery below him, all of it gleaming in the light like some million-eyed creature—and his heart did gymnastics as he realized the effect was caused by the eye-boggling array of hubcaps that covered every surface. The dip below could just barely be called a valley, Bibi thought, by comparison with how the term was used in the mountains—it was more a sort of gulch. But at this point, he figured Hope Gulch would suit him just fine.

As he walked down the slope Bibi caught sight of a man below, wearing what appeared to be a long striped nightcap, and putting the final touches on an array of hubcaps laid out upon the ground. As he looked on, the fellow stooped to make a few adjustments, then stood back to survey the result.

"Like my sculpture?" he asked as Bibi approached. "I believe I may at last have achieved the closest representation possible of the human soul!"

As Bibi looked more closely, the pattern, which had at first appeared abstract, suddenly took on sensible form: it was an enormous gleaming question mark.

"Ah," the man sighed, looking on the bright disks. "Don't you just love the way they shine?"

Despite the changes of years—the white hair sticking from beneath the incongruous cap, the face carved with canyons, the overall sagging of that once powerful frame—there was no doubt in Bibi's mind who he was.

"Uncle Otto?"

The man turned to look at him.

"It's me. Bibi."

The fellow stared at him blankly.

"Bibi Brown, your nephew. I've been searching for you all my life."

"Bibi?" The Hubcap King looked at him with consternation, then dawning comprehension. "But—I thought for sure you were dead!"

"And I thought *you* were," replied his nephew.

"God may exist," the fellow with the hair that stood on end and the grey tufts growing out of his ears was saying, "—but if so, he has clearly forgotten all about us."

"God does exist," responded a scholarly looking woman puffing at a pipe, "—but we are an experiment *she* started long ago that has gone very, very wrong."

"God isn't dead," put in a small, greyish fellow lying on his back in front of the fire. "He's merely taking an awfully long nap."

And a somewhat stunted woman in dark glasses remarked, "We're a petri dish God stuffed in the back of his underwear drawer and lost track of ages ago!"

"Perhaps," Otto said, as he stepped through the doorway, "we ought to let sleeping Gods lie." At this all eyes swiveled in his direction. "But be that as it may, I'd like you all to meet my nephew, Bibi. He's going to be staying with us for a while."

"Nephew?" said the woman with the pipe, peering over the tops of her spectacles to examine the newcomer. "I thought all your male relatives were dead."

"So did I," replied the Hubcap King.

Otto's followers—or students, or hangers-on, as he referred to them, depending on mood—were among the oddest assemblages of human beings Bibi had encountered anywhere in his travels. There was Hermit, for instance, the fellow with the ear tufts, who'd spent twenty-four years living in a mining tunnel at the edge of the desert, trading scavenged auto parts for canned goods.

"That is," he beamed, "till I met your Uncle Otto and realized there was a whole world of people out there just like me!"

Bingo, the woman with the dark glasses, had been a caller for twenty years in an all-night gambling parlor, and now found it impossible to tolerate any light brighter than fifteen watts without protection. Misty, the woman with the pipe, had undergone a dangerous transsexual operation while scarcely more than a girl, so that she might realize her true identity as a man who dressed in women's clothing. And the small horizontal fellow by the fire was known as—"Dormouse," he yawned, extending his hand to Bibi. "Because I'm exceptionally fond of sleeping."

In addition there was a woman named Destiny, whose every exposed skin surface was covered with scars, burns, and bruises she'd gained in a series of freak accidents ("What happened to you?" Bibi finally got up the nerve to ask. "You mean what *always* happens to me," came her mournful reply.)—and Otto's chief assistant, a slender black man with thinning hair, known as Word Salad Jones.

"Excellent to meet you," said Jones. He took Bibi's hand and shook it vigorously, asking, "Tell me—does gravity affect shadows?"

Bibi didn't know how to respond.

"Some say his mind's unhinged," piped up Dormouse. "But as Otto always says"—and here the others chimed in unison—"an unhinged mind is easier to keep open!"

Bibi summarized for the group his years of searching, his struggles to escape the fate of his ancestors, and his lifelong quest to understand Time, the Universe, and America.

"Time, the Universe, *and* America?" responded Misty. "Why, you've set awfully high standards for yourself."

And Dormouse put in, "Time? Perhaps. The Universe? Maybe. But America? Impossible!"

"So," Otto asked his nephew, "putting aside all that stuff about the universe and all—what did you really come here to find out?"

Bibi was silent. "Why I'm alive, I guess," he responded finally.

Without a word Otto took a hubcap from its place on the wall and rolled it across the floor to him.

"This is your answer?" replied Bibi. "A Pontiac hubcap?" He picked up the disk and examined it, but all he could see in its gleaming surface was his own reflection.

It was scarcely twelve hours after Bibi's arrival that the Hubcap King put him to work.

"Rise and shine," Otto crowed, stalking into his room and yanking the bedsheets from Bibi's still-sleeping form before the sun had gotten its head decently over the horizon. "Work's a-waiting!"

"Work?" muttered Bibi, rubbing his eyeballs. "I spent the last seven years working. I came here to understand the essential nature of the universe."

"The essential nature of the universe *is* work," replied his uncle. "Now up and at 'em!"

Bibi spent that day, and the day after that, and the following week, polishing hubcaps. He'd never dreamed there could be so many hubcaps in the world. They covered every available surface at the ranch, inside and out: walls, doors, outhouses, cabinets—even stoves and refrigerators. There were Edsel hubcaps and Tucker hubcaps and Studebaker hubcaps. There were frying pans made of hubcaps, and hubcap light fixtures. There were hubcap serving platters in the kitchen and hubcap mirrors in the showers—even the toilet lids were fashioned from oversized truck models. By the time Bibi had finished cleaning the specimens in and around The Great Hall, as the residents called the main building, the ones at the beginning were dirty again.

"They're here, so we've got to take care of them!" said the Hubcap King, wearing one or another of his trademark pieces of headgear as he took a breather from his latest project to check on Bibi's work. "Ah," he'd cry, glancing from beneath his fez as his nephew stretched from an extension ladder to reach the eves. "This morning is so grand I could eat it. Chew up the air, devour the trees, slice up the very sky for pie! Er—I think you missed one."

The others, too, took breaks from their various responsibilities to give Bibi advice.

"You're rubbing too hard," opined Destiny, who'd been painting the trim on the outhouses, as she shaded her battered face from the sun with one hand.

"Not hard enough," countered Hermit, as he headed toward the workshop with spanner in hand.

"What is the color of a mirror?" called Word Salad Jones, passing by with a tour group of Senegalese businessmen. Without missing a beat he carried on with his patter: "We have new hubcaps, old hubcaps, hubcaps through all history! Duck soup hubcaps, Bette Davis hubcaps, hook and eye hubcaps, men named Don hubcaps—"

"How's it going?" Otto called up to Bibi one afternoon, perhaps ten days into his reluctant polishing marathon.

"I feel like Cinderella—and no ball in sight," replied Bibi. "Um . . . excuse me for asking—but is there a point to all this?"

"The point," responded the Hubcap King cheerfully, "is to empty yourself out."

"I feel pretty empty."

"I'm talking *really* empty."

"O.K.," Bibi said. "I see what you're getting at. But all things being equal, I'd rather—"

"All things *are* equal," the Hubcap King replied. "And it's all that 'rather-ing' you're doing that's causing the problem."

After that Bibi began working to clear his mind of everything other than the task at hand. He stopped thinking about how much he hated what he was doing, and what he'd prefer to be doing, and what an idiot he was to be putting up with it anyway, and instead put his complete attention into his work. As his mind became emptier, he began to notice how the hubcaps caught the light at different times of the day, how each felt beneath his cloth, how every one twisted and reflected the world in its own unique way—"Like people!" remarked the Hubcap King. Bibi grew very silent inside, and after a time found he didn't mind polishing hubcaps after all—in fact, he'd just as soon be polishing hubcaps as anything he could imagine.

It was right about then that Otto changed his assignment to emptying the outhouse pits.

"Did you have to go through the same thing when you arrived?" an exhausted Bibi asked, sitting down beside Dormouse at dinner.

"Of course," Dormouse responded, slurping at a bowl of Destiny's famous leek soup. "Why do you think I still have to rest all the time?"

Bibi broke off a hunk of bread and reached for the butter. "So is there really some kind of method to it all?"

"Well," said Dormouse, "I *could* tell you your uncle's approach is based on a system of ancient spiritual-alchemical practices for self-liberation—" He scraped the last bit from the bottom of his bowl and licked his spoon clean. "Or I could just say that this is really good soup!"

Bibi was silent for a moment. "So once I'm *really* empty— what happens then?"

"Nothing," replied Dormouse. "But a very deep and significant form of nothing."

In his few free hours Bibi prowled the ranch, poking into every nook and cubbyhole; and there was no shortage of things to discover. The Great Hall had been added onto again and again until it was a maze of corridors, chambers, and alcoves—an octopus of a building, a hall of mirrors three stories high and sprawling over half an acre; and even after he'd been there for months Bibi was never sure he'd seen it all.

Otto's penchant for wordplay was illustrated by signs that hung all about the place. Over the entrance to The Great Hall was the inscription:

WELCOME TO THE OTTO-MAN EMPIRE!

The "O's" in "Otto" had been replaced with hubcaps. And in a field of daisies Bibi found a tiny sign affixed to a stake, the letters so small he had to get on his knees to look at them:

Morning has broken:

Who will pick up the pieces?

Junk of all descriptions was everywhere, not lying about at random, but arranged in a labyrinthine design of arcs, spirals, and other geometric shapes. There were turbines and farm machinery, refrigeration units and grappling hooks, cranes and airplane propellers; even a Buick with two front ends—all covered from top to bottom in hubcaps.

At times during those first weeks Bibi felt so exhausted he could barely see the ground in front of him; at others he was so exalted he could have taken wing. But studying his surroundings, he concluded that anyone who had gone to this much trouble to arrange things had to be very much alive.

Watching his uncle around the ranch only confirmed Bibi's impression. Otto, like the others—even Dormouse, who seemed, despite his frequent naps, to be exceptionally effective at any task he undertook—worked tirelessly for the better part of each day, building, tearing down, expanding, repairing. There was, it seemed to Bibi, a peculiar fluidity to his uncle's movements, as though there were no friction between him and his surroundings; as though he were coasting along on hidden ball bearings. Then there were his eyes. They were blue, like Bibi's, but more so; their blueness had the depth of the sky or sea to them, that same sense of unpredictable, elemental force.

But the most striking thing about the Hubcap King was his laugh. Other people had high, brittle laughs that lodged in their throats, or little tinkly laughs imprisoned in their sinuses, or laughs that started in the belly but went nowhere. Otto's laughter began in his abdomen and spread till it took over his entire body, reaching all the way up to his head and down to his feet, until his whole form shuddered, and his fingers and toes shook with the force of it, and great dollops of tears rolled down his cheeks. There was not one iota of control to it; it was like the eruption of a geyser or the twisting of a whirlwind—and if one did not know that he had survived such explosions in the past, one might have feared for his health. Indeed, despite his many signs of age, the whiteness of his hair and the creases in his face, Otto had the lightness and vitality of a child.

All in all, Bibi thought him the youngest old man he'd ever met.

And there was one more curious thing he noticed as he watched his uncle through those first weeks: alone among all the people Bibi had met in his life and his travels, Otto could never be drawn to defend himself, his ideas, or his position.

Bibi had been at the ranch for a week or so when the Hubcap King invited him to his quarters for an after-dinner chat.

"Some folks claim," the scrapheap sage told his nephew, "that

I have attained perfect freedom of thought and action. No one's sure whether it's true!"

As usual during the evening hours, he was seated behind his battered Wurlitzer organ, wearing a Shriner's cap and attended by several of his favorite cats. During gaps in the conversation, he was trying to figure out the melody to "Girl from Ipanema" on the keyboard.

"After many years of study in the esoteric disciplines of Bhutan, I asked my teacher what I should do next. He told me: 'Go home already! Do something ordinary. Something American.' So I did."

"I read about that Wake Up From The American Dream Foundation you started," Bibi said.

Otto nodded. "*That* whole debacle convinced me I had to start over on a smaller scale—that real change had to come from within. After I got out of prison I disappeared for seven years. No one knows where I went—not even me. I reinvented myself. I became a Hubcap King!" He chuckled and tinkled at the keys of the organ. "But the Wake Up From The American Dream movement, from what I hear, is still going strong." He shook his head. "You never know the outcome of the things you begin."

"You can say that again," Bibi responded. "But still, I can't help but wonder why—"

"Why hubcaps?" The junkyard ruler sighed. "That's the thing everyone wants to know. To which I reply: 'Why not?' If people start wondering 'Why hubcaps' maybe they'll wonder 'Why automobiles?' 'Why coats and ties?' 'Why linguine?' " He shrugged. "Everyone asks why I built the hubcap ranch. What makes them think I know?" This last comment seemed directed less to Bibi than to Mack, a calico-Persian half-breed with part of his tail missing.

Otto frowned at the keyboard. "Actually, in the first years I was so obsessed with collecting and building I never stopped to ask why. Then, on the day The Great Hall was finished, I stood back in what I'd expected to be a moment of triumph and found myself wondering: *What on earth did I do this for?* So I sat down and pondered it. I did the same thing the next day, and the next. In fact, I spent most of every day for months just staring at that same wall of hubcaps until I thought my eyes would pop out of my skull. Then one morning it came to me, clear as a shaft of light gleaming from that '53 Mercury over there: I had no idea why I'd done it. No idea whatsoever!"

He began to laugh, in great booming bursts that echoed up and down the hallways. "I know nothing," he exulted, rising to his feet as Bibi looked on and prancing about the room in an im-promptu jig. "Nothing. NO-THING!"

But suddenly his mood turned sober. "It is the goal and pur-pose of my life," the Hubcap King told Bibi, eyes turning bright as chrome, "that each of you here at the ranch will realize this same no-thing. Then—no problems." He laughed again, ges-turing into the imagined distance. "Far as the eye can see, not a problem in sight!"

Bibi recounted for the Hubcap King his many adventures: the insane asylum and the Canyons of Time, his years of dark-ness and the years of love. But for some reason his uncle seemed most interested in hearing about the anti-gravity pit.

"Ah," Otto mused, fingering the keys of the organ, "that is why, of all forms of artistic pursuit—excepting, of course, the arrangement and display of hubcaps—I love music the best. It is entirely unaffected by gravity or the lack thereof." He'd al-most figured out the entire melody to "Girl from Ipanema," but kept messing up the same note.

Visitors showed up at the ranch frequently, many bearing ques-tions of a personal or existential nature. If Otto felt so inclined, he'd entertain them himself. But often he'd pass these seekers along to Word Salad Jones.

"What is the meaning of life?" demanded a fellow who drove up one morning in a red sports car, chomping an old stogie. As usual Bibi and the other residents had turned out to see who the new arrival was.

Dormouse put his elbows on the passenger door and leaned in over the seat. "Meaning of life?" he responded. "That's right up there with the central questions of existence, like 'Who created the universe, and was his name Bob?' "

"Meaning of life?" echoed Bingo, pushing her dark-glassed face through the opposite window while Mack the cat leapt onto the hood. "Why, we don't even know the meaning of a spoon!"

And Hermit, bouncing up and down on the bumper to check the shocks, remarked: "Water is round in a toilet, but square in a swimming pool."

Just then Bibi saw Otto approaching with Jones.

"This fellow," Destiny explained, "is asking about the meaning of life."

"It's a shame to ruin these things by speaking about them," replied the Hubcap King. "But I suppose my friend and associate Word Salad Jones has as good a handle on it as anyone."

The man in the car turned to Jones. "So what I really want to know is this: what the hell are we? I mean, what's it really about, being a human being?"

Jones shrugged. "We're just mammals with jobs." Then, glancing at the motley assortment of misfits that surrounded him, he added, "—or without, as the case may be. Now, speaking as a mammal"—Jones wheeled and pointed at the heavens—"show me where east leaves off and west begins!"

The man craned his head out his window to see where Jones was pointing. "Could you, er . . . repeat the question?"

But Jones just carried on: "Is the sky separate from the air? If a fish in the ocean gets wet, why don't birds turn blue?"

The man squinted and rolled his cigar over in his mouth. "I don't see what any of this has to do with—"

Jones had too much momentum to stop. "The thing is to be natural—like an orange is natural, like a cantaloupe. Be like the cantaloupe, my friend! Return to the source. Plow the moonlight, fish the clouds!" He spun in place and pointed to a particularly large cumulus drifting overhead. "That," he announced, "is our life!"

Turning back, he stared for a long moment at the driver, who shifted his stogie from one side of his mouth to the other. Then Jones wheeled and walked off, with Mack trailing after him.

"Um—" the visitor began, still looking skyward as though the answer to his question were hovering someplace overhead. "What did he just say?"

"I think he said," replied Bingo, "that there are some things we can't know."

"Or maybe," added Dormouse, "that you're asking the wrong question."

With that the visitor drove off, chomping his cigar and trailing plumes of dust.

But no one was paying attention anymore, for Destiny had suddenly begun prancing about the driveway, holding her left foot in her hands and emitting a series of ear-piercing shrieks.

The man in the car had run it over.

"Uncle Otto," Bibi asked the Hubcap King later, "that man—he never really got his answer, did he?"

The scrapheap sage wrinkled his brow. "Remind me what his question was?"

"He wanted to know the meaning of life."

"He wanted an *explanation* for life," Otto answered, "but I'm afraid the only available ones are false." He shrugged. "Besides, maybe life has better things to do than mean anything."

"So—" Bibi persisted, "are you saying that instead of trying to explain that to him, Jones was trying to shake him loose from his ideas so he could see the truth for himself?"

His uncle squinted into the distance. "Let's just say that if that man were to sink deeply enough into his own question, to chew on it and chew on it until his whole life had become nothing but an enormous question—then he might find what he's after." The Hubcap King sighed. "But what a bunch of blather. To talk about it like this is to encase its feet in a block of concrete and drop it in the Atlantic."

The other residents, when Bibi brought the matter up after dinner, were no more help than his uncle.

"Look at it this way," said Jones. "You've said yourself that you were looking for understanding, yes?"

Bibi nodded. "Sure."

"I take it this would be a *complete* understanding you're after?"

"Well, of course," nodded Bibi, a trifle less certainly.

"So wouldn't an understanding *that* complete include—have to include—confusion?"

A few days after the man-with-the-stogie incident, Otto handed Bibi an apple. "Think carefully about this apple," he instructed his nephew. "Analyze its texture and consistency as you bite into it." Bibi crunched his way past the skin. "Now consider all the apples you've eaten in the past: Macintoshes, Red Delicious, Pippins, Granny Smiths . . ." Bibi chewed, swallowed, took another bite. "Consider which are your favorites, all the trouble they took to develop, scientific research, genetic theory. Amazing, eh?" Bibi nodded and bit again. "Not to mention apples in mythology, paintings, literature—Snow White . . . William Tell . . . Hieronymous Bosch! Why, apples aren't just apples, they're a cultural icon." Bibi, who hadn't eaten anything for several hours and had been contemplating lunch for some time, was just about down to the core. He examined it, took the last bite, and tossed the remains into a bush.

"Well," inquired the old serpent, "how was it?"

Bibi shrugged. "Okay, I guess."

"Tart? Sweet? Perfectly ripe or a bit over the hill?"

"It was—well, I—"

"You didn't even notice the apple, did you?" said the Hubcap King. "Why, you were so busy listening to my carryings-on and thinking about apples in general that the real apple passed right by you."

Bibi was silent.

"Everything's like that," said his uncle.

After this exchange Bibi resumed, at Otto's suggestion, the mind-clearing exercises he'd developed while living in Polly's trailer. "What you've been practicing," the Hubcap King told him, "is very similar to a Mongolian esoteric technique which, roughly translated, means: 'Not doing anything in the face of what isn't really there anyway.' So carry right on!"

Meanwhile, his uncle instructed him, in every hour of the day, Bibi was to practice something he called "pure presence." What that meant, the Hubcap King said, his nephew was going to have to find out for himself.

At lunch and in the evenings there were group meals, signaled by a crash on a bus-hubcap-turned-gong, and cooked by each of the residents in rotation. These consisted largely of vegetables Destiny coaxed from the hard earth of the garden (the tools she used there accounting for a significant percentage of her battle scars), along with other essentials Hermit bartered from nearby farmers for bits of still-usable junk. Every month or two the ranch sponsored a meal as a service to the local community; these required an afternoon of cooking by all the residents, and were attended by an ever-changing assortment of border-hopping Manitobans, sharecroppers, transients, and anyone else who happened by. Occasionally one or another of these visitors might stay for a while, provided they were willing to pitch in and help around the place. Destiny told Bibi that she herself had arrived through this route—and it was sometimes hypothesized that the place's rigorous work schedule was designed primarily to keep anyone who wasn't entirely serious from staying on.

Dinners were followed by games of chess or backgammon, personal study, or one of the freewheeling discussions about God, reality, and existence that Otto's students loved to participate in—although Bibi couldn't help but notice that the Hubcap King and Jones rarely, if ever, took part in these. And sometimes Bibi felt as though he'd been having the same discussions all his life and they'd been getting him nowhere.

Each week Bibi wrote Polly, but his letters, even those he sent to the diner, all came back with the same message:

"RETURN TO SENDER. NO FORWARDING ADDRESS."

In addition to their other activities, Otto encouraged a variety of body-awareness practices, which the residents performed on a regular basis. Misty and Hermit had developed a unique form of shadowboxing, using their own images reflected in a wall of hubcaps as sparring partners. "After all, the real adversary is always ourselves, ain't it?" offered Hermit in explanation. Destiny and Bingo favored an obscure form of yogic discipline that involved long periods of inversion, and Bibi periodically startled himself by stumbling on one of them, balanced on her head in some out-of-the-way corner of the building. Jones, for his part, practiced a kind of whirling-dervish system that made Bibi dizzy to look upon (and which, Jones quipped, sometimes provoked "Otto-body experiences"), while the Hubcap King took it on himself to train his nephew in a traditional form of kickboxing from Inner Dolpo—of which, it was said, he was considered a master.

But all Dormouse ever seemed to use the exercise periods for was to get an extra forty winks.

"So doesn't Otto ever assign you any . . . exercises?" Bibi asked Dormouse one afternoon, as delicately as he could manage.

"Dreaming is my exercise," responded the fellow, with a yawn.

"But—" Bibi replied in astonishment. "I thought Otto's mission was to wake us up!"

"It is. You should have seen how much I slept before I came here."

"So," responded Bibi, who was beginning to feel a little irritated at the exchange, "that's all you have to do? Sleep?"

"Perhaps there are forms of dreaming," suggested Dormouse, "that can wake us up."

When Bibi approached the Hubcap King about the issue, his uncle would only say: "Dormouse has earned the right to sleep. He's been awake for a long time!"

And Jones, who was standing by, simply winked and put in, "What is the sound of one man napping?"

Were these people self-liberated, Bibi sometimes wondered, or just plain crazy? Were any of them really gaining in wisdom or compassion, or were they just there to get three square meals and a roof over their heads? Bibi thought that certain of the residents—particularly Jones and Dormouse—demonstrated, at least occasionally, some unusual brand of freedom or understanding. But none seemed to have the vitality, the presence, of the Hubcap King.

At times during these first months Bibi's mind felt luminous, buoyant—an infinitely expanding balloon with no bursting point. At other times he felt deflated, entirely lacking in energy and understanding. At times, too, his heart yearned so much for Polly it seemed it might burst in his chest.

Still, he had no place else to go, couldn't think of a single other thing worth doing. He decided to trust his circumstances.

He decided to trust Otto.

With each passing week, Bibi's schedule and responsibilities intensified; it seemed that every time he grew particularly attached to any one job, he was assigned to something else. He'd just begun to rather enjoy emptying outhouse pits when an early storm swept in and he was reassigned to snow removal.

"But it's not even October yet!" he exclaimed to Jones, who was working beside him. Bibi paused and leaned on the handle of his shovel amidst the rapidly mounting mounds of whiteness.

Jones shrugged and plunged his blade into a drift. "Don't think of it as snow," he suggested. "Just regard it as . . . vertical water."

That night Bibi dreamed he was standing at the foot of a mountain of ice, its surface utterly smooth.

Somehow, he knew, he must reach the top.

. . .

"People say I'm crazy, people say I'm wise—guess they've got to say something, eh?" Otto laughed as gleefully as if he'd just slid down a playground slide for the umpteenth time. He and the ranch residents had joined a representative of the American Folk Art Collective in an interview for their bimonthly publication, *Folks and Their Art*.

"Well, yes, I guess they do, don't they?" agreed the interviewer, Brigid Presley, a thirtyish woman dressed all in black and wearing squared-off glasses with dark rims. She laughed politely. "Now, Mr. Brown—"

"Yes?" answered Bibi.

"Mr. *Brown*."

"He *is* Mr. Brown," explained the Hubcap King, who'd insisted on wearing his lucky Peruvian fisherman's cap for the occasion.

"Oh," replied Ms. Presley. "Then the other Mr. Brown."

"Call me Otto."

"Otto. Now, from what I understand, you consider the ranch to be as much a venue for spiritual inquiry as artistic expression—"

"They're the same," replied the Hubcap King.

"Excuse me?"

"There's no difference between the two."

"I see," said the interviewer. "So then Otto, as the director of a—spiritual center, as it were . . . could you tell us something about your beliefs in God?"

"We are all children of God," answered the scrapheap sage. "It's just that in some cases you can see the resemblance—in others you figure the real father had to have been the postman."

To which Misty added: "Every God must have his day."

And Bingo, peering over the tops of her dark glasses, put in: "Can't teach an old God new tricks!"

There was a pause. "I'm not sure we're getting anywhere—" Ms. Presley began.

"That's the point," responded Dormouse. "Once you've *really* gotten nowhere, you're free."

There was a long silence. "Well," Ms. Presley suggested, "let's take another tack. How about other concerns—say, the question of suffering. Why, in your view, is life so—problematic?"

"We're like horses," suggested Destiny. "Life is breaking us in so she can ride us."

And Bingo piped in: "Life will pinch you till you're all squeezed out of shape!"

"Well, Brigid—" mused Hermit, "instead of dwelling on suffering, perhaps we should consider all the ways we *don't* suffer.

For instance, when was the last time you had a really ferocious navel ache? A case of elbow sores? You can bet no one here at the hubcap ranch is losing any sleep over elbow sores. Nosiree!"

At which Jones, staring moodily into the distance, commented: "All the riches of the universe are nothing to one who has seen the true radiance of Teflon."

Again there was silence.

"Well," Ms. Presley struggled gamely on. "One thing our readers are always interested in is why artists such as yourselves might choose to work in such an unusual medium—using items other people regard as useless. To put it another way, why surround yourselves with garbage?"

"Garbage is God," Otto replied, "—or, you might say, God is garbage. Depends on your perspective." He chuckled and winked. "Garbage is in the eye of the beholder—won't someone get it out?"

"I see," said Ms. Presley. "Now, Mr. Brown—"

"Yes?" replied Bibi.

"Otto. We've got time for just a couple of quick ones before we wrap this up. Tell me, Otto—does life *mean* anything?"

"We want to clothe life in our conception of it—but left to its own devices, it's perfectly happy to run around stark naked!"

"What do you say to people who want to cast you in the role of guru?"

"People argue whether I'm an egomaniac or an enlightened man," the Hubcap King answered. "I say, that's all the universe is: one enormous ego. A single great self. And you can view it any way you like: it's me—it's not me—it's me—it's not me—" And he danced around the room laughing and prancing like some enormous child.

Bibi's first year with his uncle passed quietly, with few visitors; but the article by the Folk Art Collective provoked an unexpected flurry of interest in the hubcap ranch the following spring. Perhaps it was the magazine cover photo, which featured a bright-eyed Otto in his fisherman's cap, captured in mid-prance as though levitating, with a hubcap on the wall behind him hovering like a halo above his head. Or the unending highway additions under the Manifest Destination program, which made travel ever more accessible. But suddenly people were arriving from all over the country, and even the world, to visit the ranch and meet the legendary dustbin prophet. On weekends there were so many trailers the residents had to convert what had once been an alfalfa field into a parking area, and turn their makeshift baseball diamond into a campground. Still there was not enough room for everyone.

And tourists were not the only visitors. Suddenly there were health inspectors, who banished the outhouse system and insisted on the installation of chemical toilets. And fire marshals, who put the ranch residents through several months of enlarging doorways and installing exit signs in the buildings. There was even a tax agent, who showed up one day with a pile of paperwork to fill out while Otto and Bibi, with Mack the cat and several of his relatives looking on, were trying to finish the plans for a new drainage system.

"This is form 68-CAX4," the tax man announced, shooing away the curious Mack as he extracted a sheet from a file, "for income derived from admission."

"We don't charge admission," responded the Hubcap King, who by this point, Bibi imagined, had had enough encounters with tax officials to last a lifetime.

"In that case, you'll want RX-562, for donated funds—" the agent pushed aside Mack's brother, Axle, who was just settling down for a snooze on his briefcase, and pulled out another form.

"We don't accept money," responded Otto.

"Hmm," the tax man said. "Tell me, then, what exactly *is* the legal status of your organization?"

"There is none," replied the scrapyard sage.

"Well," the agent persisted, holding out a hand to fend off

Axle's cousin Rig, who was angling toward his lap, "then how do you all eat?"

"Some things we grow," Bibi put in, nodding in the direction of Destiny's garden. "Others we trade for."

"But what about materials, building supplies?"

"Look around you," said the Hubcap King. "We build with junk!"

Finally the tax man came up with a series of forms for converting bartered items into cash equivalents and, after a bit of calculation, presented them with the bill. But the junkyard ruler quickly reconverted the figures using the same formulas, and Bibi watched the agent go staggering off beneath a payment of antique hood ornaments, wheel covers, and similar paraphernalia, valued, according to blue books presented by his uncle, at several thousand dollars.

Then there was the afternoon a reeducation specialist from the Cult Extraction League showed up. Bibi, not knowing what else to do, escorted the fellow into The Great Hall to meet his uncle.

"By all means, reeducate anyone you like," the Hubcap King greeted the visitor. "I've been trying to do the same thing for years, with few results."

"What kind of League?" murmured Dormouse, who roused himself from his afternoon nap by the fire just long enough to remark, "I had a bicuspid extracted last month," before rolling back over into slumber.

"But don't you see—" the man insisted to Hermit. "This hubcap fellow—he's brainwashing you!"

"Maybe it'll rid me of some o' them dirty thoughts," the old scavenger replied.

In a last-ditch effort the fellow fastened on Misty. "Think of what you're missing—a sophisticated woman like you, living in a junkyard."

"You mean a sophisticated former woman, who is now a man in drag," corrected Misty, lighting her pipe.

"Hmm," the man responded. "Anyone know where I can find some of those trashbag saints?" And he got in his car and sped off.

To keep up with the ever-increasing demands of the visitors, Otto was compelled to start giving public talks for their benefit.

"In the beginning was the hubcap—" the Hubcap King began one of his first such addresses, delivered for a busload of Albanian tourists who'd happened in off the highway, "around which revolved the wheel of life. And at its center was reflected everything in the universe."

Bibi, who'd been roped into functioning as his uncle's assistant, held up a gleaming specimen from a '43 Plymouth Cranbrook in illustration.

"Its shape was the essential form of reality," the Hubcap King went on, "—for the sun is round, and the moon and planets; the days are round, and the seasons—and life itself is a cycle, a great shining hubcap, spinning like a wheel!" Otto paused to adjust his Ukrainian peasant's cap, which had gone slightly askew, while Bibi took a moment to gaze out over the audience members, who were looking on with a variety of puzzled expressions wandering across their faces.

"The hubcap!" proclaimed the junkyard sage. "It shines like a mirror, a great metallic moon. Strike it and it sings like a bell—" At this he nudged his nephew, who thwacked the back of the Cranbrook model with his knuckles; and indeed, it emitted the clearest, purest tone he could imagine.

"Without thinking, it spins"—Otto appeared, Bibi thought, to be gearing up for his climax—"without holding on to an image, it reflects. It is always moving forward yet always revolving in place. It has an existence of its own, yet admirably serves the whole. Yes, my friends," concluded the Hubcap King, "the way of the hubcap is the way of freedom: to move through life without friction, to live at the very center of things, forever moving, yet always at rest, reflecting the world back to itself with nary a ripple!"

Bibi never realized until it was all over, and he watched the audience members shuffle past, scratching their scalps and shaking their heads, that not one of the Albanian travelers understood a single word of English.

"You know, Bibi," remarked his uncle with a sigh, as they walked together back toward The Great Hall, "sometimes it's not so easy, being the Hubcap King."

As life at the ranch grew more complex, Bibi's responsibilities continued to multiply. In his fourth summer he received the assignment of designing and building a new bunkhouse for the burgeoning crop of summer visitors and short-term residents. Honored that his uncle would entrust him with such a task, Bibi went all out. Working ten- and twelve-hour days for weeks, he directed a team of eager seasonal arrivals who helped him erect a truly grand structure. The inside featured a spiral staircase fabricated of old running boards, while the exterior boasted the most imaginative display of automotive finery Bibi could muster: a complex, interlocking design of steering columns, bright chrome bumpers, and brake-light housings that actually turned off and on.

Otto, who'd refused to be drawn into any consultations, made no comment as the structure went up. In fact, he paid no attention to the process whatsoever. On the day it was finished, he showed up just long enough to remark: "Too fancy!" before turning and walking away.

A crestfallen Bibi went to Word Salad Jones that evening, hoping for clarification.

"So," said the chief disciple. "You're proud of your work, I take it?"

"You bet I'm proud of it," answered Bibi. "Why, this project took months!"

"Tell me, are you more proud of the effort you made, or the results?"

"Well," Bibi thought for a moment. "I'd have to say the effort was most important."

"Then if you have to do it all over again, you'll be twice as proud!" And with a broad wink Jones walked off.

"But wait," Bibi called after him, "I don't understand—"

"Ah," responded Jones. "You're making progress!"

That night, still feeling unsettled, Bibi consulted Dormouse.

"Hmm," his friend said after he'd finished his story. "I'll bet your head was just buzzing with ideas the whole time you were working on this thing. I bet you had ideas for a million different ways you might handle this sort of project, how you could improve the other buildings around here, how buildings in general might be better designed—"

"Of course," answered Bibi. "Isn't that what the creative process is all about?"

"So what ever happened," responded Dormouse, "to emptying yourself out?"

Bibi spent the next week quietly dismantling his grand creation, and several more directing its reconstruction in a more austere style.

"I don't get it," protested his chief assistant, a college kid on a summer internship, as they relaid the shingles on the roof. "All that effort, gone to waste—"

Bibi paused, hammer in hand, and looked at him. "Nothing ever goes to waste," he responded, with a quiet intensity that surprised even himself. "Everything has an effect."

"But—" the college kid began.

Bibi lifted his hammer to pound the next nail. "Besides, it's a lovely afternoon, isn't it? And after we've finished we'll have a nice, satisfying meal with our friends. What more do we need?"

And Bibi had to admit afterward, when he looked at the simple, clean lines of the final structure, its wooden walls adorned with the usual assortment of hubcaps and no more, that the effect was much more harmonious.

Over the next few seasons the number of visitors only increased. The more tourists came, the more press showed up to find out what was going on. The more press came, the more inspectors and tax agents arrived. The more *they* came, the more reporters showed up to find out why. And the more stories were printed, the more people came in from the highway.

"Hubcap Healer?" read one headline in the *National Embroiler,* featuring a front-page photo of Otto beside a young elephantiasis victim. And an article in a rival publication showed the ashcan oracle with a photo of actress Carolyn Conway pasted in beside him, and the caption: "Hubcap Hussy!"

More and more people showed up with questions about life. More and more people were assigned to hubcap polishing and Mongolian mind-clearing exercises. And although Otto resisted taking on any more permanent residents, the ranch acquired dozens of temporary lodgers, who arrived every spring and stayed until late in the fall.

"It's a certifiable phenomenon!" crowed Rex Carrs, a graduate student-in-residence doing a thesis on Spiritual Traditions of America.

Of greater concern to Bibi were the figures, whom the residents had come to call "The Watchers," who stood on the ridge at the west side of the valley most afternoons, dressed in identical dark suits and sunglasses, studying all comings and goings with binoculars, and snapping pictures through long telephoto lenses.

"Well, invite them down for supper!" was Otto's response when his nephew shared his concern—but whenever anybody climbed the slope they found the men gone, with only a few scuff marks in the dust and some crushed cigarette butts to show they'd been there at all.

If not for winter, which brought six months of snowfall and impassable roads, all the commotion would shortly have driven the permanent tenants mad. The cold months, which Bibi at first dreaded, became a blessing: the quiet season at the ranch, a time for introspection and study. Bibi spent six or eight hours a day cleaning, doing repairs on the buildings, or cooking meals, as well as an hour on kickboxing practice and several more on mind-clearing exercises—and he still had time to play back-gammon in the evening with the others.

Bibi served stints as housekeeper, cook, and construction co-ordinator for the community, and every other month devoted an entire week to nothing but mind-clearing exercises. He came to find an unaccustomed depth and ease to his life here, despite its many complications. It seemed a relief to lend his energy merely to what was needed at each moment, to dispense with dwelling on the past or the future; to surrender, in every instant, to the simple freedom of necessity. Bibi had tried to free himself from his own mind before—to let go of all that was conditioned and binding. But his old ideas always crept back in. Now, at last, a time came when he no longer knew what to think. For long moments it seemed as though he did not exist at all: there was no Bibi, only the world.

Except for occasional pangs of missing Polly, to whom his increasingly infrequent letters still came back unopened, he'd never been so satisfied in his life.

Bibi was having tea with his uncle one afternoon in early spring when Hermit, who'd been out on one of his regular trading missions into town, burst into the room in a grey-haired swirl of agitation.

"Otto!" shouted the old scavenger. "Bibi! They're planning to bulldoze the hubcap ranch!"

"They're what?" Bibi leapt to his feet. "Who—"

"It's the Hope Valley Cloverleaf Project," panted the old fellow, struggling to catch his breath. "I just heard about it down at the cafe. The Highway Department's planning to condemn the hubcap ranch. They're saying the valley's the ideal place to put an interchange!"

"Here? But why? There's so much space!"

"It's the Manifest Destination program. They say that with so many people showing up all the time, it's the inevitable destiny of the valley to have a cloverleaf."

"But," sputtered Bibi, "—the *reason* all these people are coming here is because of the hubcap ranch. That's circular logic!"

"The best kind," remarked the Hubcap King, "—under ordinary circumstances." He held the hubcap he was polishing up to the light.

"But Uncle Otto," Bibi said. "What are we going to do?"

The Hubcap King just smiled. "My teacher used to say that there are twenty-three different categories of fools in this world—and we each belong to one of them."

For the umpteenth time during his stay at the hubcap ranch, Bibi could only guess at his uncle's meaning.

The next weeks found the ranch in a whirl of new activity. Bibi contacted senators, congresspeople, and even wrote the president—who, he explained to the others, was an old friend of his, and would surely intervene on their behalf. Misty lobbied prominent citizens and civic organizations, and Jones toured the region, delivering a presentation titled "On the Central Importance of Wheelcovers" to anyone who would listen. Bingo and Hermit staged fund-raising raffles and car washes, while Dormouse took it on himself to organize an innovative series of political slumber parties. Meanwhile Destiny, who had long ago failed in an attempt to finish law school, endeavored to bring their case before the courts. As the first of the seasonal arrivals began to roll in, Rex Carrs mounted a letter-writing campaign, while Ms. Presley published a series of scorching exposes on the pervasive abuse of folk artists by the country's political system.

"Look at all this activity," exulted Bibi. "This has got to work!"

"We never know the outcome of the things we start," was all the Hubcap King would say. "We've got the rare opportunity to give this our best effort—while remaining entirely unattached to the results."

Meanwhile, as spring idled its way into summer, Bibi found his training with his uncle entering, without any particular notice, onto a new phase. Perhaps it was the uncertainty about their life here, or some intuitive sense that his nephew was ready for a new direction; but the Hubcap King appeared all at once to have gained a fresh sense of urgency. In addition to the extra political work Bibi had taken on, his uncle had him increase his practice of "not doing anything in the face of what is not really there anyway" to several times daily. In addition, Otto assigned him to a series of dialogues with Jones, in which Bibi attempted to field such questions as "Where do our shadows go at night?" and "Is a tree still green in the dark?"—generally with little success.

"So what are you learning?" the Hubcap King asked him after one of these sessions.

"I don't have the slightest idea," replied his nephew.

"Well, now," smiled Otto. "That's a refreshing development. Keep up the good work!"

And these were not the only innovations in Bibi's training. As the usual array of summer visitors looked on, the scrapheap sage had Bibi fabricate, then dismantle, a series of enormous junk sculptures—all the while striving to maintain the requisite condition of perfect presence. He had Bibi contemplate, and attempt to implement in his life, a doctrine he called the Four Freedoms—which, the Hubcap King maintained, were the foundation of any liberated existence:

Freedom from Before and After
Freedom from Likes and Dislikes
Freedom from Pleasure and Pain
Freedom from Yours and Mine

"And say, didn't you once tell me," the Hubcap King asked Bibi, "that you had an overwhelming question—one you'd pondered off and on since you were a child?"

"You mean," answered Bibi, "*Is this all I am?*"

"That's it," said Otto. "From now on, why don't you work on that?"

So Bibi did. Following the instructions of his uncle, he sank into the familiar question, devoting himself to it more completely than ever before. And as the days went by and the question took hold ever more deeply, merging inside him with all of his questions around the fate of the hubcap ranch, Bibi again found, to his dismay, his sense of calm and contentment vanishing, and his old hunger, his yearning, returning—still intact after all these years. At the same time he commenced a series of private meetings with the Hubcap King, in which he'd sit before his uncle while the junkyard sage looked *into* him, his clear blue eyes, like holes drilled into an iceberg, seeming to pass straight through Bibi and out the other side.

"Is *this* all you are?" Otto would demand, pointing a finger at the center of Bibi's chest. "Who is the real you?"

The increased pressure only drove Bibi more deeply into his efforts. "*Is this all I am?*" he'd ask the mirror before his evening bath. "*Is this all I am?*" he asked the night sky. "*Is this all I am?*" while kickboxing. "*Is this all I am?*" while using the toilet. It became the last thought in his mind as he went to sleep at night, the first when he woke in the morning.

Meanwhile, his uncle had become his shadow. When Bibi did his kickboxing practice, there was Otto: "Higher! I want the leg higher. Left leg bent, not rigid. No, that's too much. No, not enough! No, no, no, no, no!"

When he was working:

"Is that any way to leave a work surface? You missed these crumbs. Have you finished that letter to the governor yet? You left the ladder out in the rain. Who taught you to hold a hammer like that, anyway?"

In the kitchen:

"That's what you call a quiche? Why, the center's all sagging. There's too much salt. This fork is dirty. Haven't you been paying attention? Attention, attention, attention!"

When Bibi groaned about how difficult it all was, his uncle just answered: "There are no problems. Only things that *look* like problems."

When he protested that he couldn't keep up the pace, the Hubcap King responded: "Do you want to be driven by your inclinations your entire life? If you never go beyond yourself, how do you expect to go beyond yourself?"

And when he complained about his inability to answer his question, Otto replied, "That's because you're still asking with your head. When you've learned to ask with your belly—then you'll find what you're looking for!"

So Bibi dropped all his concentration into his abdomen. And as the weeks passed, as he sat motionless and cross-legged during his daily mind-clearing exercises, he felt the question beginning to inhabit his body, as though his entire being had taken on the form of a question mark—the single dot rooted in his lower belly, the shaft of the mark rising along his back, curving over the top of his head to end between his eyes. Until finally the words fell away and there was only questioning—raw, ceaseless, and burning. Until he lay constantly within the curved shape of mystery, nestled closer than a child to its mother's womb.

And it was in this state of ripeness, as the mystery burned continually through his being, that Bibi was cleaning out a storeroom in the basement of The Great Hall one morning. He was piling up a stack of dusty boxes when he backed against a side wall and felt it, to his surprise, slightly give way. Tentatively pushing and probing about the surface, he found that with just the right pressure in just the right place, he could cause the entire panel to swivel open. Bibi peered inside to find a long passage, dimly lit by several bare lightbulbs. Curious at finding any part of the ranch he didn't know about—for he'd thought he knew it all—he entered.

Bibi followed the corridor for what seemed like several minutes—reckoning, by distant clankings as though of pots and pans, that he must be roughly beneath the kitchen. After several sharp turns and swivels the passage gave, to his astonishment, onto an enormous hidden chamber. And there, suspended at eye level by wires from the ceiling, Bibi found the most stupendous array of hubcaps he'd ever imagined. There were Eldorados, Firebirds, Mercuries, and Triumphs, to mention just a few—each shined to perfection and reflecting back from its surface a slightly different image of its viewer: enormous, shrunken, refracted this way or that; fat, thin, twisted to the left, squashed to the right. There were Bibis with gigantic heads and tiny bodies; Bibis with enormous legs and pin-sized heads. Bibi strode amongst them, studying his endlessly receding reflections, weaving in and around the images of himself, until his brain was spinning like a hubcap.

He'd paused, overwhelmed, and was just standing in place trying to take it all in, when one of the images stepped suddenly from amidst the others and greeted him with a robust: "Good morning!"

It took several long moments for Bibi to realize that he was looking at the Hubcap King himself.

"Congratulations," his uncle said. "At last, you've stumbled upon the inner sanctum. I call it 'Otto's Cave.'" He swept the beret from his head and bowed deeply. "And this, of course"— he indicated the enormous hubcap apparatus hanging from the ceiling, "is the Otto-Mobile!"

The Hubcap King began to stroll about the chamber as he spoke, passing between and behind the shining orbs, while Bibi's face, depending on which one Otto stood behind, topped his shoulders, torso, pelvis. "As you've no doubt guessed, each of these beauties was chosen for its reflective qualities, and poised in just such a way that anyone who enters the room might get a very thorough look at himself." The hubcap sage laughed. "It's enough to drive a man mad, eh?—or sane!" At this, his head cocked out from behind a particularly grotesque image of his nephew, twisted and splintered into dozens of tiny faces—a Bibi medusa that made Bibi shudder to look on it.

"One might picture the entire universe this way," said the Hubcap King. "A vast matrix of spinning hubcaps, each reflecting and containing all the rest." He smiled. "I suggest that now that you've found this place you spend a bit of time contemplating it." He directed his nephew to a raised platform that appeared to have been placed there for just such a purpose. "When you've found which is the *real* Bibi—and not before—you may feel free to leave." With that, Otto turned and exited the chamber.

So Bibi sat there. He spent the whole day sitting there, in fact, and long into the night, staring hour upon hour into the ever-dividing images, while the question, the great single question—renewed, purified, and formless—built within him. At last he came to the point where he could no longer feel a difference between the reflections and himself. The images were the countless moments of his lifetime, the countless Bibis he'd been: there was the Bibi of his childhood, the Bibi of the asylum, Bibi on trial, Bibi seeing into the nature of time—each a moment like the rest, a moment that had passed. There was no continuity other than what he cared to provide, nothing whatsoever at the center, not a single thing to hold on to—for he saw now that to hold on to any of them would be to kill all the rest.

Finally Bibi settled so deeply into himself that the chamber, the reflections, and even the sense of sitting there faded away, until all that was left was the barest sliver of consciousness shimmering in a luminous void. Then that too fell away, and he could not have said what happened afterward, for there was no one left to notice it.

It was that moment the Hubcap King chose to slip back into the room. Creeping through the labyrinth of hubcaps, he made his way to the rear wall, where a thick cable stretched from a hook to a network of wires in the ceiling that suspended the entire apparatus. And all at once, in a voice like the roar of the universe he cried:

"WILL THE REAL BIBI BROWN PLEASE STAND UP?!"

With that, Otto released the cable; and with a tremendous crash all of the hubcaps went plummeting to the floor.

Bibi did stand up. In fact, he leapt several feet off his seat in a moment of near-levitation. And when he came down, he found that for the first time in his life he was, indeed, real.

Bibi landed on his feet amidst a chaos of tumbling hubcaps, each bearing a reflection of—who? No one! The sound had shattered everything in his mind; and all he'd ever known or felt or dreamed—the countless Bibis in the countless moments of his life—had fallen away. There was no Bibi anymore. And because he was no longer Bibi, he was everything. Every hubcap rolling about the floor, every space between them, the objects they reflected, the walls that echoed their clatter. He was the cable that had held them suspended, lying slack on the floor now like some enormous serpent, and he was the platform he'd leapt from. He was even that white-haired old madman on the opposite side of the room, holding his belly now in convulsions of laughter: the freest human being he'd ever met. He crossed to his uncle and the two embraced one another, laughing and crying uncontrollably—for laughter had become sadness and sorrow was the same as happiness; everything was mixed up together and it was absolutely all right that way.

. . .

Bibi stumbled out of the chamber and back down the corridor, up the stairs and out the door of The Great Hall, across the now-darkened yard, past all the machines with the grass growing up in tufts around their bases, out to the meadow, where he cried and laughed and laughed and cried for hours.

Bibi walked about for the rest of that night in a state of exaltation; the things of the world had forsaken their names and forms, and rejoined the flow of pure, undifferentiated being. Nothing was separate anymore: the world was a patchwork quilt where every object was joined to the next, and none could be divided from the whole. In the glory of his deliverance from himself, Bibi spoke to the hills and trees, delivered sermons to piles of stones— and sometimes, it seemed, one of them nodded in reply.

The moon hung in the sky like—what else?—a great gleaming hubcap.

"Hmm," Dormouse greeted him sleepily, rising from his place by the fire and looking Bibi over when he finally came inside, just after dawn. "What on earth happened to you?"

"The universe—" Bibi managed to spit out finally, "is one enormous mind!"

"I know," Dormouse said, looking at his friend for a moment with fond affection. Then he rolled back over to resume his slumbers.

Life carried on as usual in the weeks after Bibi's awakening. He worked about the ranch as always, making the usual end-of-summer preparations for fall. He saw off the last of the seasonal residents, and helped shutter up the bunkhouse in anticipation of the first snows. He was looking forward to the long quiet of winter, the opportunity to work closely with the Hubcap King, to spend time with the other residents, to sink ever more deeply into his new state of being—which, his uncle had warned him, was still fragile and had to be dealt with carefully.

"Real freedom has to be won step by step," his uncle told him. "You're only half baked as yet—but never fear, one day soon you'll be the whole pie!"

And Bibi had to admit that no matter how free he felt from himself, no matter how complete he felt in his connection to the universe, somewhere in the core of his being there still lurked a tiny sliver of something not yet completely resolved— the gleaming, curved mark of a question.

The only thing that really worried him however, was The Watchers, whose numbers seemed to have increased with each passing week. There were sometimes more than a dozen of them on the ridgetop, looking through binoculars and snapping pictures; they arrived earlier, too, often standing in position by the time Bibi rose at dawn and staying past sunset, silent in their dark suits and sunglasses, watching, watching.

Bibi was having a meeting with Otto a few weeks later when Hermit again burst into his uncle's quarters.

"They're coming," he shouted, grey hair and beard flying in every direction. "They're coming! They're rolling the bulldozers down the road right now!"

"What do you mean 'they're coming'?" Bibi sprang to standing and peered out the front window. The long curve of dark road that led to the ranch, looping freely over the nearby hills, was as yet entirely empty. "But—it's all still under consideration by the district attorney. They haven't even given us a court date yet!"

"Tell that to the road crew. I saw them with my own eyes!"

"Uncle Otto—" Bibi turned to the Hubcap King. "Did you hear? What are we going to do?"

But his uncle was just sitting there, serenely polishing a hubcap. "I know all about it," he replied.

"But—then why are you just sitting there shining hubcaps?"

"I want the place to look good when it goes."

The next days were a flurry of panic and activity as the residents readied for disaster. Bibi made hourly, unanswered calls to the district attorney, and finally phoned the White House directly, only to get a recording saying the number had been disconnected. The others contacted or visited everyone of influence in a hundred-mile radius. Meanwhile bags were packed, photos taken, keepsakes squirreled away, and Mack, Axle, and Rig were delivered to Ms. Presley, who'd offered to adopt them.

The Hubcap King alone remained in a condition of utter calm.

"But Uncle Otto," said Bibi, examining the condemnation documents presented by the highway crew, "there must be something we still can do to fight this—"

"Did you think it would last forever?" the Hubcap King said. "Everything comes to an end. Maybe the time has come for us to give the hubcap ranch away. Maybe it's time for us—all of us—to set off into the world. See if we can do some good."

"I'll stay with you, at least," Bibi persisted.

His uncle smiled softly, a bit sadly. "Bibi," he said, "you and I—we'll carry the hubcap ranch in our bones. We'll pass on what we've realized to others. In this way—and only in this way—the hubcap ranch will never die."

Otto ran his hand fondly along the edge of one of the hubcaps on the mantel. "They call these secondhand objects," he said. "But what's wrong with that? The moon shines with secondhand light, doesn't it?"

He began to laugh, so deeply Bibi thought he would never stop.

.   .   .   .

The day before the demolition, Otto was scheduled to record a closing interview for a local television station. The bulldozers were already visible in the next field, just beyond the ranch's tumbledown fence, pushing aside mounds of earth and leveling the ground for concrete, as the TV crew set up the camera. A small group of protesters stood off to one side, carrying signs that said "Save the Hubcap Ranch!" and "Don't Give Up Hope Valley!"

There, facing the lens while the machinery roared and the dust rose in the background, the Hubcap King gave his final statement:

"I believe in many, many things. I believe the ocean is vast and salty because for millennia it has been the repository of all the tears shed by humanity. I believe cats to be the true master race, and humans to have evolved merely to serve them. I believe flowers bloom in the springtime purely for their own purposes, with no thought of us, their admirers.

"I used to have big ideas. Cover the Statue of Liberty with hubcaps. Pave the streets of the cities with them. But my visions of the paradise that might be have gradually been replaced by the paradise that is.

"Look around us—there is beauty everywhere! The marvel is not that there is wonder in hubcaps. It is that there is wonder at all."

Otto raised both arms high in the air and stared straight into the camera.

"The hubcap ranch is dead," he cried. "Long live the hubcap ranch!"

Later that evening Bibi stood in the front room of Otto's quarters, having just finished the last dinner he'd ever eat in Hope Valley. He was staring blankly at the old Wurlitzer—it looked, he thought, like it had been through a war—when he heard a door open and the Hubcap King entered the room. The junk-yard sage was wearing a red fireman's hat; his eyes shone and sparkled like twin hubcaps.

"Uncle Otto," Bibi burst out. "What am I going to do without you? I don't know what anything means anymore!"

"Hmm," smiled his uncle. "You're progressing."

"Be reasonable," Bibi persisted. "At least let me come with you."

"Ah, Bibi." The Hubcap King placed one hand on his nephew's shoulder. "You don't need me anymore. I had nothing to give you, after all, from the start. From here on out, I'm afraid you're on your own."

"But where will you go? What will you do?"

"Hoboes, politicians, and holy men have always been beggars," he shrugged. "I'll get along." He smiled. "I've been the Hubcap King now for an awfully long time. I'd like to see what it's like to just be a man again. I'm interested to see what will happen."

With that the Hubcap King embraced his nephew. The two stood for a long time looking at one another's eyes: blue into blue, like the merging of seas.

"Thank you," said Bibi, "for giving me back my life."

"Thank you," replied his uncle. "You did it yourself." As he stepped away, Bibi could see a single tear roll down his cheek. "Guess we'd better get ourselves ready, eh?" said the Hubcap King, heading into the hallway toward his bedroom. "We've got a big day tomorrow."

Just as he was about to clear the doorway he looked back. "Share what you've found," he said. "Help others. And, er . . . do keep up those mind-clearing exercises. You're never finished, you know. They're good for you."

But Dormouse had the last word of the evening, as the residents sadly packed up the backgammon board following their final after-dinner game.

"Let us sleep," he said, settling into his place by the fire for the last time, "and in sleeping, dream a perfect world into being."

The next morning Bibi rose before dawn and went to the Hubcap King's quarters to make one last attempt at convincing him not to head off alone. But the old sage had already departed, leaving a note on top of the Wurlitzer:

> *They have taken the hubcap ranch.*
> *But look:*
> *they left one behind.*
> *For high above us,*
> *that great single orb still gleams.*
> *Try as they might—they could not take*
> *the moon!*

Bibi thought to follow his uncle, for the first snow had come at nightfall, and there should have been tracks. But although he checked every possible exit from the building, he could find no sign of anyone having passed there.

Otto had left no footprints.

Later that morning, Bibi stepped out onto the porch and set down his old rucksack, now patched and repatched many times over. There he ran into Jones, dressed for the road with suitcase in hand, staring at the white, fresh world in wonder.

"You know," said Jones, looking out over the land, "sometimes I think to myself: Here I am, Jones! I mean, I could have been anyone, but here I am—me!" He stared at Bibi, a new light of comprehension dawning in his eyes. "I'm stark raving mad, aren't I?" he said suddenly. "I'm an absolute lunatic."

"No more than anyone else. The only difference is you know it." Bibi looked at his friend. "So what will you do now?"

"Maybe I'll open a restaurant," Jones replied. "I'll call it: Jones's Word Salad Bar!" With that he sprang from the porch in a single leap and bounded off across the white, open fields, shouting: "I'm insane and it's O.K.! I'm insane and it's O.K.!" Jumping in the air and clicking his heels together, waving his arms and shouting, he passed out of sight.

Bibi went inside to say good-bye to the others. He could hear the men starting up their bulldozers in the open tract beyond the fence as he took his leave of Dormouse, whom he found sitting in The Great Hall, working on a farewell poem of his own.

"So how long have you been writing poetry?" Bibi greeted him, having never seen the fellow with a pen in his hand before.

"Since the thesauruses went extinct," quipped his friend. "Now tell me, what do you think of this opening line: 'When last the Dormouse in the lilacs bloomed—'"

"Not bad," said Bibi. "Though something about it does sound a bit familiar . . ."

The two regarded one another for a long moment.

"So are you ready to go?" said Dormouse.

"As ready as I'll ever be," said Bibi. There was a moment's silence, then he added, "Actually, I'll never be ready."

"Me, either." Dormouse took Bibi's hand. "Sleep with your eyes open," he said in parting. "So you can see your dreams."

Bibi found Bingo standing in the yard, dark glasses lifted to gaze about the ranch one last time before setting forth into the unknown. Together she and Bibi looked out over the whole of it, draped in fresh snow: The Great Hall, with its enormous, hubcap-studded exterior; the grounds, with their intricate labyrinth of dynamos and derricks, windlasses and harrows; and the "Otto-Man Empire" sign above it all—the surface of which, momentarily forgetting his circumstances, Bibi made a mental note to repaint soon.

"This is what the world is," sighed Bingo. "Heaps and mounds of shapes and sounds; some of it polished, some of it not." With that she raised one hand and, with a jaunty wave, set off.

Bibi found Hermit, too, staring out over the ranch from the steps of the back porch, chin resting on one hand.

"I was just thinking," said the old scavenger. "If a hubcap falls on the highway and there's no one there to see it—will it somehow find its way here?"

With that he handed Bibi a box. "Here, I got you a present."

Bibi opened the package. "Why, it's a carburetor—Hermit, how thoughtful!"

"Original '57 Chevy," replied the old fellow. "You ever get in trouble, you can sell that thing. Make yourself a bundle!"

Misty seemed more despondent than the rest. "What is this world," she mused, as she stepped toward the door with her white patent leather suitcase in one hand and her pipe in the other, "but a flower cast in Lucite, a paperweight, a ball in which anyone can make it snow by turning it upside down?"

She kissed Bibi on both cheeks. "You know," she said, shaking her head, "I used to believe in a single almighty God. But now I look around me and realize: they've *got* to be doing it by committee."

"Take good care of yourself," Destiny told Bibi, folding him into her embrace. "And *do* be cautious out there. After all, if it's not one thing," she drew back and regarded him, "—it's another." With that, she stepped onto the porch, closed the door on her thumb and, dancing away from the pain, slipped on an ice patch. Bibi watched as she limped slowly toward the horizon, receding to a tiny, distant figure.

At last, having taken leave of everyone, Bibi made his way onto the porch, picked up his rucksack, and headed out into the clear white universe. Walking through the fresh snow along the drive, he heard the first fence posts go down as the bulldozers moved onto ranch property, felt the roar and rumble of the earth vibrating beneath his feet. Mechanically, he stopped to check the mailbox at the end of the driveway, finding a single envelope addressed to him. *Mom's news is just going to have to wait for another day,* thought Bibi, tucking the envelope into his jacket without a second glance.

Then he stepped between the twin posts that marked the ranch gate and out into the world. Again, as though his life were no more than some absurd merry-go-round, a great spinning hubcap, Bibi found himself moving out onto the road. From behind came a roar of machinery, then a tremendous, splintering crash, as what must have been a thousand wheelcovers hit the ground. He did not look back.

Rucksack hoisted into its accustomed place, he trudged along the shoulder of the deserted highway, all thought and feeling spent. The road stretched as far as he could see. At the end it narrowed to a point; at that point it was fastened to the sky. White-dusted plains flattened to infinity on either side. That was all. Bibi looked out across the creased and folded face of the planet—an old face, one that had seen many things and would, with luck, see many more before its days had passed—and he reflected to himself: there are no imperfect stones.

He'd never felt so weary in all his life.

After some time, Bibi heard the sound of an approaching engine and turned to look. The vehicle backfired as it came into view, weaving slightly; a minute or two later the oddly familiar pickup skidded to a halt beside him, spitting smoke and shuddering.

The driver greeted him, wheezing. "Still got the same old rucksack, huh?"

"And you've still got the same old truck." For some reason it came as no surprise to Bibi to find that the driver was the Man with the Terry Cloth Face.

"Year upon year," said the Terry Cloth Man, "—not much

changes. But then, you could say the same for millennium upon millennium, eh?" He looked Bibi over. "Need a ride?"

Bibi had the strong feeling he shouldn't get into the pickup. But at the same time he felt compelled, as though a knot was closing in a loop of fate. He watched his hand rise as though it were someone else's and reach for the door.

"How've you been?" Bibi asked as he climbed in.

"I oscillate between terror and boredom," replied the Terry Cloth Man, "—as usual." His breathing sounded worse than ever. "So where you headed?"

"Nowhere," Bibi answered. "Anywhere."

"I think we can arrange that." Bibi couldn't help but notice that the years had not treated the Terry Cloth Man well. In fact, he looked terrible. Beads of sweat stood out on his roughened, sallow brow, and his jaw was clenched and trembling, as though holding something enormous inside.

"So what have you been doing these past years?" Bibi asked as they pulled back onto the road.

"Making a list, among other activities, of the saddest things in the world."

"What did you come up with?"

"Oh . . . being young, being old. Rain, lack of rain. Falling in love, not falling in love. Dying, being born. Paintings of Elvis on velvet . . ."

"I think I get the picture," said Bibi.

"In fact," concluded the Terry Cloth Man, "just about everything in the world is sad, if you look at it right."

They rode for a while in silence.

"You know," the Terry Cloth Man said, "though we only met that once, I've thought of you a lot over the years—even dreamed about you."

"Me, too," said Bibi.

"So'd you ever find that—what'd you call him—Hubcap King of yours?"

"I spent the last seven years with him."

"Did he help you find whatever it was you were looking for?"

"I guess you could say that—or helped me lose what I didn't need." Bibi had never thought about the Terry Cloth Man's eyes before. He noticed now that the irises, when he glanced away from the road, showed as a fractured grey, like those of a cornered animal, while the whites were as yellowed and jaundiced as broken eggs.

"What are the chances of taking me to meet him sometime?" asked the Terry Cloth Man. "He sounded like an interesting fellow."

"No chance at all, I'm afraid," answered Bibi. "He's left town. No one knows where he's gone."

"Left town?" The Terry Cloth Man wiped his face with a shirtsleeve. He clenched the wheel and Bibi could see the muscles standing out on his jaw. "What a shame. I was hoping to kill him."

For a moment Bibi doubted his own ears. "You—what?"

"You heard right." The Man with the Terry Cloth Face was grinning, a terrible yellowish grin, dripping with perspiration. "You see," he said, "from the minute I saw you, so long ago, so filled with youth and vitality and hope, I wanted to destroy you and everything you stood for." He gasped for breath and mopped at his face. "And I must admit, I considered that option carefully. But then I figured a more elegant way to handle it would be to track down what you valued more than anything else, and destroy *it* instead—then let life finish you off, like it does everyone else." His breath whistled loudly in the closed space of the cab. "So I've spent these last years looking for the Hubcap King, too, just like you."

"But I don't understand," Bibi began, "how that one chance encounter—"

The Terry Cloth Man was hunched over the wheel, white-knuckled and intent. "Ahh, I'd gotten so bored with the daily activities of life . . . breathing, drinking coffee—wiping my rear. I needed something to occupy my time. Perhaps I should even be grateful—after all, you gave my life the only real purpose it ever had. But now it seems that, as usual, I've arrived too late."

He yanked the pickup around a bend and the tires emitted a squeal of amazement. A riverbed opened below the wheels on the passenger side as they headed up a long incline. The Man with the Terry Cloth Face turned to look at Bibi, then shrugged his shoulders.

"Ah well," he said, "I guess there's always Plan B."

With that he gave the wheel of the pickup a hard jerk to the right. Bibi felt the tire give way beneath him as the truck jounced across the low embankment at the edge of the shoulder, metal screeching and shuddering. Then he felt nothing—nothing at all, as they went sailing into space.

11.
THE
WHOLE PIE

Bibi drifts down, down like a diver, through a sea of image and memory, words coiling about him like kelp:

Hold on to nothing . . .

Will the real Bibi Brown please stand up?

The whole pie—

Is this all I am?

The universe is one enormous mind!

In his dreams he visits everything he has been, all that he might have been, everything he might yet become. He sees people, coming into being, grasping after something they can't identify, hears the minds ticking all across the buckled, heaving continent. He sees the strange curved landscape of time, across which the deeds of humanity crawl like insects. He feels the pull of the earth, drawing him down into form, into pain; imagines the long slow suffering of stones . . .

At last, letting go his hold on all he knows, Bibi glides deep into blackness. He hears words that are not words, feels sensations that cannot be said to be sensations. Then, nothing. How long he stays there, he has no way of telling.

Bit by bit, the little that is left of Bibi is being rubbed away, like a smudge on a piece of crystal.

• • •

A murmuring of voices, faint, indistinct.

"So this is the new one, eh? Any idea who he is?"

Pale light, a feeling of constriction.

"Part of a driver's license, name obscured . . ."

A coming and going; a scuffing of feet on floor.

"White male, mid-thirties, put him down as Doe—"

"John?"

"Of course, what do you think?"

Pressure above one eye; light, burning into the
    brain.

"Well, it just occurred to me how funny it is that
    there's never a Jim, or an Edward. I mean, why not give
    'em all different names—"

"Like hurricanes?"

Pressure releases; twilight again.

"Well, this one's certainly been through a storm."

Now a woman's voice, soft, encouraging. "Sir, can you
    hear me?"

"Wouldn't waste your time, hon. He's been totally
    unresponsive ever since he came in."

Touch of skin: smooth, warm. "Sir, if you can hear me,
    try to squeeze my hand."

A straining, a tremendous upwelling of effort—

"Or an eye. Just try to blink one eye!"

—like trying to move a mountain!

"Think he'll ever live a normal life again?"

A chuckle. "From the looks of him, I'm not sure he
  ever has."

The woman's voice: "There! A flicker, did you see it?
  Just for a moment—"

"Unlikely, I'd say, given his condition."

"I didn't see a thing."

"C'mon, what do you say we get ourselves a cup of
  coffee?"

In shifting, fitful sleep, Bibi relives the fall again and again. It takes place, as one might expect, in slow motion: a gradual, dreamlike dropping through space and time, locked in the vise-like grip of gravity. On his 468th replay, in the instant before hitting bottom, he finds himself suddenly, unaccountably, awake—and it occurs to him that all of life might be viewed in this fashion: a process of graceful falling, a slow-motion drop from one form of darkness to another, a surrendering in the same way that a falling object surrenders to gravity.

He sees an infinite gap open up between the past and the future: and all the Bibis that have ever been, that ever might be, tumble into it.

Falling backward into himself, he finds no bottom: he is the bottom!

This is what is real, he thinks, *this precise moment, where I have always lived.*

Could it be that this was the death of time?

"I'm afraid there's been damage—extensive . . .
  neuromuscular . . . cognitive—nurse, are you getting
  this down?"

"Yes, Doctor."

Sound of scribbling.

"And these contractions, frankly, have me worried. Rhythmic dysfunctions in the breathing, accompanied by periodic, involuntary spasms of the . . ."

"Doctor?"

". . . diaphragm. I recommend 20 milligrams of Prednosphyline, every two hours, injected subcutaneously—"

"Doctor."

Silence.

"It's laughter."

"What?"

"The contractions—they're laughter."

Again, silence.

"I believe the patient is laughing."

. . .

Bibi awakens to pain. Pain is a craggy, snag-toothed wilderness through which he toils; through which he has toiled all of his life. It consumes him, sweeping through his limbs and up his spine like fire. He feels pain as his home, pain as the great dream of life.

At last, there is no choice but to yield. At last, he allows the pain to engulf him, to sweep over him in great shuddering waves, until his body shakes with the force of it, and sweat pours down his face like the lost tears of a lifetime.

Until finally the pain bursts open, and all that holds him together collapses. Collapses completely, utterly, at last.

Collapses: yet he is still here.

A boundless euphoria comes over him—a joy so vast it includes pain.

I've had it wrong, he thinks, *all these years. It's not the* world *that's unreal—it's me!*

He spends days in uncontrollable laughter. His former life, everything that has been and everything that is to come, seems now no more than a dream, a passing thought in the enormous mind that is his true self.

But he, at last, is awake.

. . .

Light. For the first time, clarity.

Fluorescent, white, window blinds, sun streaming in.

"Well! Aren't we improving!"

A woman's face—kind. Rather pretty.

"Today we're going to try something new. Today we're going to see if we can get you to sit up. Maybe even have something to eat."

Everything is familiar. Everything has a name.

Except him.

To be sure, he now remembers what it used to be: Brown.

But the word no longer seems to refer to anything in particular.

Sitting up, as the nurse wheels the meal tray into position, Bibi fights to speak:

"There was a man with me . . . Terry Cloth . . ."

"I'm afraid he didn't make it."

Silence.

"Were you close to him?" the nurse asks.

"In a way . . ." Bibi struggles to fit words to feeling. "Closer than I ever knew."

Something passes—weeks? Months? Who can say?

For after all, what is time?

We are, he thinks.

The day comes when he's ready to leave.

"We're going to miss you," says the nurse.

Bibi smiles. Legs feel brand-new as he walks down the hallway toward the front door, rucksack lifted once more onto his back.

"Excuse me," he hears a voice behind him. "I nearly forgot—this was found in the truck. I thought you might want it." The nurse hands him an envelope, which he vaguely recognizes as the one he tucked in his jacket the morning he left the hubcap ranch. It is now marked by a rust-colored stain that spreads in a dark blotch across one end of it.

"Thank you," says Bibi, tucking it in his pocket again. "Thanks for all the help you've given me." He takes her hand, turns to leave. Then he turns back.

"My name is Bibi," he tells her. "Bibi Brown."

. . .

Leaving the hospital behind, Bibi finds himself stepping once more onto the road; and he reflects to himself, once again, that life is indeed circular.

The sky outside looks crisp and blue, and hard enough to walk upon.

He looks at the land stretching away on either side—land that is, after all, only land, topped by the sky that is only a sky, filled with clouds that are simply clouds.

"Well," he thinks to himself. "That's that."

And, laughing out loud, he sets off into the world.

. . .

Dear Bibi, begins the letter—stiff with rusty redness, its edges flutter in the wind like dead leaves as he sits reading on a stump alongside the highway:

> *Did your friend ever show up? Did he give you my other letter? I've been putting off writing, figuring if you haven't answered then you must not want to. And if you don't, I'll understand. After all it's been seven years. But then I figured, well there's no way of knowing for sure if he ever found you, especially considering the state he was in—I was awfully concerned with him looking so pale and all, and he seemed to be having some sort of trouble with his breathing. I hope it was O.K. that I gave him* (several words obscured by a rusty stain) . . . *he seemed so sweet and concerned about finding you, and I figured that way you'd be more sure of getting* . . . (a long stretch of lost words, buried in dark splotches) . . . *ry I never wrote before. I just wanted to forget, I think. But of course that's impossible with* (words obliterated) . . . *anyway I just thought you might like to know, and to know where to find us, in case you ever* (stained and illegible) . . . *always love* . . . (illegible).

Bibi studies the letter for a long, long time. But although he examines it carefully, turning it over again and again, there beside the road in the bright and blinding sunlight, he is unable to make out the address.

12.
THE LAND
OF NO SHADOWS

Late one afternoon, as the clouds bundle tightly along the horizon and the cold winds of early spring whip their way between the buildings, Bibi reenters the metropolis. He weaves in and along the streets, past the structures in a sort of rapture; for he now always sees things as they truly are. In the late, slanting sun even the tenements and alleyways are translucent and shot through with light; and the face of every hurrying citizen bears the features of an angel.

But things in America are not in good order. Gravity, having been tampered with for far too long, is beginning to wear thin, and everyone has become extraordinarily light on their feet. Growing numbers of citizens, particularly those of lighter builds, have taken to wearing weight belts, or ball-and-chain arrangements fastened about their ankles, lest they blow off the planet in a sudden breeze. Structures in sensitive zones have had to be strapped down with cables. There is even talk of building magnetic streets and equipping everyone with shoes of iron. Still, the skyscraper race has continued to accelerate: the tallest structures now penetrate the clouds; and it is said of those that dwell in them that each inhabitant speaks a different language.

Meanwhile, a religious revival is sweeping the nation. The trashbag saints are everywhere; and as Bibi stands at the edge of a garbage-strewn alleyway he hears an old woman pass by, pushing a shopping cart full of clothes and muttering to herself the one thousand names of God.

A sign on the marquee of the "First Bank of Christ" reads:

Jesus Saves. You can too!

The Wake Up From The American Dream movement is featured in the press daily, and slogans like "If you want to see clearly, open your eyes!" are splashed in bright paint on buildings and government installations everywhere.

Time is in crisis as well. Although a man who worked in the quarries once told Bibi: "there's so much time out there the day don't never seem to come to an end!", elsewhere people have squandered so much of it that there is no longer enough to go around. In some areas time is growing so short that the poorer classes, who can't afford to purchase a backup supply, are birthed, grow old, and die in less than a week. Nobody knows what to expect when it runs out entirely.

The weather, predictably, is being affected too; snow now falls as frequently in July as in December. Even history has begun to collapse under the strain: at this very moment, somewhere in France, the earliest cave paintings are being created; and it is said that in the countryside one can hear the rush and clatter of the barbarian hordes that destroyed Rome.

Everywhere Bibi goes he finds legions of the lame and diseased. Crime has become epidemic. Needing nothing for himself, he wanders the streets, devoting himself to those he meets. When people need help he does what he can; and he smiles with perfect love upon the street gangs who rob him. At last his only belongings, beyond the simplest of garments, are his coat and shoes, which he gives away to a shivering drunk on a street corner.

The next morning, as dawn comes over the city, Bibi uncurls from the subway grate where he spent the hours of darkness. Crumpling the newspapers he used to cover himself, he tosses them into a trash basket. With no remaining possessions, unburdened by hope or fear, he paces the empty, dreaming streets of the city as dawn warms the faces of the buildings and the sun casts long shadows down the avenues.

At last he comes to a place where a shaft of morning light spills along an alleyway. He stands there for a long while, basking like a lizard, letting the heat seep into his bones. He, with nothing, has become no one. He is simply a man. He watches as the pigeons peck about the sidewalks for lost crumbs, and the deserted streets come slowly alive.

"Hey, buddy," calls a ragged fellow standing in a doorway.

Bibi turns toward him.

"Hey," the man repeats, pointing. "Look at that!"

Bibi follows the finger to see the outline of his own shadow. Stretched out against the sidewalk in the low rays of the sun to several times his length, it appears vague and oddly shimmering. As Bibi watches, it lightens and seems to vibrate, until at last it pales and fades out altogether.

Bibi continues to feel the warmth against his back; but something has changed. He passes one hand before his body, and then the other. The sun still spills in an unbroken stream against the concrete.

The light is passing through him.

ABOUT THE AUTHOR

A Zen practitioner for the past fifteen years, Sean Murphy is also the author of *One Bird, One Stone: 108 American Zen Stories*. The winner of the 1999 Hemingway Award for a First Novel, he has produced and directed documentary films, founded a theatre company, and performed as a songwriter and guitarist. He teaches writing seminars in the United States and abroad, and is an instructor in writing, literature, and film at the University of New Mexico. He lives with his wife, Tania, in northern New Mexico. Visit his website at http://www.murphyzen.com.